# Long Island Executioner

## Dark Mafia BWWM Romance

### Long Island Mafia Romance
#### Book 1

## Jamila Jasper

# Contents

# A Preview 🩶

# Another Preview 🎁

ISBN: 9798355161330

This is book one in an interracial mafia romance series with dark themes and potential triggers. If you enjoy steamy and spicy BWWM romance with a black woman/white man romance, you will enjoy this story. For readers of the Pagonis family or Doukas family series, strap in... You'll enjoy this deliciously wild ride.

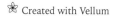 Created with Vellum

# Description

**Lucky meets her pressed against the wall of a public bathroom. Ready for him.**

Mahogany skin. Gorgeous brown eyes.

She has the voluptuous body of a goddess.

Lucky wants more than just one night…

He spends a decade tracking her down…

Althea spends that decade hiding from a dangerous man.

When he shows up on her doorstep,

The last thing she wants to do is talk to the father of her child...

She knows his reputation.

The executioner.

Good thing talking is the last thing on Lucky's mind.

# Series Titles

*Long Island Executioner*
*Long Island Butcher*
*Long Island Slayer*

*smarturl.it/longislandmafia*

# Content Awareness

*dark bwwm mafia romance*

This is a mafia romance story with dark themes including potentially triggering content, frank discussions and language surrounding bedroom scenes and race. All characters in this story are 18+. Sensitive readers, be cautioned about some of the material in this dark but extremely hot romance novel.

*Enjoy the steamy romance story…*

# Note From Jamila

**Welcome to the darkest corner of my heart and soul.**

When I'm not lifting weights for therapy, I'm twisting up the darkest parts of myself into my plots, my characters, their motivations and in teasing out brutality from the words I write.

The sex scenes, violence and darkness in this book reflect my shadow psyche and hopefully a little bit of the shadow in all of us that draws us to the **bad boy archetypes** in fiction like Luca "Lucky" Vicari, the lead male character in this story.

Words are powerful. We all know this intuitively. Language differentiates us from other species after all…

The words here may disturb you, but if you're anything like me, you have a little darkness in you — a strange magnetism towards the macabre and disturbing that you can't explain.

You enjoy the bad boys who are truly fucked up. You are the relentless optimist who finds the good in everyone — even the worst villains fiction could have to offer. Welcome, queen. You're in good company.

Be warned, the content in this story may be sensitive to some readers but if you want to walk with me on the wild side and dare to have dark fantasies about twisted alpha heroes and black female leads — welcome.

# Chapter 1
# The First Encounter
### Althea Little (18-Years-Old)

**10 YEARS AGO...**

**D**oesn't it always seem like every fucking bill comes at once when you're least prepared to deal with it? You can't catch a break these days. Rent comes on the first, car payment on the second, insurance on the third, then you need to come up with some new money for even more bullshit. It's the worst...

My mama helps when she can, but if she had the money to stay helping me out, I wouldn't have to work this job and I wouldn't have had to move out when I turned eighteen. Mama tries her best, but there's only so much she can do.

I push open the door to the kitchen after dropping off another stack of plates and head to the table of fifteen customers to check out the tips. I need those tips tonight so I can pay the back rent my stupid left roommate left me with when she dipped and moved to Los Angeles with a guy she met off some stupid dating app. Instead of paying $1,200 for my room in our two-bedroom apartment, I have to come up with $2,000. Yeah, she had the bigger room too, so I found out her ass was scamming me. Bullshit. It's all bullshit.

I hurry over to the table I just cleared, gleefully searching for the tip. Fifteen customers sat here for hours ordering glasses of wine, entire bottles, entrees, dessert, the whole works. I search for the tip and then I finally see it. I snatch the bill. Five dollars.

I want to scream. These people left a fucking five-dollar tip on a dinner they spent over $1,856.78 on. There were fifteen people and they could only come up with five dollars for the tip? I want to scream and punch the fucking wall in this place. There's no way I'll make enough in tips the rest of the night to cover rent. I'm so screwed.

I hate this job. I hate this job so fucking badly and I don't know what could make this job any worse.

The bell at the front of Il Pappa's rings and a man stumbles into the restaurant. I hope Mike's ass doesn't expect me to wait another damn table tonight because I swear to God... I'm done waiting tables. I'm sick of people treating me like dirt and even when they don't treat you like dirt, they don't tip. You can't pay the bills with fake ass politeness.

I don't care if the man stumbling into the restaurant is the fucking mayor of New York, I'm not doing shit for the rest of the night. My manager can take it up with me if he wants to, but I just worked my ass off for hours, carting bottles of wine, entrees and desserts back to this bullshit table to only get $5. I'm hot. Upset. Livid.

I glance at the man who walks in and quickly avert my eyes. When I catch sight of a neck tattoo, I know it's in my best interest to look away. The thug life ain't for me. Once I save up enough money, I'm headed to beauty school.

# The First Encounter

The man glances at me, and his eyes linger. Damn, they're really green. He's not bad looking either, except for the next tattoo.Too bad he looks like the typical guido scumbag you see around here, like he would crack someone's face in for looking at him wrong. I'd better stop fucking looking at him. I avert my eyes and continue wiping down the tables in my section, which doesn't stop the man from gazing at me. It's not like he's waiting for me to take his order or anything. He's just staring. Hmph. His ass can stare all he wants — I'm not going over there.

I might clean my tables, but I'm not fucking serving anyone.

Another server takes the man who just walked in. He's tall, well over six feet, and he has tattoos everywhere including a freaky ass neck tattoo with a demon face carved into the knife's reflection. He has thick brown hair, tight black jeans and a white t-shirt underneath his leather jacket. There are patches all over his jacket, but I can't read the language written on the patches. Italian? Probably.

This is a high end Italian restaurant and a lot people in this part of town are from the old country. I don't know though. This guy looks American, just pretty fucked up. The man glances over at me and he keeps staring. I can feel his eyes on me, but I know better than to look twice at any white boy, especially one who walks in here covered in tattoos looking like that. He's bad news, and he looks drunk. It doesn't matter if he has those pretty green eyes, a man like that is nothing but a lot of fucking trouble.

I finish cleaning up my table and head to the back kitchen. I don't make it ten feet when my manager grabs my arm, seemingly out of nowhere.

"Damn, Mikey! What the fuck?"

"Hey. You see that guy out front?"

"What guy? I'm finishing up my table. Those fifteen assholes tipped me five dollars by the way so I don't know how the fuck I'm going to keep my apartment. I'm not doing shit for the rest of the night."

I don't know how my boss puts up with managing a bunch of teenagers, but Mikey handles it well. I'm not the first person to have a mental breakdown this week. In the service industry, there's always somebody having a dang breakdown.

"Hey, hey, hey, Althea, relax. Okay? I need you to relax."

"Relax? You're asking me about bullshit and I don't have any fucking money, Mikey. I've worked here for two years and I can barely keep a roof over my head. You need to find a way to make these cheap ass guidos leave better tips."

I know I shouldn't call them guidos to Mikey's face but I'm so pissed off I can't control myself. My mom's always telling me I need to get my temper under control, but I don't know if I ever will. Mikey handles my insults well.

"Hey! Hey, no need to get personal," Mikey grumbles. "And money? You need money? I've got a way for you to make some fucking money if you chill the fuck out."

"How? I need the money tonight Mikey and I don't want to be here anymore. I want to go home."

"Althea, honey, you can't go home. Wait here three minutes, I'll talk to Lucky outside."

"Lucky? Who the fuck is Lucky? I don't want to wait for anything, Mikey—I—."

Mikey doesn't answer because he heads out of the kitchen. I'm desperate enough for money to do whatever the

4

hell he asks as long as it's not too crazy. I'm about to head out of the kitchen and give up on Mikey's ass when he comes back in, a bright look on his face. He pats me on the back.

"You want that money, head into the employee restroom back there and just do whatever he asks you to do, okay? Whatever money you need, he'll give you as long as you do what he says."

"What? Mikey, who are you talking about. What are you talking about?"

"Christ, Althea. Do you want the fucking money or not? Lucky Vicari is in this fucking restaurant and he's willing to pay big bucks, okay? The girl who I had to meet him bailed on me and I swear if you do this, you won't regret it."

"Do what?"

"Christ, Althea, what do you fucking think? Do you need the money or not?"

The realization of what Mikey's asking me hits me like the LIRR. He wants me to sleep with this guy. Or this guy wants to sleep with me. Or something. Rage courses through me, rushing to my face. I might need money, but I don't expect my boss to suggest I sleep with someone to get it. This is a restaurant, last time I checked, not a brothel.

"Mikey, I'm not a hooker."

Mikey shrugs as if he's not exactly sure. Bastard. He responds to the increasingly angered look on my face with unflinching calm, which makes the situation even more annoying.

"Althea, do you know who the fuck Lucky Vicari is?" Mikey asks as if this guy is on a teen show or something. I shake my head. How the hell would I know a guy like that? I

5

mind my business, I keep my head down, I don't get involved with gang shit. It's not the life I want.

"No, and I don't care," I tell Mikey firmly, meaning it at the moment and desperately suppressing a million anxious thoughts rushing through my head. "I'm not having sex with some guy in the employee bathroom."

I need the money. I need the money so badly that even if my stupid patrons had tipped properly, I would still be short. I just thought some money would be better than none while pleading with my landlord for mercy. The Italian landlords around here are ruthless, but you can always beg your way out of trouble if you try hard enough. I think.

"Look, how much money do you need?" Mikey responds like he can read my mind. I hate that about him. He's managed so many teenagers that he can practically read our minds.

"$1,400," I mutter, utterly embarrassed at my destitution even if Mikey clearly doesn't give a crap. I have some of the money, but there's no way that I can come up with all of it in such a short space of time. I'm absolutely screwed despite my best efforts.

My boss confidently responds, "Ask him for five grand."

Sex for five grand? Does Mikey think I'm Rihanna-level-hot or something? I'm a plus-sized teenager working at a restaurant who last took a shower over sixteen hours ago. I'm not worth five grand. A guy who looks like Lucky wouldn't pay five grand for a few minutes with me. This has to be some sort of scam.

"Mikey! I'm not doing that," I tell him. Who knows what freak shit a guy like that would ask me to do. But five thousand dollars? Can I say no to that? My heart pounds and my palms feel really gross and wet. I can't touch some guy with gross, clammy hands.

"Come on, Althea. I don't give out these opportunities for free. I'm telling you, five minutes, it'll be over, you'll have all the money you need. I swear, this won't get back to you. I promise."

"Mikey..."

"Five grand, Althea. Five minutes for five grand. Think about it."

I DON'T NEED LONG to think.

I DON'T KNOW his name, but I know he's waiting for me in the bathroom. I knock four times in a row on the door in rapid succession, just like Mikey told me to do. A thick Long Island accent slurs from the other side.

"Fucking hell, open the door." That must be Lucky. Funny thing is, I don't feel lucky at all.

I open the door and there's a man bending over the sink. He's large. He looks larger than he did when he came bustling through the restaurant door, but he's even bigger up close. The man has to be at least 6'4" and he's muscular. He could throw me across the room with two fingers. I try to hide the nervous gulp that struggles its way down my throat.

I shut the door behind me but he doesn't stand until he finishes those three lines of white powder on the mirror. Fuck. I've heard you see some shit when you work the night shift, but watching a giant Italian man shove his face full with cocaine isn't exactly what I expected when I walked into the bathroom.

When he turns around to look at me, he grins. Those green eyes size me up again and make me feel very fucking nervous. He's way older than eighteen, maybe a whole decade older than me. That makes me nervous too. What the fuck is he doing here and why is he doing coke off a bathroom mirror and trying to get his rocks off in an Italian restaurant?

Lucky runs his tongue over his smooth lower lips. His lips aren't grossly thin. They're pretty full for a white boy and I hate myself for even looking at them and tell myself I only looked because he licked them.

"Fuck, you look good for a hooker," he says after several minutes of sizing me up. It's not a big romantic compliment, but then again, he tells me exactly who the fuck he thinks I am — a hooker. I'm not worth a better compliment. Shame courses through me, but I'm too far to turn back, stuck in the bathroom with a giant guy who could easily overpower me and damn, five thousand dollars could make a difference in my life.

"I'm not a hooker," I say to him, trying to sound tough. I sound like a nervous toy poodle instead, which doesn't make me feel any better.

"Tonight you are," Lucky says. "Don't matter. I don't judge."

He takes a black credit card out of his pocket and pours white powder onto the mirror. He divides the powder into three lines with precision. There are no words between us as Lucky cuts his lines until he finishes. Five minutes. This feels a hell of a lot longer than five fucking minutes.

Lucky finally makes me an offer. "Want a hit?"

He points to the mirror balanced precariously on the sink. I don't do drugs and just because I'm here in this bathroom tonight doesn't mean I have to lose all my morals. This is a one-time thing. I'll never be in this situation again, not like Lucky Vicari gives a crap. He hasn't even asked my name. There's a spot of white right under his nose and his pupils dilate so wide the man's eyes look black.

He smiles at me and it has a handsome smile but that doesn't change the fact that he's a monster for what he wants from me.

"No thanks," I tell him. "I don't do drugs."

My desperate clinging to morality sounds pathetic out loud, but it's the only dignity I have in this bathroom with Lucky where we both know exactly what I came here to do. I try not to act humiliated, but I already am.

"Bend over then," he says. "Get against the sink and lift your dress."

He says it matter-of-factly like he's ordering a cheese-burger from the dollar menu. I want to be treated with a little more respect, but like Mikey said, if I do this in five minutes, I can get out of here. If he wants to treat this like business, so will I.

"You need to wear a condom," I respond sharply, trying to be tough again and ignoring how fucking degraded I feel by the way he talks to me.

He grins. "No, I don't. They call me Lucky for a reason."

"I don't care," I say as forcefully as I can muster.

"What's your name?"

He doesn't really care. He just doesn't want to feel like an asshole while he pays to use a woman's body.

"None of your damn business. Wear a condom or–

"Stop fucking with my high," Lucky interrupts. "Bend over or leave the money on the fuckin' table. I like fucking when I'm high and I'm getting some tonight."

I step forward, legs trembling. I don't know what keeps me going forward, but I do it and I bend over the sink. I lean forward, my face far too close to Lucky's white-powdered coated mirror.

"Fine," I snap. "But if you knock me up, I'm coming for child support."

Lucky snickers, and my body responds with a strange spread of goosebumps. I don't want to be here, but my body feels weird. Lucky eases his body behind mine and I know there's no way out of this and absolutely no letting go. I bite my lip and look down as Lucky stands behind me. He runs his hand over me like he's petting a horse from the base of my neck to the base of my spine. His hand wanders over my ass and he groans.

"I just love a black woman's ass," he whispers. "You fine ass black women never want to let a white boy fuck unless we pay."

I want to punch this smart-mouthed Italian in the face, but I can't if I want this money and I don't just want it, I need it. He runs his hand between my ass cheeks and the strangest feeling swells inside me. I feel dirty and fucked up for letting this happen. If I don't look at myself in the mirror, maybe I can pretend it's happening to someone else. Unfortunately, Lucky has other plans.

He squeezes my ass and groans again. "It's a nice, big chocolate colored ass, isn't it?"

It's like he's talking to himself. I can't believe I agreed to this. I've never had a guy talk to me like that before. I've never been with a white guy.

"Just fuck me..." I breathe, hoping it will encourage him to stop talking and put his dick inside me. I don't want to hear anymore of his dirty talk. Lucky chuckles and lifts my dress high. He can see my entire ass and underwear. I'm gross from a whole day working the floor. He can probably tell that I've been sweating my butt off in this restaurant but if he can tell, he doesn't care.

"What are you, eighteen?" He grunts. I doubt he cares.

"Yeah."

"Good," he says. "Don't plan on going to jail just to get a piece of black pussy..."

I squeeze my thighs together in silent protest, expecting Lucky to put his hand or fingers between my legs. Instead, Lucky drops to his knees. I wriggle my ass nervously, or to get away from him. My body moves of its own accord, but Lucky stops me with his hands. It's the first time I feel his bare hands on my skin and I suck in air sharply.

"Quiet," he murmurs. "Let me lick your nice black pussy while I'm high..."

He peels my panties to the side and the struggle to move away. My underwear feels cold and wet. My wetness humiliates me but Lucky's tongue sliding between my legs only makes it worse. OMG. I'm all sweaty and gross up there but Lucky doesn't give a crap. His tongue slips all the way to my clit as he buries his nose between my legs. I make the situation even more embarrassing by moaning.

Lucky spreads my legs apart and pushes his tongue deeper. He keeps moving his mouth down there and I lose control of myself. I tell myself my body doesn't want this, but there's so much squishiness down there that I don't feel like I'm in control.

There's a sharp tightening in my core, and I lose control of everything. I cum hard all over Lucky's face.

Humiliation courses through me along with pleasure from climaxing and the confusing rush of emotions causes me to stumble forward slightly. Lucky chuckles and rises to his feet, wiping his face off. He's so warm and his mouth moving away from me exposes me to the cold bathroom. I shudder and press my hips back against him.

He gives my ass an unceremonious slap.

"Good pussy," Lucky grunts after smacking my ass. Holy shit, this man is like an animal. That slap sends a tingle through me.

Lucky unzips his pants and pulls his cock out. I really want him to use a condom, but I also have to check out what he's working with. A guy who does coke and has sex like this has to have the world's smallest dick. I glance behind me to make sure I'm right and nearly choke on my own spit.

"What the fuck is that?" I blurt out.

"It's a cock, princess. You didn't taste like a virgin. I think you've seen one before."

He doesn't care what I think. He doesn't care how I feel. I have to tell myself that even as he slowly slides his fingers between my lower lips to get me ready.

"Tight pussy like that has gotta get real fuckin' wet to take my dick," he mutters incoherently. I grip the ceramic sides to the sink, closing my eyes to avoid bearing witness to my humiliation as I allow a strange Italian man to bend me over the bathroom sink I just cleaned puke off of last week and enter me. His body provides a warm cover as he hovers over mine and I wince as he rubs the head of his cock against my wet entrance.

Lucky growls authoritatively. "Look in the fucking mirror."

I whimper as he slides the head past my entrance. Holy fuck, it hurts. He doesn't even have more than the head in but his enormous cock hurts like hell. I whimper, but I can't bring myself to obey his instructions. Lucky won't take no for an answer. He wraps his hands around my braids and tilts my head so I can see myself in the mirror and more impressively, his tattooed, muscular frame hulking over mine. His chest heaves with lust as our eyes connect in the mirror. Holy fuck, his eyes are green.

There's a tattoo of a pair of dice on his torso and the image contorts as Lucky slides forward, pushing more of his dick inside me. I gasp desperately for breath because Lucky's dick is wine-bottle-thick and I might not be the smallest girl, but his big Italian cock could still break me in half. Tears pierce the edge of my eyes and Lucky grunts as he pushes his dick forward.

"You're tight," he grunts. "I'll be quick. Black girls always get me off quick."

I don't dignify his racially charged comment with a response. Lucky's big dick feels like it's going to break me in half. He pushes his hips forward, and the pressure builds up into pleasure, forcing me to moan. Lucky groans and moves forward again, bending over me and reaching between my legs to touch my clit. He whispers, "fuck", in my ear as he finds my clit.

"You have a pretty little clit down there," he whispers. "Soft…"

Lucky rubs my pussy in slow circles as he eases the rest of his dick between my legs. It hurts so much that I wriggle and push my hips back because it's the only way my body can find to get away from him. It doesn't work. Lucky pumps his hips into me, forcing me against the bathroom sink and keeping me gazing at our bodies as he enters me from behind.

He's hot, and he has a lot of tattoos. They're all random, like they tell a story. Probably a fucking serial killer thriller.

When our hips join, the worst mix of shame and pleasure surges through me. *I'm not a hooker. I'm not a hooker.* I bite my lower lip as Lucky massages my clit, as if I have a chance in hell of holding back the orgasm about to burst out of me.

His dick hurt like hell at first but with his thumb on my clit and the slow movements from Lucky's hips, pleasure replaces the pain.

"I want you to cum," he growls. "Fuck, I want the cum from your black pussy."

Why does he keep talking like that? I hate that his gross words get me really wet and it doesn't help that Lucky knows exactly how to turn me on with his thumb and his big dick. He moves behind me in slow strokes and when I can't bear to look at myself in the mirror, I gaze at him instead. He must be crazy as fuck to look this good but pay five grand to have sex with a waitress in a bathroom.

Lucky kisses my shoulder as he fucks me from behind and his steady rhythm and slow massages around my clit threaten to push me to an orgasm. I struggle to resist the mounting pleasure, gripping the sink to steady myself. I can't help it. Lucky's dick is too big, and he's too fucking good at what he does with his fingers. I cum hard and my breasts press into the sink as Lucky's weight presses into me and he pushes his dick even deeper to make me cum harder.

Juices explode from between my legs over Lucky's dick and dribble down my thighs. He makes an animalistic growl and pumps between my legs a few more minutes before I feel his cock stiffening.

"Please… I don't want a baby. I don't…"

"I'm gonna cum," He growls, ignoring me entirely. "You know what you signed up for."

Lucky pushes his hips forward and empties his seed inside me. I freeze as the reality of the situation hits me. He's doing it. He's cumming inside me and he doesn't even know my last name. Lucky swears enthusiastically as he finishes. His body pulses and tenses against mine. His chest leans against my body and I get an intense feel of his muscles. My stomach tightens and I climax again as my body has this involuntary pleasurable response to Lucky filling me with his seed.

"You are fucking good," he whispers. "My white cum looks so good dripping down those sweet brown thighs."

I shudder, too ashamed and terrified to respond. Money. I need to think about getting my money. Lucky pulls his dick out of me and I turn around quickly, smoothing down my dress and ignoring the degrading sensation of his thick cum slipping out of my pussy and sliding down my leg.

"I need my money."

"Sure thing. Wanna do this again?"

"I'd rather die," I snarl at him. I sound defeated because I am. This man had his way with me for money and I never thought I would sink this low. I wanted to make something of myself, maybe start my own hair salon. But this is how it goes for poor black girls, huh? This is what we have to stoop to. I fight back tears.

I don't want this asshole to see me crying. I can't show anyone my pain.

"Whatever. Need coke?"

"I don't do drugs," I respond calmly.

Lucky chuckles. "You would if you were me, princess. Here's your fucking money."

He throws his wallet at me like he expects me to take out however much I need. I pull out the cash and ignore how much more he has left in there. I just need to get out of here. My heart races like crazy as I race for the door the second I have the money. This guy could follow me and kill me if he wanted to. He could do anything to me because he already has.

As I run to my car with the money burning a hole in my handbag, I make myself one promise—to never go back to that stupid fucking job again.

# Chapter 2
# Wise Guys & The Casino
### Lucky Vicari

**Present Day.**

J ohn's late — as fucking usual. I don't know why the fuck he has this meeting in a casino when he knows I'm sober and these places have more cocaine than a stripper's ass crack. I hate being in places like this alone. I'm not the same guy I was eight years ago and I don't plan on being a menace to society in some restaurant bathroom after tonight. I have to fight the urge to become the fuck up I used to be. Junkie. That's the worst fucking thing you can be in the mob. It's shameful. I have to deal with my problems like a man now... I have to change.

We're still cleaning up our cousin's messes and apparently, that little fuck made a big one. I might as well play the slots if I'm going to be stuck here waiting any longer. I get a few hundreds out of my wallet and stuff them into the machine. Doesn't matter if I win or lose, the money's all ours. I hold the security contracts to the casino with Lucky

Security LLC and John owns the place. He's better at running numbers and dealing with bullshit than I am.

I win fifty dollars and lose twenty-five in one go before the other member of our crew arrives. We're still waiting for John but at least Sammy's here. He doesn't notice me at first until I whistle and his eyes meet mine across the room. Everyone looks at Sammy when he enters a room and starts whispering. Nobody in Long Island moved past the arrests last year and it's all anyone talks about when they see our cousin, Sammy Zagarella, walk into a room.

Sammy rakes his fingers through his slicked back dark brown hair and points to a table near my machines and I get the rest of my money back, accepting the loss so I can join him at the table. It's been a fucking minute since I've seen Sammy or his kids. Crazy motherfucker, crazy fucking kids. Sammy looks stressed as fuck, which is normal for him. He needs a new girl.

Sammy whistles for a cocktail waitress and a plain girl with dark brown hair and a scowling face takes his order. John must be doing one of his buddies a favor to have a chick so uninspiring working the floor. Even Sammy appears visibly disappointed as he orders a gin and tonic. He respects the fact that I don't drink and shoos the waitress away before she can ask for my order and disrupt my apparently tenuously held sobriety.

"Where the fuck is John?" Sammy grunts impatiently. He's older than both of us and chock full of the bullshit that comes with the life. He hasn't slept through the night in a decade and he drinks way too fucking much. At least he's never been like me and gone to the dark side. I'm lucky I pulled myself out of that shit before I got myself whacked.

"Fuck if I know," I mutter to Sammy. "I've just been losing money."

"Any hot chicks in here tonight?" Sammy asks, scanning the room and determining the bleakness of the situation himself. Women. My throat tightens at the thought of women. Would he believe it's been eight years for me? I haven't touched a woman in eight painfully long years and I won't change that tonight.

I learned my lesson when I woke up in my puke at the train station with my wallet gone and all my coke stolen. I learned my lesson when the vivid nightmares of what I did to that woman stole my sleep for weeks. Lucky Vicari doesn't need hookers or waitresses or hot chicks. I stole something from that woman I can't ever give back. She never told me her name. I bet she had a pretty name. She sure had a pretty pair of tits and a great ass. Her moans were so sweet, I remember that night like I was fucking sober.

She fucked me up.

"Who cares about hot chicks?" I snap at Sammy bitterly. "What about John's news? Did the stupid motherfucker give you any clues or anything?"

"Ask him yourself," Sammy grunts, gesturing to a corner of the room as the waitress returns with his gin and tonic. Sammy slides her a tip and gestures to John entering the room. He dresses like the boss tonight, attracting attention from the casino patrons who recognize John Vicari for who he is — one of New York's most powerful men.

"Sorry I'm late," John says, but he sounds more impatient than sorry.

"Lucky won't stop twitching," Sammy says. "He's

thinking about coke or booze or whatever the fuck. Let's get this shit over with."

Something about Sammy's tone tells me he's the one who has to go. It's probably some fucking trouble with his kids. Sammy's a terrible fucking father, honestly.

John gives me a stern look. "You're staying off that shit, right? We can't deal with anymore fucking junkies. You get back on that shit, you know what's going to happen."

"It's still been eight years. I'm fine. Can you get to the point of why we're here?"

John outranks me, but we're still brothers. I can get away with some shit I couldn't pull on anyone else. Shit I definitely couldn't pull on Sammy.

"One of you stupid fucks has a kid out there," John says matter-of-factly. "And I don't know who the fuck it is."

"Uh, I have a kid who I'm pretty sure you know about," Sammy says, finishing the rest of his gin and searching desperately for the waitress. For a guy who drinks and fucks as much as Sammy, you would think he would show more concern. He has his hands full with his kid though and if he's smart, he's wrapped it up ever since bringing that little shit into the world... no offense to Enrico.

"Everyone knows you can't keep it in your pants," John shoots back at Sammy with thinly veiled bitterness. What the fuck is pissing my brother off tonight? He's normally grouchy, but whatever he has to say to us has nearly pushed him over the edge. It dawns on me that he suspects the fuck up belongs to me. Shit.

The cocktail waitress reappears, and we silence our personal conversation. No one in this place would dare talk about anything they overheard at a Vicari table if they wanted to keep their life and this waitress is no different. Still, given Sammy's arrest last year, you can never be too safe. You can never know exactly who to trust.

"Can I get you boys any more drinks?" The waitress asks in a slight attempt to add some pep into her voice because of John's presence. Fuck's sake, these people show up at your table at exactly the wrong time. I don't want to think about waitresses because every time I think of waitresses, I think about her…

I don't think he's buying it because he raises a curious eyebrow and orders a spiced Barclay rum on ice. Sammy orders three more gin and tonics. I order a seltzer. I miss booze, but I definitely don't miss what it did to me. I don't miss how much I fucked up my morals. I don't miss the asshole who used a waitress in the bathroom of some unknown Italian restaurant because he was so fucking high. I can't stop thinking about her and this terrible knot forms in my stomach. What if she had a fucking kid? I would be so fucking fucked.

I can remember everything about what that woman looked like. I could have tracked her down if I wanted to, especially if she stayed in New York. If she has a fucking kid… Fuck, did I mention how much I miss booze? I'm tense and my tension clearly makes John suspicious.

When the waitress disappears again, John leans forward, glowering at me even if he's trying to act like he's talking to both of us. Hot shame courses through me. My fuck up got me into this and John knows it.

He reaches into the breast pocket of his fancy blazer and pulls out a letter in a red envelope that looks like a Valentine's Day card.

"Look at the fucking letter I got," John says. "Straight to my office. Whoever sent this knows what the fuck they're talking about and they mean business. I don't know who the fuck did this or what the fuck they want but it's pissing me the fuck off."

John probably sets a world record daily for how often he uses the f-word. It's the only reminder left I used to be the good brother, and he used to be crazy, drunk ass Johnny.

Relief releases some of my tension when John slides the letter over to Sammy, like that'll straighten out my guilt. Maybe he still thinks both of us are equally to blame. What could be in that letter to piss John off so much? I'm burning to snatch the letter out of Sammy's hands, but I can't. If I don't act cool. I'll bury my ass so deep in trouble with John that I won't be able to get out.

John gave my company the casino contracts even after my many screwups. I owe my brother respect. I owe him peace of mind. Sammy unfolds the letter. Sammy never seems impatient, and he never seems in a rush. He carries himself with total control he gets from his Zagarella side. Everyone knows the Vicari boys are crazy, the Zagarella boys are both withdrawn and terrifying.

Sammy snickers after reading the letter. "Come on. It's clear this is Lucky's problem. Weren't you fucking a detective a few years back?"

Sammy's the only other person who can get away with talking to John like that. Sammy's comment is apparently the least of John's concerns. John's eyes flicker to mine. He barely conceals his outrage before turning his gaze back to Sammy for an explanation. Why is it Lucky's problem? How can you prove to me what's in the letter was about him? I know what my brother's thinking. I drove a wedge between us, but there's still a part of me that knows John way too fucking well.

"So you're saying the kid isn't yours?" John says calmly.

The lump in my throat expands, threatening to choke me on the spot. I wish I still drank. My head swims as I try to keep it together for the rest of the conversation. Cousin Sammy's entirely too fucking cavalier about the whole thing. My stomach turns as he explains. I still haven't read the fucking letter.

"Yeah," Sammy says, snickering. "I am saying the kid ain't mine."

Sammy has kids—no reason for him not to claim this one.

He continues, "Put it together. The kid's almost ten years old. Guess who hasn't had sex or a drink or a fucking bump of coke in ten years? Almost like he did something that he regretted… like he knocked somebody up."

"Knocked who up? Who the fuck are you knocking up?" John growls. He's taking this shit way too personally. John might be the boss, but he doesn't get a say in who I get to fuck or knock up. He's right to be upset. Bastard kids cause more problems than they're worth. Hot shame courses through me even thinking the word bastard. If this kid is mine, they're my blood. Italian.

Sammy slides the letter across the table, and I don't want to open it. Sammy scoffs as he hands me the letter. "Don't ask me, John. Ask Lucky."

I try to sound cool, like I can somehow convince John this isn't a mistake I made even when I believe him. "I don't have a kid. How the fuck could I have a kid? You guys are messing with me."

I don't sound like I believe my bullshit. John sees right through me which only makes things worse. I still can't bring myself to touch the letter. John notices the hesitation. Fuck. I betray myself.

Bile rises in my throat. They don't know the real reason I stopped partying. I told everyone I liked my nickname, and I didn't want to run out of luck. That was another bullshit story quickly unraveling before me. Sammy and John don't know about the girl in the bathroom. My family doesn't know about the shit I said to her or the fact that I pushed her face into the sink and fucked her hard.

They don't understand my attraction to her and to women like her with smooth, forbidden brown skin and walls a mile high around them. I never told my brothers I came inside a stranger and gave her enough money to make the problem go away.

Drugs took away my dignity, and they made me take away someone else's. That's not cosa nostra. If word got out… I'd be in deep shit.

I slowly unfold the letter, knowing it will be my undoing.

Dear Mr. Vicari,

I hope this finds you well.
We are familiar with your family and your work in
New York.
We wish to establish business alongside the Vicari
family.

We do not expect this to be any trouble.

If there are any problems, your daughter, 9-year-old Chiara Little will suffer.

She lives nearby where we hope to establish business and we are monitoring her closely for you.

If you attempt to stop us, your entire bloodline will suffer.

You will know us when we come.

Sincerely,

Your Future Business Partners

I SHAKE my head as I re-read the letter. I don't believe anyone could be so stupid as to send this to John. It's just not humanly possible.

"Where the fuck did you get this?" I ask him.

John doesn't want there to be any mistakes about who's in charge here.

"Who the fuck is Chiara Little? Do you have some fucking kid we don't know about?"

"If I've got some kid, I don't fucking know about her."

John looks like he wants to punch me in the face. I struggle not to seethe. It's not any of his business what happened in my past. My stomach tightens into a knot. Getting pissed off at John won't make any of this shit go away.

"If you have a kid? What the fuck, Lucky?"

"I did a lot of fucked up shit a few years ago. I don't know. I don't think I have a kid."

"Chiara Little. Read the fucking name and tell me right now if you have a fucking kid. Do you recognize that fucking name?"

Chiara Little. It's a pretty name, sounds a little Italian. And Little. I mean... That name I recognize. I tracked her down after that night. Mikey told me to stick it where the sun don't shine and leave the chick alone, but I remember her last name now that I see it written down. Althea Little. She's the one. My stomach sinks into my ass and then threatens to come out my fucking mouth. I get that "you're in deep shit" feeling I thought I left behind when I turned twenty-five and vowed to let go of this shit and put the past behind me.

You can't always make amends for the fucked up shit you did. All you've got half the time is a promise to do better and the hope that in the end, God sees your heart and has it in his to forgive. John isn't a damn thing like God or Jesus. Forgiveness doesn't come easily to my older brother.

I can feel John's anger rising to a peak. He's a dick when he loses his temper and now, he's a dick with power. Once we returned from Matteo Doukas' big fat Italian wedding, our father gave him leadership of our family in his absence, a move every mob family on the east coast approves of.

John doesn't need something like this to threaten his leadership and he also doesn't need it to come between us. If John can't control his temper, it's my job to talk him down a notch and help him chill the fuck out. We can't fight here in front of people. Sammy glances around the room nervously and sticks his hand out to calm the fight he senses brewing between us. If John wants me to beat myself over the head for what I did a decade ago, I won't do it. If I have a kid, I'll take care of it.

"We have no proof it's my kid."

Sammy grunts. "Don't we? You turned all red and there has to be a reason Long Island's worst party animal turned away from puking his guts out every fucking weekend."

I offer a lame excuse about the security company taking all my energy that neither my brother nor my cousin believe. John continues to fume over his spiced rum which the waitress finally brings over.

"You need to take care of this," John says to me. "Find the kid, get the truth and get the kid the fuck out of the way. We need to protect that part of New York. No one starts a business on this side of town, threatens the Vicari family and gets away with it."

Sammy snorts. "It's like we always have to remind people who we are, eh?"

"We'll do that," John mutters. "We'll fucking do that. Lucky? You sort this shit out. Got it?"

"YES, BOSS," I mutter to my brother, a plan already forming in my head to find this mystery child and the woman who I hurt all those years ago.

"Do you have any suspects for who sent this? It didn't just turn up."

"I have suspects," John mutters bitterly. "But I'll follow my leads on my own."

"Clue us in," Sammy insists. John gives him that funny look again. I wonder if this has something to do with

Sammy's side of the family. The Zagarellas and the Vicaris have been long intertwined, but that doesn't mean shit can't change. In the mob, shit can always change.

I must be wrong because John sighs and gives an equally worrisome response to Sammy's question.

"Whoever did this might be working with or otherwise affiliated with the two Murray assholes who broke away from Padraig Murray out in Boston. We don't want to fuck with the Irish."

Sammy snorts. "There was a time we used to love fucking with the Irish."

"Not these motherfuckers," John says. "If they have anything to do with this... we're in trouble and Lucky's fucking kid is in trouble too."

"Which Murray boys?" I ask him. I've met Rian and Darragh, but none of Padraig Murray's other sons.

"Padraig's nephews," John says. "Not his sons. Don't know their names or why the fuck they think Long Island is weak enough for them to take over, but we'll get that shit fucking sorted."

"Yes, sir," I mutter, finishing my seltzer and lime.

"Blackjack, anyone?" Sammy grumbles. We never finish a meeting without a round of blackjack. I grin and John's expression instantly sours. He hates losing to me, but he can't turn down a round just in case today's his lucky day instead of mine.

"Sure," John says. "One round and then you bozos get the fuck outta here and get to work."

# Chapter 3
# The Father Returns
### Althea

Chiara runs across the field with her new stick, tossing the ball to the tallest girl on the team with a swift flick of her wrist. Her legs are so long and every step she takes, I swear she'll go flying. Hm. She didn't get her height from me and she definitely didn't get her interest in this dang sport from me. Lacrosse. I never thought I would see my little black girl playing lacrosse, but she found her way onto the team and she loves it.

I don't know who or what convinced her to try out for the team, but she found a way and had me searching all over the city for lacrosse sticks and knee pads and cleats, plus watching videos about the rules all night long. If my baby wants to play lacrosse, she plays lacrosse, even if that makes me the only black lacrosse mom in the whole damn school.

Chiara's the fastest and watching her play makes me feel so fucking proud, like all the shameful shit that happened in my past is nothing because I get the joy of having her in my life — my precious baby girl. Everything I've sacrificed in my life is worth it to have her.

29

"GO CHIARA!" I scream. "You can do this!"

Adrenaline courses through me like I'm the one on the field with her. I scream again and I feel like one of those crazy ass sports dads. I have to be the mom and the dad sometimes, that's all it is.

Chiara runs to the other end of the field and catches the ball in the net of her lacrosse stick. My throat catches. I want her to make the goal. My fists clench to stop myself from screaming and making an even bigger fool of myself for my daughter.

All the parents watching cheer as Chiara sprints down the field faster than all the other girls and effortlessly flicks the lacrosse ball into the net. I cheer in the loudest, most ghetto ass way because my baby girl just scored and I am happier than a bear at a barbecue.

"THAT'S MY GIRL!"

Chiara's teammates crowd her and hug her as the referee stops the play. I pull out my phone to text my best friend Shana and my mom about Chiara's amazing goal. Unfortunately, finishing those text messages let my guard down for way too long. I hear a man clearing his throat behind me and from the annoying phlegmatic throat-clearing, I know exactly who it is.

How the fuck did he find us here?

I swing around, ready to throw hands at my ex-boyfriend Drew for showing up at another one of Chiara's games. He's one of the many crazies who hasn't stopped flocking around me since I returned to New York with my daughter to open the salon.

"Hello, sweet cheeks," Drew says. "I showed up for our daughter's game."

## The Father Returns

I broke up with Drew when we were both sixteen. Since then, I had my encounter with the Italian in the bathroom, gave birth to my daughter, left New York and came back. Drew has still been hanging around the same block, hanging onto the same bullshit that happened all those years ago.

We never even slept together because Drew couldn't exactly find where he was supposed to put it and he finished too soon. I literally explained this to him several times. His obsession with me terrifies me, but nothing terrifies me more than Lucky, so I put up with Drew always "accidentally" showing up wherever I am, convinced that the worst thing has already happened to me. Drew is a harmless stalker. That's all. There's such a thing, right?

I'm just a high school crush he can't let go of. Eventually, he'll have to face the truth. I hope that day comes today.

I screw up my face to look extra serious but I swear, nothing short of a foghorn would work to scare Drew's annoying ass off. "Drew, Chiara isn't your baby. I already told you that a thousand times."

He shrugs and sticks his arms out for a hug. "Stick to your story, baby. Whatever you have to do. But just know... you don't have to push me away."

He whispers the last part. Drew is a chronic cornball. I wrinkle my nose in disgust, hoping to chase him away. It's bad enough that my mama's obsessed with his annoying, churchy ass. I don't want him telling Chiara he's her father and confusing her. She doesn't need to know the truth about her father—at least not until she's way older and her father's finally in jail for tax evasion or however the hell mobsters get caught up these days.

"Drew, Chiara isn't your kid. She's mixed. You're black as

night and I'm dark. How the fuck could we get a kid the color of a caramel latte?"

"The Lord works in mysterious ways," Drew says. "I asked your mama to pray on both of us."

I could scream at my mom for continuing to entertain Drew, but what is she supposed to do when he shows up at her house every Sunday and offers to do the washing up? She's a black mother. Helping her with the housework is basically a shortcut into her heart. Drew manipulates her and I'm sick of it.

"Yes, the Lord works in mysterious ways, but he isn't a geneticist. He can't make two black people have a white baby."

Drew acts like he isn't listening to any of the words coming out of my mouth.

"I won't let you keep me from my daughter, Althea. I'm not a deadbeat," he says. "I'm part of your family. How long will you push me away, Althea? Don't you think Chiara needs a man in your life?"

Did this dumbass just say my daughter needs a man in *my* life? I want to smack Drew across his bulbous face.

"Drew. She's not your daughter. The game's gonna start again soon. Skedaddle."

I fold my arms and turn away from Drew so I don't have to deal with his annoying ass. Next time, I ought to pepper spray him. That's what he really deserves.

Drew ignores my commands and stands up next to me, folding his arms to watch the game as the ref starts the whistle. I want to push him onto the field so fucking badly. Gossip spread fast in our community and it was easier for me to tell people I didn't know who fathered my child than to tell the truth.

Only fast girls and hoes do shit with Italian men. These Italians don't marry black people. They don't fuck with us unless they need to use us for something. We stay on our side of the city and they stay on theirs. I never meant to have Chiara. She's a blessing, but I know her father's identity could put her in danger one day.

But maybe not today… Drew's cheering knocks me out of my train of thought as Chiara gets the ball again and sprints full throttle towards the goal. My baby girl scores again, extending her team's lead even more. When I'm about to give up on Drew's ass, my homegirl Shana finally gets to the game. I can hear her coming a mile away because Shana doesn't play about anything.

"Drew, is that your big ass head bothering my homegirl again?!"

Thank God she's here… I don't want to cause scenes at my daughter's games but Shana doesn't mind causing a scene anywhere.

Drew turns around with an unusual look of shame on his face. Shana's the one person in the world Drew fears more than anything. He gives me a stern look. "I'll be back to say hi to Chiara after practice."

"Don't bother, Drew. She's not yours."

Shana smirks, simmering in the essence of her power as Drew mumbles a greeting and then slinks away. I'm utterly relieved that he's gone. The last time I fought him at one of Chiara's games, the referee threatened to kick me out and ban me from future games. I have to keep this shit together for my daughter, you know?

"What was Dustavious Jackson doing here?" Shana says, punctuating her greeting with a loud, "GO CHIARA!"

Chiara waves to her Aunty Shana from the sidelines. She's been playing almost the entire game, so she's taking a much needed water break.

"I can't stay long," Shana says, shaking out the new sew-in I installed for her last week. She moves her head like a flamingo all day long whenever she gets a new sew-in.

Shana kisses both my cheeks, bouncing her 24-inch hair intentionally. "How are you? How's everything going with the salon? Did Roxanne finally pay her rent?"

I nod because yes, Roxanne finally paid her rent, and I didn't have to pimp her out to get money for that chair...

"It's great," I tell Shana, really meaning it. Things are going well for us. Chiara passes the ball and we both clap as another player takes it down the length of the field in a full-on sprint.

"Chiara's doing better than ever in lacrosse," I continue to my bestie. "Maybe you'll see another goal."

Shana enjoys Chiara's lacrosse games almost more than I do. She loves the idea of a black girl breaking out of traditional roles and insists I need to put Chiara in a commercial.

"Maybe," Shana says, a mischievous smile crossing her face. "See any hot single dads today?"

"There are never any hot single dads and if there are any, they're crazy."

Shana stands up straight and towers over me. She's already pretty tall and then she wears these 6-inch heels everywhere that make her even taller.

Shana puts her hands on her hips and offers wisely, "Crazy has the best dick."

"I have a daughter, Shana. I have enough crazy in my life and I can't be adding any crazy to hers."

Shana shrugs, but she won't stop smiling at me in the way she does when she knows she's going to ask me a question that I won't enjoy answering.

"Stop giving me that goofy ass look."

"If you told Drew who her daddy was, he would leave you alone," Shana says. "The truth will set you free, Althea."

Shana desperately wants to know the truth and I'm not telling her because I can't trust her. I know enough about Lucky Vicari—I found out enough about him after what happened—to know that the fewer people who know about this, the better. Telling her could put her life in danger and it's bad enough that she's come close to guessing he's in the mob several times.

"Nobody knows who her daddy is and I'm keeping it that way," I say firmly.

"Why not?" Shana whines. "What's the big deal, Althea? I told you when I fucked our history teacher. I told you when I fucked dorky Mike! I told you when I fucked my doorman. I told you when I fucked—

"Damn it, Shana. I know. You tell me every time you get dick. In detail."

"Even if it's just the tip," Shana adds seriously. "I wouldn't keep shit from you. Even if he only put the little ass tip in me, I would text you about it."

I close my eyes and sigh. Shana doesn't need to update me every time she gets dick. The nearly constant updates are frankly hard to keep track of. She could give Carrie Bradshaw a run for her money with her constant slew of dick appointments.

"The only thing anyone needs to know about Chiara's daddy is that he's crazy," I tell her, hoping to get her off my back. Shana rolls her eyes, but I can tell she's ready to give up and get back to enjoying the game. She went to a prep school in Connecticut for high school on a scholarship so she actually understands lacrosse and entirely supports Chiara "occupying the space" as she says.

"I'll beat it out of you someday," Shana says playfully, turning her attention back towards the kids on the lacrosse field. The other team looks tuckered out, which hopefully bodes well for us. Thankfully, Chiara's back on the field, distracting Shana from her questioning. I can't imagine how she would react if she knew the truth about Chiara's dad.

Shana knows about one shady underbelly of the city from her modeling work in Manhattan. She may have even come across a Vicari or two in her time working for Vogue or her year with Betsey Johnson. I don't want to risk endangering her or having her freak out and demand I assert myself when it's just better I shut up about this.

She would want me to do something crazy like go after Chiara's crazy white daddy for child support. I don't fuck with the mob. I got the money I needed that night and I left that shit behind me. I'm never going back to that world and I never want to see Lucky Vicari again. It's weird that I never forgot his name. I've been on several dates since then with a few men and I've even forgotten some of their names.

I never forgot Lucky. Isn't that weird? I guess that's trauma for you. Or something.

Chiara's team dominates the field easily. The last minutes of the game are riveting. Shana and I can't look away and we can't stop making a scene with excited screaming for Chiara.

# The Father Returns

A few parents pay Chiara hushed compliments as she steals the ball several times and makes some incredible passes that even some of the older kids couldn't make (apparently).

Chiara scores a final goal and Shana gets a text from a photographer she's meeting up with that she has a meeting ASAP all the way in Manhattan if she wants to snag a last-minute vodka ad contract. At least she didn't miss the end of the game.

I give my best friend a hug and wish her luck as she sprints to her car so she can get to the station and catch the train into the city. After saying goodbye to Shana, I catch sight of my daughter on the lacrosse field in the middle of the crowd of her friends. The game just ended and her team won. Woo!

As my eye spies my daughter, I catch notice of one person standing on the other side of the fence on the opposite end of the field.

I would recognize his face anywhere. My instincts take over and as soon as I see him, I look for my daughter. I need to get her out of here. I don't know if he's noticed us yet or if he's just looking. I duck and rush over to the field, grabbing Chiara by her hand and whispering a quick goodbye to her coach as I rush her away from the field with her gym bag in tow.

"Are we in a hurry or something?" Chiara says.

"Yes. We're in a hurry. Come on, sweetie. Get in the car. You had a great game back there."

I have to try my best to sound normal but I don't feel fucking normal. Terror courses through me and the only thing keeping me the fuck together is Chiara and my instincts to protect her first and put her life ahead of mine.

He's seen her. He knows about her. Even if I get away from here, if he suspects or knows Chiara's his... he can fuck with our lives.

The man who bought my body in a restaurant bathroom could have custody of my child. My head swims and my grasp on my daughter's hand tightens enough for her to give me a nervous look. She's never seen me freak out like this. After my "Lucky" night, I lost all sense of fear. The worst thing in the world already fucking happened to me. What else was there for me to worry about?

"Thanks," Chiara says, pulling her car door open and shoving her gym bag in. My heart won't stop pounding. A decade later and he looks the same—devilishly handsome. Looking good was never his problem. He's fucking evil.

"Get your seatbelt on, Chiara," I say nervously. My efforts to sound calm are futile and I hate that Chiara has to hear me like this. I just don't want her to figure out who's chasing us. I don't want her to know she has a mobster for a father.

My daughter fastens her seatbelt, and I kick my car into immediate motion and speed away. I don't look to see where Lucky Vicari ended up, but I hope he didn't see us and I hope he's not following me.

"Geez, mom. You're driving all crazy," Chiara calls from the backseat.

"Don't worry," I tell my daughter. "I have everything under control."

I don't have everything under control. My heart races as I pull up at the intersection and glance in my rearview mirror out of panic. I didn't escape him fast enough, and he's following me. Lucky Vicari's in a fancy fucking car and he's right behind me. My heart jumps into my throat. Our eyes lock in my rearview mirror and my neck tightens.

I try to go through all the steps to calm a panic attack but nothing works. The panic will win because it's Lucky, the man who pushed me over a bathroom sink and had his way with me like I was nothing. He's back and I don't know what the fuck he wants. If my daughter weren't in the backseat, I would have run the red light and risked it all to get away from him.

He can't touch her. Nothing can happen to her.

The light can't turn green fast enough. Chiara breaks down her game from the back seat as I try to keep my voice steady. She loves talking about game strategy. I swear this kid treats this sport like she's going pro. I glance in the rearview mirror and he's still there. At least Chiara's blissfully oblivious.

I can't lead Lucky to my house, but he's following me and I need to take Chiara somewhere she'll be safe. Mom's house. We can get to mom's house and call the police from there. The light turns green and I slam on the gas zooming through the intersection. Chiara grabs the door and squeals as my car speeds up. I can see Lucky's car behind me, but I have to stop looking. I just need to lose him.

I take a sharp right turn and then take another right after while Chiara squeals.

"Mom! Why are you driving like this?"

My daughter knows me too well. I normally drive carefully but she's seeing the side of me I had to set aside when I had my baby girl. The light up ahead turns yellow and I just know I can make it. I step on the gas. The light turns red. I'm close enough. If I can just make it through the intersection, I can escape Lucky Vicari and get the fuck out of here.

"MOM!!!" Chiara shrieks. I feel a hard impact on the driver's side of my car. I scream my daughter's name as the car spins out of my control, flying across the room as I call out to her. When the car finally stops, my head flies forward with a sharp jerk. That's the very last thing I remember about the accident.

*CHIARA… No… He can't get to Chiara.*

# Chapter 4
# My Daughter
## Lucky

Holy fuck, *my daughter*. Traffic vents around the crash. The SUV that hit Althea's car remains in the middle of the road relatively unscathed. I pull over and hurry out of my car. The driver of the SUV revs and drives off. I catch the plates. You get to my age in the mob and you can memorize plate numbers like it's fucking nothing..

I pull out my phone and text the number to John immediately. He won't understand right away but once he hears about this, he'll know what to do. Right now, I can't afford to stay panicked about the SUV hitting the car and fucking off. My daughter's in that car. I can't lose her the first day I lay eyes on her.

That kid is fucking mine, I can tell. Althea wouldn't have reacted that way if the kid weren't fucking mine. I can already hear sirens which means thankfully someone called 911. I run into the middle of the street through honking horns. I don't care what the fuck happens... I have to get to them.

Her car's a fucking mess and honestly, I don't want the

cops to get here and have anything to do with taking Althea or my daughter away from me. I glance at the car that hit them suspiciously as I approach the driver's door. Althea's slumped over the wheel, her head pressed into the airbag. Her chest moves, which is a good sign.

There's a thump from the backseat. Two hands press against the window and the most beautiful kid I've ever seen presses her face to the window next to her hands. She's even more beautiful up close than she was on the lacrosse field.

"HELPPPPPP!" She shrieks.

Her voice activates something deep and primal in me. She's my daughter. After all those fucking years, I have a daughter and this is how I meet her.

"Hold on!" The car must have child locks on it. I grab Chiara's door and nothing works. I'll have to break the window. Thankfully, I'm always ready for shit like that. I pull my pistol out of my jacket and double check the gun to make sure it's unloaded. Chiara's eyes widen as she watches me slam the base of the pistol into the car.

Sorry, kid. This isn't how you should meet your dad but… I gotta do this. I hit the window with all my might, applying several sharp blows to break the glass. Chiara wisely scoots back to the other side of her mom's sedan. Once I break the window, I gesture to her and she scrambles over, real careful not to cut herself. I pull her through the window as the sharp smell of gasoline fills the surrounding air. Chiara clings to my neck even if I'm a stranger and the biological part of me that knows my child understands exactly what to do. I hold her against me and run across the road back to my car.

The smell of gasoline isn't fucking good and Althea's still in trouble. It's Long Island, so cars don't stop for help. The sound of sirens get closer as I set Chiara on the hood of my car.

"Hey kid, you stay here. Don't move for anyone, got it? I'm going back for your mom."

She's bug-eyed with worry and she has a few minor cuts but I think the kid will be okay. Althea… What the fuck was she thinking? I just wanted to talk to her. I just wanted answers about the kid she hid from me all those years. She nearly killed herself to avoid me. My stomach tightens with guilt and I nearly get hit by a Mercedes E-class Coupe as I cross the street again back to Althea's car.

Steam or smoke or some shit like that fizzes up from Althea's car in a giant cloud. You aren't raised in 'the life' without getting really fucking good in a crisis. With a father, brothers, uncles and cousins like mine, you learn early that the only way to win is to become entirely fucking fearless. I don't want to leave Chiara across the street, but it's the only way. I fight the driver's side door open and Althea appears to be slightly conscious, but not conscious enough to fight me.

Who knows, whoever hit her could have done it on purpose. This might not have been just an accident. She groans something unintelligible as I sling her body over my shoulder. I haven't touched her in eight years and fuck, I was high back then, but the second I grab her forearm to fire-fighter carry Althea Little's body over my shoulder, our first and only night together rushes back to me. It's like the high never happened and instead of that hole in my fucking head, I have her.

At first, there's shame from the way I spoke to her, how fucking drunk and drugged out I was, and all that. Then I feel the magic, the memorable flush of desire from my hand brushing the skin of a beautiful woman, a beautiful woman I should know better than to fuck with. Her people don't fuck with my people — that's the rule of the city. Times have changed for the rest of society, but not for our people, not for Italians on Long Island.

She groans in a manner I interpret as frustrated as I race her across the street. Two cop cars pull up next to hers, searching for whoever placed the call. I open the backseat of my car and toss Althea into the back. My cousin patrols this part of the city and he's young, normally one of the first guys out. I hold my breath and cross the street again, intercepting the officer talking to an old lady who ain't making a lick of sense.

"Officer? It's Lucky Vicari. Maybe you know my cousin, Harvey?"

The officer's face brightens and I know I'm all good. I talk to the cop a little and cousin Harvey shows up. I convince him to talk to the EMTs about Althea and Chiara, and the cops and everybody else allows me to take them both away.

"What about my lacrosse stuff?" Chiara asks when I buckle her into the back seat of the car. She's pretty little and I don't have one of those kid seats, which makes me fucking nervous.

"Don't worry, sweetheart. I'll get you new lacrosse stuff," I say to her, trying to comfort her. I feel like a fucking idiot and I'm no fucking good at this dad shit at all. Chiara appears content, if not excessively quiet. She doesn't know who the fuck I am or where I'm taking her, but she doesn't ask questions. Not at first.

"Are you mommy's boyfriend?"

"Uh... no. Just a friend."

I feel like I have a fucking peach pit stuck in my throat. I don't know what questions this kid will ask next and although I don't want to lie to her, I'm not here to be her father. I'm here to keep her safe until John and I figure out what the fuck's going on here.

"Is she dead?" Chiara asks, glancing to her left at her mom's body, leaned against the car door. My stomach tightens. Almost. I came way too fucking close to losing her before I had a chance to make things right. That's what this fucking blackmail must be — a chance to make things right. I can't screw this up.

"No. Just hurt."

"Are you taking her to the hospital?"

She might be unconscious, but she doesn't look too bad. I've seen Sammy and John pull through with worse.

"No. She just needs to rest," I promise the kid.

"Oh," Chiara says, satisfied that she figured it out. "You're taking us home."

She's been through a lot and even if she's a kid and unscathed, she knows something's wrong. Chiara leans her head on the opposite car door from her mom and they both stay asleep until I drive them out to my place in Westhampton, over an hour from the site of the accident and probably ninety minutes from where Althea lives. Chiara's asleep by the time we get there. I'm glad her lacrosse game tired her out because I am not fucking ready to explain this shit to her.

I'm barely ready to explain it to her mom.

I get Chiara out of the car once we get to my place and call a couple guys out from the tennis courts to help get Althea up the stairs without me whacking her head on any of the paintings or anything. Chiara slips her hand in mine as we wait for my men to get downstairs. I don't know why she does it, or why she doesn't seem the slightest bit afraid of me. I'll have to give Althea a lecture on her mothering. Rule one, teach your kid not to trust strangers.

If she'd grown up like me, she wouldn't trust anyone.

I let the kid's hand nestle in mine so she ain't too scared. Mike and Vinnie ease Althea out of the car and carry her gently towards the house. Chiara glances at me. "She doesn't look so good."

"She just needs rest. You'll be safe here and I'll have my family nurse come in the morning."

Chiara glances at my house for the first time, taking it in with wide, curious eyes. Her eyes are the color of cinnamon and her black hair whips around her head in loose, untamed curls. She's a pretty little girl. She's mine. I can see myself in her, even if she looks so much like her mother.

"Is this a palace?"

"No."

"Where are we?"

"Long Island."

Chiara smiles. "Don't be stupid. There aren't any palaces on Long Island."

"Come see for yourself," I tell her, gesturing towards the house and leading the little girl inside. She vigorously moves forward, her curls bouncing with each step. It occurs to me that perhaps she's bold and unafraid because of my influence. She's the sort of child I was — impulsive, energetic, and inherently proud.

"What's your name?" She asks. "Sorry. My head was all fuzzy because of the accident."

Hm. She'll need a doctor tomorrow. I'll arrange that once

her mother wakes up. It's not safe for them to be out there right now, especially not after tonight.

"Lucky."

"That's a weird name," she replies.

"It's a nickname."

"I didn't ask for your nickname," Chiara snaps with a sassy little tone I can't help but feel amused by.

"Luca. Luca Vicari. But everyone calls me Lucky."

"Chiara. But I'm not telling you my last name."

Maybe she's more perceptive than I thought.

"Okay."

"I want to see my mom," Chiara says firmly.

"Okay, I'll take you there, but she needs to rest."

Chiara's bossy tone intensifies. "Once I make sure she's okay, I'll let her rest."

There are those curious eyes again. Maybe this little girl is smarter than she's letting on. Maybe she's not relaxed at all and she just wants me to think I trust her. I nod and take her upstairs to her mother's room. Vinnie and Mike have Althea sleeping in my West Wing guest suite — one of the semi-circular tower rooms overlooking the tennis court. Chiara won't stop gawking at the house as we make our way to Althea's bedroom. Once I open the door, she seems visibly relieved that her mother's in bed.

Chiara rushes to her and presses two fingers to her mom's neck. Yes. She's definitely much smarter than I expected. I don't know any kids and I definitely don't know how smart they're supposed to be. John's right to be pissed at me. I don't know what the fuck I'm doing.

"She's alive," Chiara says with relief. "You pass the test."

"Glad to hear it."

"I'm hungry, Lucky. You're the adult around here. Do you have any food?"

"Why don't we go downstairs and I'll have Vinnie and Mike get you pizza for dinner. Does that sound nice?"

They may not be the world's best babysitters, but they'll keep Chiara occupied while I tap my connections to find out who the fuck hit Althea's car and if they have anything to do with our enemies and the people stupid enough to send blackmail meant for me to John. Nobody should have known about that night at all. How the fuck did they track down Althea? How the fuck did they know about a daughter I didn't even know I had?

*I hate that this person feels close.*

Vinnie and Mike negotiate a pizza order with Chiara. She gets along easily with men twice her size and covered in tattoos, which surprises me. If she's scared, she doesn't act scared. I wonder if this is another way she's like me. Then again, perhaps not. I learned to be fearless. A younger Lucky couldn't walk to Althea's room without a bump of coke. I had no courage that I hadn't found at the bottom of a whiskey glass.

Tonight, it's just me and the powerful feelings I had ten years ago, strong enough to drive me into sobriety. I'd fucked so many times before Althea, but what I had with her wasn't fucking. What I had with Althea snapped me out of my dreamworld and brought me down to earth and the ethereal power of a woman with a beautiful body and spirit.

Touching her changed me. Touching her saved my fucking life. I don't care what it takes, I won't let anyone hurt Althea, even if it means never letting her go. Even if it means allowing her to think I'm still a monster.

# My Daughter

# Chapter 5
# The Executioner's Captive
### Althea

**P**anic surges through me as I realize I'm in a bed. My mind twirls a million possibilities in my head. He got me. He got me and he's made me his sex slave. He probably killed Chiara... and ate her. My panic goes into overdrive. I have to get out of here and get my ass to my baby girl. NOW!

The door to my prison swings open and I almost scream because my nightmare came true. The monster from a decade ago stands in the doorway with that sharp jawline and slender Italian nose. The monster with the fatally attractive stare and the soft pink lips that sucked inappropriately between my legs, forcing me to orgasm for his own pleasure. He's here.

I leap out of bed, my next instinct to rush for wherever the hell Chiara might be, and I lunge for him without thinking. I scream as loudly as possible and swing my fists at him with all the strength I wish I could have mustered years ago. I want to kill him for what he did to me. I love my baby girl, but that was not how she was meant to be brought into this world. This man robbed me and now, a decade later, he must have rammed his car into mine and captured me.

I don't remember the accident, but I know there must have been one and my body feels like hell. He grabs my fist, but I swing again, forcing my other hand free as I surprise him with my weaker hand. Lucky ducks my swing, but he doesn't hit back. Fuck him, he's a monster. I want his ass to hit back. Knowing he's the sick fuck I think he is would give me even more motivation to beat his ass.

"Stop fighting," he says calmly.

"Where's my daughter?!" I scream, my motherly instinct overwhelming even my sense for self preservation. It really doesn't matter if I survive this as long as Chiara does.

"She's safe. She's downstairs and so are you. I got you out of the accident and no one is going to hurt you."

I ball up a wad of spit in my mouth and hurl it at Lucky. It lands at his feet. A momentary flash of anger crosses his face and I smile once I realize I pissed him off. Good. I want to piss him off. I ball my hands up into fists but before I can swing at Lucky's face, he yells. This damned man has the audacity to raise his voice at me?!

"Why didn't you come find me after she was born?" He snaps, as if he's the one who has a reason to be angry about something between us.

"Fuck you, rapist."

I've waited years to say that to his face, but it doesn't feel as good as I thought it would. I have to think of another way to twist the knife in and let this motherfucker know he's a piece of shit.

"I'm not a rapist," Lucky says, his cheeks reddening. "I

paid you. I gave you more than enough money to get you out of your situation."

I want to kill him and I'm doing a bad fucking job of holding back my facial expressions. He knows how badly I hate him right now and it hurts him. Man, that feels good. I've wanted to hurt him for so fucking long.

I tell Lucky exactly what I wanted to tell him every night for years. "Don't you dare act like paying for it changes what it is. You hurt me. You used me. That's not sex, and it's sure as fuck not making love."

"People don't normally make love to hookers," he shoots back. The words still sting even after all this time.

I can tell he just wants to hurt me, but I'm not the naïve teenager he used in a restaurant bathroom. I've changed my fucking life and I can look this man in the eye and stand up for myself now. That night changed me.

"I wasn't a damn hooker," I respond, trying to sound tough instead of exposed and embarrassed, which is exactly how he made me feel an entire decade ago. "You know I wasn't a hooker. I was an innocent, stupid teenage waitress who really needed money. That money was nothing to you, but you just had to have my dignity that night."

The fire of rage within me cools with those unplanned words. I'm standing in Lucky's face saying words I never thought I could. His face doesn't twist in anger and he doesn't lunge to attack me. I feel nervous, like I've gotten away with something.

"Sorry," he says and I hate that he sounds sweet and genuine. I know this man and he's anything but sweet and genuine. He has me here for a damned reason and it ain't a good reason, my body knows that. I need to see Chiara. I need to play his psycho fucking game until he lets me see her.

Lucky's expression steels. "You kept Chiara a secret and doing that could have had her killed. Maybe you don't deserve custody of our daughter."

See? He's exactly who I thought he was. A monster. The thought of Chiara growing up away from me makes me sick. I don't know what kind of life she would have in wherever the fuck this is. It's a bedroom — and a fancy one at that — but money ain't the only thing kids need. They need love and they need parents who don't do lines of cocaine in small Italian restaurants.

"What's your fucking point?"

"Your actions nearly endangered Chiara. I brought you here because there have been threats on her life and someone nearly carried them out. This is your fault for keeping her from me. If I hadn't showed up today… our daughter would be dead."

His words cut. He's calling me a negligent mother without saying the words out loud. The attack feels cheap and cruel.

Dead? Chiara? Who the hell would want to hurt Chiara and how the fuck would that be my fault and not his? He's the one involved with killers. I don't know any monsters except for him.

"My fault? I don't know anyone who would threaten my daughter's life because I'm not a fucking thug," I say to him. Lucky might be a thug, but it's painful how much he doesn't look like one. His eyes are an intense blue-green color and he has features that would draw any woman's attention across a room.

I was never foolish enough to fall for his looks. When I saw him in that restaurant, I knew he was trouble. Getting that close to Lucky was a choice born out of desperation. I'm immune to him and his tricks. Whatever he wants with me in this stupid house, I'll give it to him and then get the fuck away.

"I'm not a thug," he says, his voice getting low and dangerous. "You know who I am. You must have figured it out by now or you would have come looking for money the way all of your type do."

"My type?"

An entire decade later and he's still a fucking asshole.

"The gold digger type."

"Fuck you," I spit. I don't know why he's being such a dick, but I hate him so badly I want to push him down a flight of stairs. I'd do it too if I had a flight of stairs to push him down.

"You can see Chiara if you agree to my rules," Lucky says.

His arrogance and entitlement send rage coursing through me. Who the fuck does this man think he is? He's just a gangster, not a god. I don't have to listen to his ass and he doesn't get to tell me if I can see my daughter or not. There was an accident, a police presence and there's always Shana. We can't just disappear. People will find us. Even my mama will realize I'm missing eventually when she glances up from her small town romance novels.

"You can get a charge for kidnapping for what you've done," I snap. "Give me my daughter and I'll do what I've done her whole fucking life, keep her safe. Send us back to my place, my neighborhood and we'll keep ourselves safe."

Lucky completely ignores my demands to leave his house.

Judging by the size of this bedroom, his mansion must be huge. That doesn't stop a place from being a prison. I don't want to be trapped in some creepy rich mobster's house. Lucky broods for a few minutes before answering me or answering the conversation he's having in his head. I can't tell which.

"That's my fault then?" He growls. "That you've done it alone? I would have been there for Chiara. She's my blood and I would have been there."

The way he says her name sends a weird sensation through me. I wanted to give her an Italian name since I thought it would be the only connection my daughter would have with her heritage. Lucky sounds fiercely possessive and his eyes harden in a way that makes his face look way more handsome than even seems fair. His good looks are an absolute act of cruelty because he has the worst fucking attitude and somehow even worse morals.

I can't believe him. He's a career criminal which makes him a liar and a manipulator. Not like it's relevant now, but I also know he's some type of sex freak. I can't let my guard down around Lucky Vicari. My body stiffens as I prepare for verbal warfare.

"You're a liar. If you knew about her now down to the damn GPS coordinates, you could have found out any time. You didn't want to know you had a daughter."

"I wasn't looking," he says. "I swear, I didn't know. Now stop pestering me with the past and agree to my terms. Six weeks and I'll find out who sent the threats, I'll stop them, and you can leave."

So much for verbal warfare. I hate how he easily dismisses me and acts like there's a chance in hell I'll let him keep me prisoner in this damn place. I don't care if there's an incredible view which I just noticed from the bedroom window. I'm going home.

"I can't spend six weeks here. I have clients to braid. Shana has a runway show for Lilly Pulitzer in Miami in six months. Chiara has lacrosse practice. I have shit to do."

Lucky looks completely bored at my list of responsibilities.

"None of that matters more than your life," Lucky says imperiously. He talks like a man used to being in charge of everyone. So basically, an asshole. I don't like that he thinks he can command us to halt our lives for him. But there's something caring in his voice that gives me pause.

"Why are you doing this? Seriously. Did you hit my car and what the fuck is going on? You give me one hint of the truth and maybe I'll agree to your stupid terms."

"I didn't hit you. I saved you and got a family member of mine to approve taking you away. I didn't want whoever hurt you to come back with another car and possibly bullets. I didn't want to leave Chiara alone. I brought you here to keep you safe, I swear."

I search his face for signs of lying.

"Swear on something big."

"I swear on Jesus Christ's name," Lucky says.

He seems serious, but I don't allow my facial expressions to relent to him. He's still terrifying, but he doesn't look like he aged much since that night in the bathroom. He looks like he's been clean and sober. There's meat on his bones and muscles. Lots of thick, bulging muscles.

"I'm telling the truth. Once I received the threats, I wanted to find you to warn you. I didn't know they would strike so soon. Now that they have, I can't let you out there. My life would be over if anything happened to my daughter."

That sends another weird jolt through me. My daughter? He barely knows Chiara. Even if he's had her downstairs for hours, he wasn't there when I gave birth to her. He wasn't there for her first steps, her first words, her first cuss words... any of that. But I can tell something from looking at her that nobody could fool me about. This man cares about her. For some fucking reason, this monster genuinely cares about Chiara. I didn't know mobsters had hearts for their bastard kids.

"Okay. I believe you," I respond tentatively. "I think. Will you let me call people? Go anywhere?"

"Friends and visitors must pass through security, but I can't allow you to leave on your own."

"We're trapped then?"

This man has problems. He can't kidnap American citizens and keep them in his home just because of some danger he can't show me any proof of. Lucky grins. He has a cute smile, but that doesn't make up because he's an annoying psycho who thinks I'm going to chill out in his damn house with my daughter for no discernible reason.

"It's a thirty-thousand square foot home with a pool and a tennis court. I hope I can keep you entertained."

What the fuck? I thought Lucky was a broke ass thug, and that this was a hotel room or something. I hadn't looked out the shaded windows or set foot out of the room. If he's serious, he must be rich as hell.

"Okay." I give a simple answer because I need time to think. I take a step back from him deeper into the bedroom. "Is that it? Are those all your terms?"

Lucky's face turns red, and he hesitates before slowly running his tongue over his lips.

"On rare occasion, I want what I wanted before," he whispers. He sounds embarrassed, but not too embarrassed to keep the question locked away.

"I told you I'm not a hooker," I say sharply.

"I know," he says. "But I'm very fucking lonely and I'm willing to pay. And if you're lonely too... We could both benefit."

He's twisted. I knew that the second I ran from that bathroom in tears.

"THAT'S IT?" I tell him. "Those are your terms?" I'm quaking with rage. How dare he ask this?

LUCKY NODS. What the fuck does he want me to say to those terms? *What the hell does he expect?*

# Chapter 6
# I'm The Fucking Bad Guy
## Lucky

I'm a fucking idiot. John would definitely agree. I just can't help myself with her. I try to be the good guy, but I'm always the fucking bad guy.

She agrees to all of my terms except the one I want the most. My foolish arrogance will get me in trouble again, my lust for her will ruin everything. She doesn't know how fucked up I am. She doesn't know that before I walked into that restaurant, I watched her for weeks. She doesn't know how I thought about her. She doesn't know how badly I wanted to ask her out. That simply wasn't something you did publicly ten years ago.

Italians don't date blacks. It's not just the law of the jungle, it's the rule of my family and our people. I was already fucking with my family's honor by abusing drugs and alcohol, making a fool of myself while my father begged me to settle down and take control of the business he gifted me on my eighteenth birthday.

I went in that night and had my way with her because I

59

was young, drunk, high, rich as fuck and I knew I could buy any woman I wanted. Back then, I behaved like a fucking coward. Tonight, that same demon comes back to haunt me. She was the most beautiful waitress on Long Island. I had to have her, and I did—I emptied my fucking wallet for a chance with a waitress I watched for a few weeks. I sunk lower than I ever had before and I almost thought it was worth it because of how fucking good it felt. There's something so fucking blissful about pure unadulterated hedonism. There's something even better about touching a woman you aren't supposed to have and you definitely aren't supposed to want more than anything in the fucking world.

I didn't mean to bring a child into the world or do anything other than satisfy my desires. I was selfish. It hurt like fuck to accept I was a monster, that she had no desire for me, that she ran from the room hiding her face in shame while my seed spilled out of her.

My stomach tightens with guilt. I ruined her. While my memories of that night involve change and transformation, for Althea, all I invoke is pure terror. She reminds me of what a monster I was and how easy it is for us monsters to romanticize ourselves. As Althea rejects one of my terms, she implements another more painful condition on her protection.

Chiara can't know who I am.

Althea isn't trying to be cruel. She wants to protect her daughter. That's all it is, but she doesn't know what the fuck she's asking me. From the second I laid eyes on that little girl, I knew she was mine. From the second I heard she was out there, I loved her... I know I hurt her mom, but there's a kid in the picture. It's time to make my foolish past right.

There was one other concession.

I knock on Althea's door early in the morning. Chiara's downstairs with Vinnie who stopped by early to cook her breakfast. This is the last time I'm letting them leave the house, but Althea won't budge until I let this happen. It's for Chiara. That tugs on my heartstrings a bit, I won't lie, so I agree.

"Lacrosse game, let's go!" I call out to Althea through the door, who I can hear shuffling behind the door in her bedroom. She mutters a few words (most likely swear words by her tone) and flings the door open in frustration.

"It's early," she grumbles with a yawn. How is it possible for her to look this fucking hot when she just rolled out of bed? I reposition my legs to hide my growing arousal. My dick chooses the wrong time to act like I'm a fucking teenager again.

"One last lacrosse game before your vacation," I tell her with a warm smile to meet her grouchy expression. "Chiara's downstairs getting breakfast."

Althea's scowl deepens intensely, and she gives me a disgusted look, like I'm worth less than shit. What the fuck did I do wrong? The kid needs to eat and I'm her fucking dad.

Althea doesn't see it that way. She prattles on, upset, "You woke her up? When did you go into her room? Let me see her. I don't need you going anywhere near her."

She still hasn't seen Chiara since last night. No particular reason for that rule except to teach her the tiniest smidge of a lesson. Althea keeps me from Chiara for years but can't handle a night without our daughter... How the fuck does she think I feel?

I'll never get that time back and all the money in the

world can't help. She grew up without a father and I'll have to live with the guilt of never having been there for her. Althea won't ever give me a second chance. She clams up or gets pissed off the second I come near her. It feels good to get one up on her for a fucking change.

She catches a whiff of my pleasure and hits me in the stomach. Hard.

"Get out of my way. I want to see her."

"Fine, fine. You can see her. I got a call from the shop, they'll have your car fixed up in a couple months but you must have shitty insurance 'cause it's going to cost you five thousand dollars."

"A couple months!? Five thousand dollars? I don't have five thousand dollars."

She glances at me and then quickly glances away. I don't know why the fuck she's worried about a car or a bit of money. Holding onto her forearm, I look her dead in the eyes so she knows I'm fucking serious.

"Whoever hit you wanted to kill you, Althea. I'm serious, you're in trouble."

She wrestles her forearm away from me, ending the blissful moments of contact between us.

"Whatever. I don't know what type of bullshit you're involved in but you keep it away from my daughter. Let her go to this lacrosse game and we'll tell her your stupid vacation story to keep this shit under wraps. I'm going to need some proof though."

"Was nearly losing your life in a car crash not significant enough proof?" I grumble.

"Nearly lost my life and you haven't called a doctor? I'm a

little bruised, but I'm fine. Hit and runs happen all the time. I need concrete proof."

"Fine," I mutter. "I'll get it to you."

"Good. This game is important to Chiara. She's worked hard on the team."

I want to know everything about her, but I don't want to scare Althea off or push her away. I've already taken too many fucking risks with her.

"Is she any good?" I ask. I never played lacrosse, but before working for my dad, I played basketball, a little baseball… lots of football.

Althea rolls her eyes. "Not like it's any of your business, but she's great. The team can't function without her. I don't want anyone getting suspicious if she misses a game, and she deserves to have this before you keep us locked up in here."

She pushes past me and struts towards the stairs like she owns the place. Locked up here? It's a mansion, not a fucking prison. Althea doesn't appear to be impressed.

I watch her leave curiously. A decade ago, I remember a woman trembling in fear as I slid inside her warmth. This woman ain't scared of shit. She doesn't act like she fears me at least. Althea calls out Chiara's name and runs towards her in the kitchen.

Running? It's a bit dramatic. I follow her downstairs. Why the fuck do I find it so hard to talk to her when I'm not laying down rules or commanding her around? She'll never want me to be a dad to Chiara if I can't soften up my edges. I want to keep them safe, not drive them away from me forever.

Althea has Chiara squeezed in a tight hug as Vinnie makes some fresh-squeezed orange juice for both of them.

"Are you sure you don't want the doctor to come by before the game?" I ask Althea.

"Chiara? Do you feel okay? Do you still want to play?"

"Uh huh. Uncle Lucky told me it was fine."

"Uncle?" Althea squeaks. Listen, I did not tell the kid to call me uncle. Althea glares at me like she just found out I shit in her cereal.

"I didn't tell her to call me that."

"They're my adopted uncles," Chiara says proudly. "Uncle Vinnie and Uncle Lucky. Duh."

"I see. Well honey, he ain't your uncle so don't call him that. Do you want to run some drills this morning?"

"Uncle Lucky already ran drills with me."

Now Althea looks like she's going to kill me for real.

"Hey, kid, why don't you finish your breakfast in front of the TV."

"She will not be doing that," Althea says sharply. "Chiara, stay right there, okay? I'll have some breakfast too."

"Will you?" I mutter.

"Yes," Althea says. "Uncle Lucky's making me breakfast."

Chiara giggles and offers her mom a piece of bacon. Vinnie glances at me like he's awaiting further instructions. I dunno what to tell him. I'd better take over in the kitchen. If making fucking breakfast is what it'll take to make Althea see I'm a different person. If saving her life ain't enough, I'll make some eggs and bacon.

AFTER BREAKFAST, Althea gets Chiara ready for the game with a shower, her uniform and her hair done in a high ponytail with a long braid that nearly hits the middle of Chiara's back. Her hair reminds me of my Italian cousins' hair, straight from the motherland. There's a bit of kinky, thick texture to her curls too, but that wild free hair makes me think of Italy. My little girl's Italian…

We get to the lacrosse field and Chiara joins her team. Althea guides me to her favorite spot on the sidelines. Eyes are on both of us and I assume Althea doesn't notice but once we situate ourselves, she chuckles. "The moms at this school love them some gossip. I'll have to kill rumors that I'm dating a mobster all weekend."

"A mobster?" I mutter. What the fuck does she mean by that? Althea must've guessed more about me than I realized. Maybe we're just that notorious around here. I don't know what to think about it.

"Whatever you people call yourselves," she responds harshly.

"Great."

My collar feels hot. I'm not any good at this dad thing. Should I be cheering for the kid yet? Althea glances at me and snorts. "If I didn't know better, I'd say you were nervous."

"There's someone trying to kill you and my daughter and you want to stand in an open field all morning."

"It's a quick game," she says. "Then we'll go back to your ridiculously excessive mansion prison."

"Excessive? Most women are impressed by a $1.8 million Westhampton home."

"A man who didn't attract assassins would impress me far more. My daughter and I have nothing to do with you. Why the hell would someone threaten to kill us? I didn't come

65

looking for you, Lucky and I didn't come looking for your money."

I wish she had. I fucking wish she had because I would have stepped up for my daughter. She made that threat ten years ago and fuck, I wish she followed through with it. I missed so much of my daughter's life and I'll never get rid of the guilt. It's bad enough I carry around all the people I killed. The hearts I broke make my outcome at St. Peter's gates seem pretty fucking grim.

I must've broken my daughter's heart a million times just by missing out. There's no way in hell I'll keep screwing this up.

"When people want to hurt you, they go for the people you care about," I remind her. She has to know that I care about her too. She looked after Chiara for ten years and never came for a fucking dime. She was too proud and too good at her job to need someone else. Fuck, it must be hard to be that independent. I want to reach her, but Althea's a million fucking miles away from me.

Her response is too quick and it stings deep. "You don't care about some chick you raped at Il Pappa's eight years ago. Don't be ridiculous."

How can she be so cold about what happened? Did I do that to her? That's how she sees it then. Rape. My hands feel cold and clammy. There's so much guilt for what I did for her and nowhere to fucking put it. I thought money would be enough. I thought money and paying for it could make her want me. Young, dumb, and too fucking rich for my own good.

I was so fucking stupid. She's right to think I'm a monster. If Althea wants me to feel deep, unyielding shame, she's done it successfully. My face probably can't hide a thing.

Is there any fucking chance I can make up for being the type of man who would buy another human being's body? I don't want her to think I'm a monster, but nothing I say seems right. It's bad enough that I don't know how to talk to chicks like her… They're off limits in New York unless you want a bunch of crazy gangbangers putting holes in your walls for messing around their sisters.

You stick with your own kind if you want to survive in New York. I don't know when I stopped caring about my survival, but it was a long fucking time ago. I just want to live now, experience every raw fucking moment of life. I want the pain. I want the pleasure. I want all of it.

"I care about Chiara," I say to her with the purest honesty. "If I'd known about her, I'd have done right by her. I swear. I know I was a piece of shit, believe me. I know I hurt you. But Althea… I thought about you every fucking day. I got clean because of that night."

"I'm glad I could be a sacrifice on the altar of your personal growth," she quips.

Althea's the type of chick to always have a smart fucking answer, isn't she? I'm always going to feel so fucking dumb and tongue-tied around her.

"Yeah, well. I thought about you. I'm looking after you now and… I'm sorry."

She raises her eyebrows at the word "sorry", but she says nothing. I'm sorry about hurting her, but I'm definitely not sorry about Chiara. I love this little girl and I hope Althea can see that. You can't fake this shit. You can't fake this feeling.

The game starts. Althea doesn't respond to my apology,

and the game starts after a few moments of her silent contemplation. I watch Chiara race onto the field and Althea cheers loudly for our little girl.

She's right—Chiara's damned good. Our daughter is the fastest girl on the team and she has skills with the stick too. Damn. Althea said she was good, but she didn't mention Chiara was fucking amazing. Who knew kids' sports could be this much fucking fun? All the kids are enjoying the crap outta themselves, especially my girl. She fears nothing and my chest swells with unimpeachable fatherly pride.

I almost can't stop watching her, even with no scoring and with the other kids fumbling miserably when it's their turn to hold the ball. Althea's answer knocks me out of the game.

"You caused someone to come after us. So technically, you're not looking after us," Althea says after several minutes of saying nothing at all. "If anyone's after us at all, this is your fault, your problem, your thug life coming to fuck with me."

"Not exactly," I mumble. This isn't just personal to me, it's about my family. If there's a problem with the Murray family, the entire Northeast could go up in smoke. They keep Boston running smoothly — an enormous band of hulking Irish fuck ups — and they keep the scumbags from running here and causing problems for us. They clean up their streets, we clean up ours, and every so often, we do business.

Murray rebels tearing up Long Island could fuck with a decades-old alliance. We had to put the past behind us for a reason. At some point, it's not about the cops or the money. When too many of our brothers and sons and fathers and uncles die, we lose the most important part of cosa nostra —family.

I don't want to believe the Murrays could sink that low—even the Murray boys out of favor with Padraig. The Irish have powerful clans in Boston and the Northeast, and they stick to their own kind. They understand the importance of family.

Why threaten Althea? That part feels personal and too close for comfort. John has suspicions, but he won't say any names until he has answers.

"It's complicated," I mutter to Althea, fighting the urge to confide in her. "Our family attracts a lot of enemies and sometimes the people closest to you are the ones you have to worry about the most…"

If there's a member of our family involved in this shit, John could lose Long Island, we could have another war. New York gets dangerous when the mob can't hold the peace. Althea doesn't give a crap about all that and forget confiding in her.

"I don't want to hear about your mob problems," Althea says huffily. "I just want you to promise that we'll be safe. Promise Chiara will be safe."

She's right, of course. I can leave getting answers to John. I owe Althea and my daughter their safety. As long as I follow John's commands, he'll take care of them, no matter what happens to me.

"Of course she'll be safe," I mutter. "Always. She's my family."

Althea's suspicious look gives for a moment but then the walls between us spring up again and she pulls away from me. I can't smell her perfume anymore and holy fuck, I want to live inside the scent. I want to get close to her again.

"She's my everything, Lucky," Althea says sternly. "Got it?"

"Yeah."

"Good."

"Is there anything I can do to change things with us?" I murmur. Althea looks pretty standing out here. I won't deny having ideas about how I want to change things.

"You offered me money for sex last night," Althea hisses disapprovingly. "You're still scum, Lucky. You might care about Chiara, but you're still scum."

She's right. I'm a fucking dirtbag and I can't explain myself. Maybe if I explain how this all got started, that would help. Feelings don't come naturally in my line of work. You learn to bury them, to suppress them, to hide them all in liquor or drugs. We don't mind liquor but drugs will fuck with your mind and drug addicts are the scum of the earth in the mob. Scum.

Hearing her say that word reminds me of how far I fell and how fucking hard I'll have to work to earn her trust again and maybe even earn her heart if I'm lucky.

"I'm sorry, Althea."

"Really? You didn't seem sorry last night. You seemed... desperate."

Ouch. This woman really doesn't hold her tongue.

"It's been ten years for me," I grumble. "Ten fucking years."

"Ten years? So... that night."

"Yeah," I mutter, shifting uncomfortably because having this conversation and allowing even the tiniest part of my mind to return to the night I first touched Althea gets me rock fucking hard.

"Neither have I," she says. "But at least I can keep it in my pants."

"So can I," I grumble. "I can definitely keep it in my pants."

FUCK, I hate trying to be the good guy sometimes. *I want her so fucking bad.*

# Chapter 7
# Broken Glass
## Althea

I watch Lucky watch the game out of the corner of my eye. I've seen hundreds of Chiara's games and it doesn't make me a terrible mom if I lose focus, especially since my survival's at stake here. I don't trust Lucky. His devilish eyes make me want to trust him and his looks have never been an issue. He's fucking hot, I'll say it. But that doesn't mean he doesn't have just a glimmer of Satan in him.

He was hot at the lowest point of his addiction, but he's even more attractive now that he's healthy and standing outside in the sunlight where I can look at him. His skin was made for the sun. It's a gentle olive color and his hair brushes his pale neck with thick brown curls.

Lucky has tattoos everywhere and the moms staring at us will definitely notice how tatted up he is. He looks more like a gangster than a typical Long Island dad. Knowing people around here, they're probably already whispering rumors about who he is or what he does. The last name would be a dead giveaway, but thankfully there's no way for them to find that out just by staring.

Lucky gives me a suspicious look, and I pretend to be intently engaged with my cellphone. The way Lucky's biceps bulge out of his shirt and the black ink swirls around his musculature with artistic beauty... ugh. Why the fuck did I tell him I hadn't had sex in a decade? What the hell about a handsome man with magnificent hair and better biceps makes you volunteer all types of stupid ass information?

I text Shana the updated score to Chiara's game and search Lucky for signs of deception, trickery or anything else. There's nothing. Outside of his addiction, outside of the fucked up thing he did to me... If I knew nothing about him except what I saw in front of me, I would say he was a totally normal guy who happened to look just a bit thuggish.

It should scare me that he looks normal. I know that he isn't. Lucky Vicari might try to keep us safe for now, but he's still dangerous, and it's still my job to keep my daughter safe.

Near the end of the game, Chiara's on the field again, but she looks exhausted. Her team is down three points and the other kids on the team just aren't doing enough to support her. One kid can't carry the entire team and I know my baby. She's not at her best and I can tell she's struggling to keep up for the sake of the other girls. Lucky grunts and leans in to whisper to me, "She's carrying the whole fucking team."

Apparently white men come with an intuitive under-standing of lacrosse. I'm surprised he has any damn idea what's happening since it took me ages to understand this game—a hell of a lot longer than it took Chiara.

When he leans in, he smells delicious. I've never actually

smelled a man that good before. I fight the urge to grab onto his shirt and press my face in it.

"Uh huh," I manage, despite a strange weakness at the knees. Chiara lunges forward to pass as I utter the words and she trips. Hard. She goes flying into the air, losing the lacrosse stick and one of her shoes as she lands face first on the grass with a hard thud. Fuck. Before I can drop my bag in Lucky's arms and race onto the field, he's gone. He's by her side before I even step over the white line and he's yelling at everyone. Loudly.

Oh my fucking God. I don't even care about what the other moms will think because I'm convinced his shouting will scare anyone away from calling an ambulance. Chiara's groaning loudly on the ground as I struggle through the quickly assembled crowd to get to her. Lucky yells at everyone to back off and then pulls his cellphone out himself. I hope to God his Italian ass is calling the police...

When I finally burst through the crowd, I get to Chiara's side and my stomach sinks. She's unconscious and holy fuck, this looks bad. My fears of losing her escalate and I want to be that mom who is good in a crisis, but Chiara's my everything and the thought of losing her, the little girl who saved me from the event I thought would ruin my life... I can't handle it.

"CHIARA BABY, WAKE UP!"

I'm not self-aware enough to realize that I'll be embarrassed by how loudly I'm yelling and getting on later on when this all dies down. I just want her awake. I scream her name again and Lucky covers his ears.

"Calm down, Althea. She's fine. It's just a bad fall and—

"Can you shut up?" I snap. Before I can tear into Lucky,

the team's EMTs finally drag their raggedy asses over to Chiara. I tell them off when Lucky clamps his hand over my mouth rudely and suggests I let them do their job. What the fuck? Who does he think he is putting his hand over my mouth and trying to silence me...

I whip around to give Lucky a piece of my mind when Chiara makes an audible sound. She calls for me.

"Mommy! I want mommy!"

Her voice comes out raspy, but it's still loud enough to get to me. My heart pumps aggressively.

"BABY!" I shriek, forgetting Lucky's entire existence. "I'm right here."

Lucky crouches down and holds Chiara's hand gently. She smiles when he touches her, and my heart does something funny and forbidden and totally fucking weird. I push the thought out of mind. I don't want to make a scene, so I let him keep holding her even as I silently seethe that he would be so bold.

He's not really her father. I don't want to indulge in that fantasy for a damn second. He's a mobster, a playboy, and he hurt me. Lucky doesn't love her the way I do. He can't. This monster can't possibly feel what I feel for our little girl. I don't want to look at the evidence and entertain the idea that I might be wrong for even a second. She's my daughter, not ours. We share nothing but one fucked up night—that's it.

It's a mess for the next twenty minutes. Chiara has a concussion, her team loses the game, and Lucky's paranoia mounts the more time we spend in public. Does he really think we're in that much danger?

We take Chiara home with strict instructions for her to rest for six weeks. Great. At least I can use that excuse when she asks why we're still at Uncle Lucky's house. My skin crawls whenever I hear her calling him that. It's guilt, fear and all my emotions about Lucky and my daughter mixed into one. I thought I'd never see him again, honestly. Foolishly, I believed we could get away and forget every damned thing about that night.

All I ever wanted was to keep my daughter safe.

Every day, I fear her asking for the truth or finding it out some other way. I don't want her to find out about Lucky and risk getting attached to some asshole who does drugs and probably won't stick around.

It's not her fault I agreed to sleep with him all those years ago. She doesn't need a deadbeat dad in her life. Today at least, he didn't act at all like a deadbeat. He acted like someone who cared.

Once we get home, I put Chiara to bed. Her head really hurts, and she doesn't have much energy left, even if it's only shortly after noon. Lucky lingers in his kitchen noncommittally, certain that I'll return eventually to search for food. He's right, of course. Chiara's accident slowed down my hunt for treats at the lacrosse game snack table. Some of those moms can throw down one hell of a cookie.

"Hey, how's the kid?" Lucky asks.

My stomach does that little flip again. He always asks about her. He always cares. It's weird. I guess I don't know him at all, so it's strange that we share this thing with Chiara and it's strange that he cares about her when he doesn't know either of us. It's just about her, I remind myself. That care doesn't extend to me.

"Sleeping. Tough game today."

"She played great. Need water?"

"I guess."

Lucky fills a glass from his fridge and grins at me. "Come and get it."

"I should have known there was a catch."

I walk for the water and Lucky keeps smiling until he hands it to me. I screw up my face when I take it.

"Did you poison this?"

"No. You just totally lost your shit today, and it's fun to know you're the type of mom who loses your shit. I'm curious. I want to know more about you."

I don't want to play Lucky's mind game. It's bad enough he has my paranoid ass convinced I need to stay in this mansion with him to stay safe. Getting any ideas about him and his feelings toward me could only be a mistake.

"What type of dad are you then?" I grumble, a million insults flooding into my mind.

"A new dad. When I'm sure you're safe… if you wanted… you two could stay. No pressure. I figure I've been absent the past ten years, I could take a load off for you."

I snort. "Are you fucking crazy? You don't know me."

The only reason I don't have work in the morning is because I finally transitioned out of a hairdressing role into just managing the salon. Aside from collecting rent from my chairs and taking private clients, I don't work crazy hours anymore. I army-crawled and dragged my ass over the coals to get this damned comfortable and I don't need Lucky waltzing into my life and telling me what to do. I'm ready to fight.

Lucky, apparently oblivious to my mounting rage continues, "I know you ain't a junkie or a criminal. I know you've done a damned good job with our daughter."

Fuck. There goes my resolve to hate him permanently and to think that he's the worst fucking person ever. I hate that he says that. It's like the one thing every single mom wants to hear, seriously. It's so fucking hard and there are so many things you seem to always get wrong that you just want one damned person to tell you that you're doing a damned good job.

Act cool, Althea.

"Yeah. Cool," I mumble, sounding ditsy instead of aloof. Fuck. Why do I always make a fool of myself in front of him? I keep trying to act like I ain't scared of shit and I can handle myself but the truth is… Lucky scares the ever living crap out of me.

"I'm serious," he says, closing the distance between us. I hate feeling him so close and I hate noticing his delicious fucking cologne again. A dirty tingle shoots straight down my thighs and what was initially guilt turns into full-blown self-loathing.

"Thanks," I whisper, my voice hoarse and sounding desperately dry. I should really drink that water. Lucky takes a step closer to me and I move back. The water sloshes and gets my hand slippery. I drop the glass. Shit. Water drenches Lucky's pants and my shirt on the way down. The glass shatters on the ground between us and the heat of humiliation courses through me.

I couldn't have picked a worse time to be a klutz. Lucky steps over the puddle of water and sticks his arms out. "Stop right there. I've got this. Don't need you getting glass in your foot."

"Lucky, I'm fine. Let me clean it up."

"Nope. No way."

I try to get past him and he darts into my way, forcing me to land against his broad, excessively muscular chest. Damn. That felt like running into a brick wall. I scowl and try to take a step away from him. Lucky takes a step toward me, forcing me to take another one back. There's a counter behind me and Lucky's body traps me against the counter. My heart quickens.

Even after all this time my body knows getting this close to Lucky Vicari ends in danger. But he won't move and he won't take those cold, dangerous eyes off me. Where am I in greater danger? Out of Lucky's grasp, or twisted in his web?

"Your shirt's really wet," he says. "Let me help you get it off."

"I won't stand shirtless in your kitchen," I protest. My voice sounds weak and we both know it. Lucky knows exactly what I'm going through. That's the problem right now. We both know the pain of abstaining from the one thing other humans long for most.

"Okay," Lucky says. "Then get up on the counter. I'll bring you a shirt."

He doesn't wait for me to respond. Lucky grabs my hips and I bite my tongue to avoid blurting out how inappropriate it is. He sets me up on the counter after lifting me like I'm weightless. A man hasn't handled me like that anywhere but my dreams.

I bite down on my lips and tell myself to fight back as Lucky reaches for my shirt and takes it off. Instead, my stupid body responds by willingly raising my arms over my head and giving Lucky the easiest access possible to taking my top off. I don't want him to think I'm a hooker. I hate knowing he'll always see me that way.

When he has my shirt off, Lucky smiles. He has an odd, mysterious smile like he's laughing at something you couldn't possibly understand even if he tried to explain it to you. Lucky runs his tongue over his lips and doesn't hesitate to check me out.

"I always liked seeing a black woman's boobs," he says. Then he runs his thumb boldly over my bra, his finger swiping over my nipples. "I like the lace."

Heat gushes between my legs, and my cheeks warm up instantly. What. The. Fuck. I can never predict the words that will come out of this man's mouth. I can never let myself forget how Lucky talked to me when he had me bent over the sink in the Il Pappa's restroom. He had the dirtiest tongue and talked the filthiest race talk. I never heard a man say all the things he liked about black women and get all specific like that.

Lucky doesn't look like the type either. He doesn't have a fake ass white rapper persona or anything like that. He's a clean cut, extremely attractive Italian American with warm olive skin, oceanic eyes and dark, lush hair. I've never even seen a guy like him with a black woman on his arm. Maybe it's sad to some people, but to me, it's just honest. Guys like Lucky don't look twice at women who look like me and they definitely don't stare at our chests like that.

"Take the bra off," Lucky commands. My stomach lurches. He told me he was getting me a shirt and nowhere in that awkward verbal contract did anyone mention anything about removing my bra. It's bad enough that it's lace and my nipples are sticking out getting rock hard in Lucky's excessively breezy kitchen.

"Are you crazy? I just got my shirt wet."

His demands are untempered by my reluctance. Lucky's body stiffens, and he commands me again. "Take the bra off, Althea. It's wet."

"It's not that wet."

Lucky spreads my legs open and stands between my thighs. Even if I wanted to scramble off the counter and run away from him, there would be no way for me to push the massive mobster away from me. He's much too large and much too strong to resist. I can feel just how muscular he is as he stands between my thighs.

"I'll get the clasp for you," Lucky says, and he reaches behind me, pressing his warm delicious smelling body over mine as he unhooks my bra boldly, without caring for permission. Lucky wants to see tits, he gets tits. He shudders as he pulls away from me holding my lace bra in his hand like a trophy.

He runs his tongue over his lower lips slowly and then presses my lace bra to his nose, inhaling deeply. He's fucking crazy. I knew that years ago when I first had the misfortune of stumbling into him at work. This is different. He tracked me down. He found me and Chiara and he still wants this from me. Sex.

"It's not what you think," he murmurs, setting my bra and shirt on the counter beside me. He kisses my forehead, practically pinning me in pace with his hips.

"I want to make up for what I did. I want to taste your cunt."

I tell myself that he's been a good father today and even if he hasn't done much, for today he did well for Chiara and that deserves a reward. I tell myself there's a completely unselfish reason for wanting to say yes to a maniac's tongue between my legs.

There are a million reasons this is a bad fucking idea but I can't remember any of them. I just want to feel more than Lucky's insanely firm hands on my thighs.

"We can't do that," I muster, with the last shred of dignity inside me.

"Why not?"

"I don't want to fuck you to earn your love or your respect. I don't want to do this to give you a sense of power over me. So we can't... Because you're the guy who bought my body and I'm... your victim."

It sounds strange acknowledging that I'm his victim while Lucky presses his weight between my legs. His throat tightens and makes a strange, nervous movement like the words that came out of my mouth finally got to him. His brows furrow for a moment but the mobster quickly regains control.

He pushes his tongue into the front of his mouth, and then sighs.

"I want to eat your cunt because it's been years since you had an orgasm. We have a kid together. We've been very chaste for a long time. I'm done with that now. You should be done with that too. Stop punishing yourself, Althea. What happened back then was my fault. Give me a fucking chance."

No. That's my first reaction to what he says because I don't want to believe that somehow, in this fucked up situation, Lucky admits he did something wrong. Men don't do that, especially not men like Lucky who can make men tremble just from hearing their name.

"Shut up."

I don't need him to lie to get into my pants. I'd prefer if he didn't lie at all, funny thing. I want the real Lucky, if there's even a real Lucky beneath the mafia bravado, the tough guy ink etched all over his skin, and behind those terrifyingly blue eyes.

Lucky gives me an expression that feels real and feels warm.

"I don't want to take anything from you tonight," he says. He rests his hand on my thigh with self-assurance. "I want to put my tongue between your legs and make you scream. That's all."

"Why?"

"Because it's been a long fucking time since I tasted a woman and I've always been a giver. Open your legs wider for me. Now."

That dominant voice is entirely unforgettable and impossible to ignore. Completely against my better judgment, I spread my legs for Lucky. His cheeks darken with his desires. It's impossible for him to hide his body's response to me no matter how hard he tries. It's not like Lucky's really trying to hide how he feels.

"I remember exactly how you tasted," he whispers. "All those years I never forgot the sweetest black pussy I ever had."

He edges closer to me. Titillating me. Terrifying me. Lucky bends forward and kisses my neck with a slow, possessive kiss that sends a jolt of energy straight between my legs. He pulls away from my neck and takes his position between my legs, still tall enough on his knees to fit his face easily between my legs. There's only the trouble of a couple layers between us, but that doesn't appear to bother Lucky in the slightest.

He kisses the tops of my clothed thighs.

"Do you remember what my tongue felt like inside you?" he murmurs, drawing his nails along the fabric as if he's toying with the idea of ripping my pants off. He's such an irresponsible, beastly slave to his lust. His warm breath spreads through the fabric of my pants and despite my outward desire to protest, my body wants nothing more than Lucky's lips against my bare thighs and anywhere else he might see fit to put his tongue.

My body might want Lucky but my barely functional upstairs brain doesn't want to talk about what happened between us all those years ago. I don't want to remember anything about the big man who got down on his knees and made me cum on the worst night of my life. He doesn't need to know he was the first man to do that for me and he definitely doesn't need to know how much it fucked me up that a stranger cared about making me climax more than any boyfriend before him.

"Tell the truth," he urges. "I won't judge."

"I don't remember that night fondly," I warn him. "But I remember."

He kisses the top of my thigh again. "Were you scared?"

His controlling hands roam possessively over my body. I remember that part too. This must be the way he fucks – he always has to be in control. He likes it. What normal woman wouldn't fear a man that damn primal?

"Obviously. I was eighteen." I'm not trying to sound bitter. Lucky peels away my pants slowly, pulling them over my thighs and baring my legs to his touch. His hands send pulses of warmth through me and even if I'm nervous and angry at him and want to resist him, I can't help but sink into his grasp.

He furrows his brow and takes his position on his knees again, still intent on getting his tongue between my legs, I suppose.

"I'm sorry," He murmurs, pressing his lips to my bare thighs for the first time. "I'm really fucking sorry for hurting you. I was an asshole, and you still gave birth to my daughter. You still cared for her. You must be an angel, Althea. I'm sure of it now."

His intense blue-green gaze flashes to mine and I don't know what the hell to say to him. I don't feel like an angel. I feel dirty and cheap and like I should be much stronger at resisting Lucky Vicari. My thighs tremble in his grasp and for the first time since Lucky brought me to his mansion, I can't think of a response to him.

# Chapter 8
# The Rat
## Lucky

With each kiss I plant on her thigh, I feel her melting. She spreads her legs further apart and blood rushes to my cock with misplaced excitement. I won't have that tonight — not until I prove to this woman that she only saw one side of me that decade ago. There's more to me than my mistake, just like there's more to her than one act she did for money.

I don't judge her the way she thinks I do. Blaming her just makes it easier for me not to blame myself. But I do, of course. I hurt her, and I brought a little girl into the world who needed a father and I wasn't there. My brother John might stop speaking to me for that crime alone.

I slip my finger inside Althea's underwear and she gasps as my rigid index finger explores her outer lips. Her soaked panties stick to her outer lips and it takes movement from my fingers before I can separate her sticky underwear from her juicy outer lips.

Quickly, I slide her underwear to the side and run my tongue over Althea's outer lips. My quick, urgent movement surprises Althea who gasps and sticks her hand into my hair instantly. Her legs spread apart wider to allow my tongue access and her fingers grip my hair tighter as my tongue makes smooth circles on the way to her clit.

I suck on her outer lips and pull away for a moment to collect myself.

"You're wet," I murmur, running my tongue over her inner thighs and then kissing Althea's most ticklish spots just to watch her react. "I like tasting a wet, black pussy."

She has a nervous, unconscious habit of biting hard on her lower lip when I say something dirty that mentions the fact that she's black. I like what the fuck I like and in bed, I don't see the point of apologizing for my desires.

I slide Althea's underwear most of the way off before my tongue returns between her thighs. Althea squirms and makes a desperate moaning sound as I grab her thick, fluffy hips and bury my tongue between her legs. There's no hesitation this time. Teasing her isn't part of the plan. I don't want her to feel teased or confused.

My tongue should tell her how many fucking years I spent remembering the perfect black pussy I found in the most unexpected place belonging to the most beautiful woman who I could have never had the courage to approach without a fuck ton of coke or a fuck ton of money. Everyone knows black women don't fuck with Italians. They don't like white boys, it's the truth.

My tongue can change that. I tell myself I can convert her, keep her far away from any guy in her neck of the woods, claim her as mine. My tongue moves in slow circles around Althea's clit. Her moaning gets louder. She wants to cum so fucking bad...

My fingers spread her lower lips and I focus my attention on Althea's very sensitive nub. She whimpers and moans as I suck on her clit and her moans get louder when I cease direct contact and tease the area around her clit with slow circles. Her pussy drips with desire to cum and her thighs tense as she gets closer to that endpoint.

I don't care if I drown in the wetness between her thighs, every fiber of my being fixates on making Althea cum with no other distractions or direction. My fingers sink possessively into her thighs as I spread her legs further apart and suck purposefully on her clit alternating between a pulsing suckling of her hardened nub and slow circles with my tongue and lips.

"I can't…" she gasps as if begging herself not to cum could stop the train of pleasure. When she releases her inhibitions, my grasp on her tightens. Althea cums harder than I've ever made a woman cum before and watching her writhe with pleasure in my grasp is fucking beautiful. Her beautiful brown thighs clench around me and I run my tongue over her inner thighs as Althea enjoys the pleasure of climax.

When she finishes, I lick up her juices and stand between her legs to take a much needed break from kneeling and admire the freshly fucked look on Althea's face. She responds to my gentle smile with an almost infuriated look.

"That was… too damn good," she gasps. I take pleasure in the fact that she can't meet my gaze, but her refusal to admit that I'm not completely monstrous gets under my skin more than I'd like to admit.

"I know," I whisper. "I'm even better in bed. But… you must remember that part at least."

I run my finger over her lips, shocked that Althea doesn't try to bite me. She scowls and pushes my hand away.

"Stop being so cocky. And you haven't fixed everything with one orgasm."

"Right. I'm fixing things by showing up for Chiara, keeping you safe for the next six weeks and starting with one of many, many future orgasms."

She sticks her foot out, pressing her adorable painted toes against my thighs. Fuck, she gets me hard.

"Many, many orgasms? Who the hell said anything about that?"

She thinks this was a one-time thing? Fuck no. If I can't sleep with her, I can at least fall asleep with the taste of her pussy on my lips. It's been a decade—I'll fucking take it.

"I hurt you pretty fucking bad, didn't I? Don't you want me to make up for it?"

She pauses for just a beat too long.

"I don't know."

Her rejection hurts, even when I don't want it to. I know it's her right to push me away, but I'm not a scumbag and it sucks that she thinks I am. She'll never let me be there for Chiara if she doesn't think I'm a good person. I might not be perfect, but I'm Italian. The most important thing to Cosa Nostra is family… Chiara's my family. Althea's my family. We'll always have that precious connection between us.

I need Althea to accept that. I can see from the look on her face that she won't and that the orgasm in my hands was nothing more than a release for her. I feel foolish for thinking I could win her over. My face fixes into an impenetrable scowl.

I shouldn't make it so fucking easy for her to get under

my skin. I'm the mobster here as she calls it. I have to stay in control.

"GO UPSTAIRS," I tell her. "Before I lose control with you."

"I thought you were going to get me a shirt," Althea protests. I shake my head.

"No. Get upstairs and out of my sight. If you need me to be a monster to feel better, that's what you'll get."

"I never said you were a monster."

"I'm trying," I sneer, knowing that Althea doesn't deserve the brunt of this frustration, but unable to stop myself from taking it out on her. "I want to be a good father but you won't let me. I would give anything to have her in my life. Anything. I forgive you for keeping her from me. I will always forgive you, but nothing I do could make you forgive me."

"You hurt me," Althea says. What the fuck can I say or do to make her understand that I'm so painfully aware of the hurt I caused and that I so deeply regret it? It feels like there's nothing I could say that she might believe. She has her mind so set against me that I don't have the slightest chance.

"I want to make it better."

"You can't," Althea snaps. "So you'd better stop trying."

She gets me so fucking angry sometimes, but my wrath will do no good here. She's not part of the mob. She's not Italian. That overblown, overemotional Italian way of dealing with things won't work at all with her. Althea's too tough, too stubborn to react to my temper.

"My only job is keeping you safe," I mutter. "Understood."

# The Rat

.  .  .

I LET her get deep under my skin. Althea and Chiara whirl around my mind as I head to the casino to check on my guys and meet up with John to discuss the accident and his discoveries. They're safe at my place for now. I have cameras, a great security system. Althea's a great mom. I know she'll look after Chiara for me.

John broods at a table near the back door to his office hallway. He has a bottle of wine on the table. Halfway done. Good night for John. I relax visibly although I wish I hadn't once I slide into the chair at the table next to him. The celebratory sound of the slot machines fades into the background as I focus all my attention on my brother, who looks deeply upset now that I consider him up close. Great. Another night of dealing with John's fucking moods. I don't need a fortune teller to tell me he's totally pissed off today.

Is it about the kid? Who am I kidding? It's John, so it's definitely about the fucking kid.

We haven't had a proper conversation about Chiara yet. I don't know what John will say about her. Dad's the boss, but while he's away, everything falls into John's hands. No one knows when the fuck dad plans on coming back. He left to handle business with the Doukas brothers six months after Matteo's wedding and that was the last we heard from him.

John calls the shots and if he tells me to send Chiara and Althea away… I have to listen to the boss. I don't want to be the type of dad who sends a paycheck and thinks his job is done. I want to be there for my kid. You don't need to be a fucking paycheck if you show up and be a father. If there's anyone who's going to give Chiara the world, it's going to be me.

If he commands me away from her, I'll never forgive him. John appears entirely oblivious to my internal plight. A waitress brings over a seltzer and lime without me asking anything. John's getting better at managing the place. My guys are hanging around the entrance and a few in front of the back office.

It's not exactly a busy night, but it's not dead in here.

"Sammy's coming," John grunts. "Thirsty?"

The temptation to join John in polishing off a bottle of wine heightens. I shake my head. With Chiara and Althea at home, saying no to temptation has been easier.

John shrugs and throws back another giant gulp of wine before adjusting his collar. He clearly has a lot on his mind and it would be easier for both of us if John spit it the fuck out.

"How's the wife and kid?"

"She's not my wife," I grumble, although thinking of Althea as my wife doesn't exactly offend me. She's the one who would feel disgust at the very notion.

John shakes his head disapprovingly. "What the fuck were you thinking Lucky? You knocked up a black chick from God knows where…"

"She's from Queens."

"I don't give a shit where she's from. Is she involved with any gang bangers?"

"No."

"Good," John says, relaxing visibly. "We don't need those fucking problems from messing with their women."

"That's it? That's all you care about?"

John half ignores the question. "Is she coming after you for child support?"

It's a reasonable question, but I loathe even the hint of an implication that Althea's a gold digger. I'm the fuck up. I'm the one who screwed up and left her alone to deal with a kid ten years ago. It would be her right to ask for child support and I would happily pay whatever she asked. She's too upright for that. She wouldn't ask for a fucking dime if she thought it would cost her dignity.

I've already had too much of her dignity to deserve asking for any more from Althea.

"She doesn't care about that. She's a good woman. A good mom."

John raises an eyebrow and stares. I hate when John stares 'cause it's usually when he wants to put you on the spot and crack you wide open to get some information he already knows.

"What do you want to know, John?"

"You fucking like her," John announces, an annoying grin spreading across his face. My brother doesn't know what the fuck he's talking about. I don't have a chance to tell him to fuck off. Sammy saunters into the casino, drawing attention because of his height and his new black leather jacket which John and I both notice at once.

"He finally ditched the fucking denim," John mutters. Sammy raises his hands like he's encouraging a cheer from the crowd as he walks towards us.

"Somebody's in a good mood," I grumble as he sits at our table, already armed with a flask of whiskey.

"Nope," he says. "I know what this meeting is about. You don't. I'm in a horrible fucking mood."

John's smile vanishes and his lips purse into a thin line.

"Drinking was a bad idea," John says critically.

"Hit me with the bad news," I say, struggling not to grab Sammy's flask of whiskey off the table now I know my brother has bad news. I could never tell based on John's facial expressions alone. When he wants to play his cards close to the vest, he can.

John finally announces the bad news and I understand why Sammy showed up to this meeting drunk. John probably didn't want me to do the same. This is terrible fucking news.

We have a rat.

"How the fuck do you know we have a rat?" I push John. Sammy doesn't question him, which means if John has proof, Sammy already knows and he believes it. Shit. Sammy might even have his own reasons for believing we have a rat. John doesn't like what he's about to tell me which means I definitely won't fucking like it.

Before John can give me his explanation, Sammy drunkenly blurts out, "It's a fucking Zagarella. One of my people. We know someone signed the initials 'EZ' on a note to Kyle Murray, and we know they gave money and information to the renegade Murray cousins from Boston."

"Renegade Murrays? Since when are the fucking Celtics struggling to keep their people in line?"

"I don't know," John says, sounding concerned, but not yet panicked, which bodes well. "They could say the same of us. There are only three Zagarellas on our suspect list."

# The Rat

I glance nervously at Sammy. His son must be one of them. Sammy's always struggled to keep the kid in line and sending him to work on construction sites with dad out in Brooklyn only ended in more family drama, more fighting at Thanksgiving. More bullshit. Bringing Eddie Doukas out here didn't help improve Enrico's moral character.

Sammy doesn't want to think the kid could be crooked, but we can't rule it out.

"Who are the suspects?" I ask John.

"We can't take the word of a few Irish rats," John mutters bitterly. "We have to conduct our own investigation. Three names came up as potentially having involvement—Enrico, Emilio and Early."

Enrico is Sammy's some. Emilio, his second cousin and Early, his nephew. We're related to Sammy on our mother's side, so we don't share his intimate knowledge of the Zagarella family.

Sammy shifts uncomfortably. "I want to clarify that I'm not a fucking rat, John and if any of my people are rats, I'll do what has to be done."

Everyone in the life knows what happens to rats. Extermination. Execution.

Doesn't matter if you rat to the NYPD or to a bunch of low-life Irish fucks.

"I need both of you to talk to them," John says. "Investigate the accusations. Let 'em know that if they've gone and fucked with us, they won't be safe out here."

It won't be the first time we've had to hurt people close to us, but there's somber energy at our table as we come to terms with those people being the Zagarella boys we grew up with. Sammy polishes off his flask and shakes his head as if clearing it from the liquor.

"We'd better start this weekend," Sammy growls. "Whoever did this must've known about Lucky's kid ten years ago. That has to be where it starts."

"That's your job," John says. "Not mine. I have to make sure the house wins tonight and tighten my grasp on this whole fucking city. We know what could happen if the wrong people talk to the wrong people."

COPS. More arrests. More jail time. FBI sniffing down every fucking street in Long Island. It's the last fucking thing any of us want. John's right — we need to end this and we need to end it soon.

IF ANYONE GETS HURT, it won't be us and it definitely won't be Chiara or Althea. My girls.

"We can handle this, John. If there's a rat, we'll find them."

"Agreed," Sammy responds, polishing off the rest of his drink in one gulp.

# Chapter 9
# Three Weeks of Luca
### Althea

I stay up all night waiting for Lucky to come home. He doesn't know I'm up, but I know he's up to something and I don't want him to think he can pull the wool over my eyes.

We've been at his house for three weeks, and it's been awkward. We avoid each other whenever Chiara's not around and she's a buffer between us when she is. There's so much tension, I don't know what to do with it. I miss my freedom and a part of me hates Lucky for taking it away from us.

His worry about us seems genuine, but he's still hiding something from me and I intend to get answers. I don't want to be his prisoner and Chiara's asking more questions than I know how to answer. If Lucky isn't in it for the long haul, I don't want to tell her more details about him. My daughter's feelings come before anything.

When Lucky saunters through the door at two in the morning, I pop out of the living room — clearly far too wide awake for him. I've waited for him for hours, concocting my lines for what I would say when I confronted him.

Lucky's eyes snap open and he gives me a surprised half-open mouthed expression. I enjoy having the element of surprise for a change.

"I didn't expect you to be awake," he says, almost stammering over his words with guilt. The thought crosses my mind that he might have been seeing another woman. He has his daughter to worry about.

I snap at him, "Where were you? Does this have anything to do with Chiara and the threats on her life? You keep saying you're taking care of it, but nothing happens around here and Chiara has to miss practice. I want answers, Lucky."

If he was out with another woman, this would be his time to tell me. I know I shouldn't care, but I'm only looking for more reasons he needs to stay out of Chiara's life.

He gives me a strange look which has the unfortunate effect of reminding me exactly what it was like to have him on his knees between my legs and to have Lucky's smooth pink tongue slipping between all my folds. Lucky calmly runs his tongue over his lower lip and then shakes his head.

"This isn't any concern of yours," Lucky says his voice filled with stubborn determination, which only freaks me out more.

"It's my daughter's life. You can't even tell me who the hell would want to kill my baby girl. Lucky, I'm trusting you, but maybe whatever the hell you're dealing with might be a better job for the police."

My heart pounds nervously. I know Lucky's in the mob, but there's still a part of me that thinks that shit is for the movies and maybe Lucky's not the type of mobster to carry a gun or kill somebody. Maybe it's different. The steely expression in his blue eyes quickly disavows me of the notion that

Lucky would be hesitant to kill. Apparently mentioning the police was a huge fucking mistake.

"Never mention the police again," Lucky growls.

"There's someone allegedly trying to kill me and my daughter. The police sound like a good idea."

Lucky takes a step, closing in on me. I can't tell if it's just his passionate energy or if he's trying to scare me, to remind me that he's a terrifying mobster who can drag me back to his mansion and tell me what to do with my little girl. My throat heaves but I hold steady. I can't let him scare me. I'm not the same woman I was in that restaurant all those years ago.

As he closes in, I can smell his cologne and the scent overpowers me, makes me feel weak compared to the brawny man hovering over me. Lucky's muscles pulse with anger. His tattoos make his outrage even more terrifying. It feels like there's a cotton ball in my mouth.

"I can protect my family," Lucky growls.

I want to tell him we're not his family, but there's something deep and primal his words activate in me. He sounds possessive and protective in the best way. He sounds like a father — the father I never dared to hope that Chiara could ever have. Lucky takes another step towards me. He's not trying to scare me.

He's trying to show me how much he cares. He takes my cheeks into his hands slowly, pressing his thumb and index finger into either side of my jaw so I'm forced to look him in the eye.

"You are my family, Althea and I will protect you. No need for police."

The slightest touch from Lucky makes me weak, but this

strange, possessive act sends me into a full-blown panic. I try to say something but my tongue hangs limply in my mouth as I submit fully to control from Lucky's hand. Is that what he really wants from me? Is that what he always wanted? Not sex, not a chance to experience a fetish but... connection?

My hands press against Lucky's torso but I can't make myself push him away. His brow furrows and before I can ask him what caused the reaction, he kisses me. It's a nervous first kiss and then he gets more confident that he can take what he wants. He holds my cheeks firmly in his grasp as he kisses and kisses me like I belong to him.

"You're mine," he growls. "Do you understand?"

If I hadn't just kissed him and tasted the mint on his breath, I would think Lucky was drunk or on drugs again. He sounds desperate. Romantic. This is a side of him I've never seen before and I don't know what the fuck brought it out. I grab onto his shirt and pull him against me so we can kiss more.

We already have a kid together. He gave me head in his kitchen. A little kissing can't possibly hurt. Lucky grunts and moves me towards the stairs as we kiss. I struggle not to fall backwards, but Lucky holds onto me tightly, allowing me to trust that I can move with him and won't topple over. He grabs my hips once we're close to the stairs and thrusts me up against the wall.

I don't fight him this time. I run my hands under his shirt, touching every inch of his muscles and after a nice long feel, I drag his shirt toward me so Lucky's body presses against mine and I can feel how fucking hard his muscles are. Lucky takes my lower lips between his teeth, drawing me towards him more. I don't want to stop myself with him anymore.

Lucky grunts as I reach between his legs and allow my palms to clasp around the outside of his trousers. The lump in my throat expands. What the actual fuck? I've never felt anything this big — at least not that I remember — and my hand instantly jumps away from Lucky's crotch as my heart pounds a million miles a minute.

Ten years isn't enough time to forget a dick that big, right? I would remember a big dick…

"What?" He whispers, a smirk easing across his annoyingly handsome face. "Did it bite?"

"I don't remember you being that big," I blurt out. I could curse my horny ass brain for the dirty things that come out of my mouth. I hate myself for saying it even more once I see the cocky ass smile spreading across Lucky Vicari's face.

He must notice the fallen expression on mine because he holds my cheeks again and forces me to look at him. Why the fuck is he so obsessed with eye contact?

"Hey, princess. Don't look away. I took something from you all those years ago. I get it. I want to make up for it. I want to be… I want to be a father to Chiara."

"Sleeping with me doesn't make you a father to Chiara," I shoot back. Even as badly as I want Lucky Vicari, protecting my daughter comes first.

"I know," he whispers. "But I don't need you scared of me and I don't need you scared of my dick. I want to make you feel better…"

A dick that big could make anyone happy. I bite on my lower lip, trying to stop myself from saying something stupid which fails miserably.

"It's enormous."

Lucky grins, his shiny eyes glimmering with desire and the sense of a close victory. He leans forward, hands still possessively grasping my cheeks, and he gives me another deep kiss. I taste his tongue back with all my passion in return. Ten years without touching a man is a really long time and none of my other suitors, none of the other men who even came close to me could kiss like this.

Lucky pushes me against the wall with his hips, pinning me there entirely under his weight. I'm breathless, utterly powerless against him.

"I want you so fucking bad," he murmurs. "Not to hurt you. Not to use you. I just…"

He trails off. I want to know the end of that sentence. I do something I never dared to do before we breached this impossible to define closeness.

"What do you want? Because you have me here. I'm basically your prisoner. You claim I'm in danger but… I don't know if that's true. I don't know why you want me here."

Lucky turns red. I forgot white men did that — got all red and weird when you try to get real with them. I forgot white guys like to keep their emotions close, sharing nothing, and getting anything "real" from a white boy is a fucking fantasy that will never come true. There's a reason we don't mess with them and it has nothing to do with dick sizes or other silly stereotypes.

It's about the real shit. Can we really be real with each other, even if we're from two different fucking planets?

"I want you because… I think… I fell in love with you ten years ago and you're back and you have my child and it's really fucking hard for me to think this isn't my second chance."

My heart stops. My body wants to give Lucky a second chance. My body definitely enjoys the way his firm hands linger on my hips and how I can tell he wants to glide his hand to my ass. Once he touches me there, it's on, so his hand hangs cautiously in the balance on my hips. We're still in that in-between space where anything could go wrong.

Love me? I don't want to believe that Lucky could love me but there's a look in his eye I haven't seen before, a look that stirs something instinctive and primal in me. His emotions are mine and every emotion inside Lucky becomes one of mine. I've never shared this closeness and intensity with anyone. My hand clings to his chest. Lucky takes my hand and holds it there. With his hand firmly covering mine, I can't deny to myself how good this closeness feels.

I want to pull myself away from it, but I just can't. He makes me feel too much. It's not love yet, but it could be.

"Okay," I whisper.

Lucky makes a low grunt in the back of his throat. "I need you upstairs. I can't survive another minute."

"Okay," I whisper.

"You aren't making me beg?"

He sounds surprised. I don't want to make him beg tonight. I don't need more friction getting between me and what I want. He loves me. He loves Chiara. Maybe there's a chance this isn't a nightmare, but a blessing a decade in the making. Maybe this man really loves me or he did and he wants to make things better. Maybe this is a chance to let the past go.

Then again, maybe I'm just really fucking horny.

"I'll make you beg if you make me wait," I whisper.

Lucky chuckles and moves his hands from my hips to my ass. There it is, the point of no return. His face visibly reddens as he cups my ass and draws my body against his. Lucky grunts as he lifts me off the ground, holding me against the wall for another kiss before he carries me upstairs effortlessly.

Lucky sets me down at the top of the stairs and pushes me against the wall again. He can't stop kissing me and I haven't stopped wanting him to. His body rests firmly against mine and I run my hands over the rippling muscles. I didn't touch him a decade ago.

When a man buys your body, you exist for his pleasure, not the other way around. His tongue between my legs was his attempt to make the situation more human, less transactional, and it worked by twisting my mind into knots for years over what happened between us. He fucked with my head so badly and now, I can be with him—not to be used by him.

It feels like healing but it's fucking terrifying. It's been three weeks. We keep trying to ignore our feelings for each other. Actually, I'm the one running away. Lucky has been quite clear about how he wants to make love to me and make up the past to me. He wants sex. Not just sex — making love.

The deep, sensual connection Lucky wants from me scares the fuck out of me. Three weeks. Surely I could make it longer than three weeks around Lucky without succumbing to his lust.

Yeah... I run my hands over his body and wrap my hands around his cock. Lucky grunts and his body stiffens as I grasp the most vulnerable part of his body. My hands can barely wrap around that dick, but I can feel it throbbing and pulsing in my hand. His cock is so fucking warm. I run my hands slowly up the length of the smooth shaft and Lucky grunts loudly.

His cock stiffens in my hand. I don't know how the fuck I got that thing inside me back then and I don't know how it's going to happen tonight. He's enormous. I glance down at the bulging, dusky pink member growing in my hand. Lucky's body pulses again and he gasps desperately, "Stop."

I release his cock, and he immediately grabs my hands and pins them over my head. Lucky eases his hips forward to pin me against the wall again and he kisses my neck before running his tongue along the length of my ear.

"I fucking love watching you touch my white cock," he murmurs. "I could cum just watching your pretty dark skin."

I don't know why the fuck he talks like this, but he doesn't seem to mind that all I do is squirm awkwardly beneath him and struggle against his grasp. His hips and hands keep me pinned against the wall, entirely submissive to Lucky's desires.

"I waited ten fucking years for this," he whispers. "I know you're worth it. I dreamed every night about your pussy but before I take you to my bed, I need your mouth around my cock."

His grasp on my wrist tightens. Lucky should scare the fuck out of me, but his hands and his kisses made me so wet that I'm not in control here. His tattooed arms hover over mine as his deep, shuddering breaths pulse his muscular body rhythmically into mine.

"Please," he whispers. "You don't have to make me cum. I just… I'm begging."

The thought of this giant, terrifying man covered in tattoos and rippling with thick muscles begging *me* for something amuses me. I run my hand over his muscular chest and wrap my hand around his dick again, taking pleasure in the way he grunts and stiffens from desire.

I enjoy watching him beg. He deserves to feel this desperate. He deserves this torture. I push him away from me and keep pushing him back up the stairs until his back lands against the wall at the top of the stairs. His back hitting the wall should have hurt him, but Lucky just has a devilish smile on his face. I run my tongue over my lips. What the fuck is wrong with me?

"I'll do it," I tell him. "But you have to agree to let me bring someone here."

He sticks his tongue into the front of his lip like he's trying to stop himself from saying something stupid and cheating himself out of the blowjob I now know he desperately wants.

# Chapter 10
# Princess' Tongue
## Lucky

I feel compelled to agree to whatever Althea wants. This infuriating woman has me exactly where she wants me and the simple concession she requests... I just want her lips around my cock and I'll say anything she wants me to say to get her lips there.

"Whatever you fucking want, princess."

I just want Althea on her knees. She approaches me slowly, like there's still a part of her that fears my desire for her. That's my fault. I hold her close to me and kiss her again.

"Kneel," I whisper. I can't control my excitement. My cock is so fucking hard, I swear the slightest brush of her lips will make me cum hard. She's so fucking beautiful and I remember those pillowy lips with every dirty detail.

Althea's eyes flicker nervously to mine, but she slowly drops to her knees. Anticipation courses through me as my cock jumps to attention. Althea's hands slowly graze the outside of my trousers and my dick wants her so bad I nearly rip my pants. She eases her soft hand to undo my belt and the anticipatory sound of my buckle sends a cascade of desire through me.

I want her to work faster. I want to take her urgently. My craving for her lips turns me into a fucking animal. Her skin color makes it so much better. I love watching her brown skin, her pretty big lips and after a decade of dreaming of this woman, wishing I could touch her again, wanting to atone, I finally get to have her.

I struggle not to rush her as she slides my trousers over my ass and my belt drags them to the ground with a crash. Her hands grip the sides of my thighs and Althea's eyes widen considerably as she stares between my legs.

"Something wrong, princess?"

"I don't remember it being that big."

There's nothing like having a woman appreciate how big your cock is. Makes you feel like the fucking man. My dick size apparently doesn't scare her away. Althea slides my underwear off quickly and my dick juts forward, the tip immediately finding Althea's lips. She slowly draws her face back and glances up at me from that sexy position on the ground.

There's something so fucking gorgeous about her on her knees gazing up at me with those large, brown eyes. A thick spurt of pre-cum oozes from the tip of my cock, drawing Althea's eyes away from mine as she suspiciously eyes my member.

"That won't fit in my mouth," she says. I push my hips forward eagerly. No. This isn't the time for Althea to resist me.

"Open wide. We'll test that theory."

Althea slowly juts her tongue out curiously, running it

along the tip of my dick and slurping up my pre-cum. Fuck. The soft touch of her tongue is nearly enough to make me cum. Mercifully, she pulls her tongue away and swallows the pre-cum. I inhale slowly, forcing myself to stay in control as the slightest touch of Althea's tongue puts me at her mercy. I groan as her tongue darts out again, moving in a slow circle around my dick.

Ten years. It's been ten fucking years, and I missed every sensation of a woman's lips working my dick.

"More," I grunt.

Althea's lips close around my cock and I face the challenge of not cumming in her mouth too soon. If there's anything better in the world, I haven't felt it yet. She slides her tight lips down the length of my cock as far down as she can take it. A loud, shuddering groan courses through me as Althea makes a gagging noise, only taking a third of my cock into her mouth before I fill her up.

She attempts to force more into her mouth until tears pierce the corners of her eyes. I withdraw my dick and Althea takes a deep gasp of air.

"I don't want to choke you."

She coughs as politely as she can manage before rasping out, "Your dick is huge."

I probably do a bad fucking job of hiding the cocky smile on my face. I press my finger beneath Althea's chin and tilt her head up so she looks me dead in the eye. My thumb finds the tears and I wipe them away before giving her a kiss on the forehead.

"You don't have to get the whole thing in there, princess. Just get my dick wet with those pretty big lips."

My dick jumps forward, nearly hitting Althea in the face.

She wraps her hand around my shaft and again I want to cum instantly. It won't take long for her perfect lips to work their magic on me. Althea swallows before inhaling slowly and sticking her tongue out again.

She already soaked my dick in spit, so her tongue working on the head of my cock and her hand slowly pumping my shaft makes me feel fucking incredible.

She takes the head of my cock deeper into her mouth and slows down her hands' movement at the base of my shaft. I can't take my eyes off her perfect lips sliding over the length of my pale shaft. Her mahogany-colored hand wrapped around the base of my cock, nestled in the trimmed thatch of my hair nearly pushes me over the edge.

I slide my hips forward instinctively again and Althea takes more of me. She runs her tongue along the underside of my shaft and then flattens it there as she draws me deeper into her throat. Her full perfect lips tighten around my shaft and pleasure surges through me again. My body tightens into a tense knot as my release draws closer.

"Deeper," I murmur, halfway between a commanding a pleading, desperate call for her mercy.

Althea obediently takes more of my cock down her throat. She doesn't gag this time. My cock's sufficient lubrication makes it easier for me to take my pleasure from her mouth and tongue. Althea bobs her head slowly over the length of my shaft, taking special care to pleasure every inch of my cock with slow swirls from her tongue as she gently sucks me off.

Deep. Slow. Tight. Everything about her fucking mouth is perfect. My body stiffens as a climax approaches and I have to finish in her mouth. I need it more than anything.

"I'm close…" I warn her, expecting that she'll pull away and expecting that I'll have to beg. Althea slowly eases her lips even further down the length of my shaft. When the tip of my dick touches the back of her throat, I can't hold myself back. My cum spurts out of my dick straight to the back of Althea's throat and euphoria grips my body as my climax hits me hard.

I've never cum this hard in my life and my dick keeps spilling seed into the back of Althea's throat as this warm sense of relief spreads through me. Fuck, that was good. Fuck, it's been forever.

Fuck, there's no way I'm letting her out of my sight before I get my dick in that beautiful black pussy.

Cumming that hard reminded me I don't give a fuck about what's proper. I just need to feel Althea's warmth and wetness. I need to claim her and cum inside her and find a fucking way to keep her here.

Althea pulls her lips away from my dick and slowly lick them with an eager, pink tongue. It won't take long for me to get hard again if she keeps this shit up.

"Get up," I command her, hoping I sound more forceful than out of breath. She listens, regardless of my tongue and gives me wide, pleading eyes as if the cum sliding down her esophagus wasn't enough of a customer review.

"Fucking good," I grunt.

Before Althea can say something sassy or too fucking smart for her own good, I pull her against me and kiss her hard. That was a damn good blowjob, and it deserves a deep fucking kiss. I grab her hips and pull her against me, enjoying the soft warmth of her body and the pillowy texture of her lips. She smells like me. I like that.

I spread her lips apart with my tongue and kiss her deeper. Althea resists at first, but I hold firmly hold her in place and kiss her exactly the way she deserves to be kissed after making love to my dick like that.

"Really fucking good," I grunt again, holding her firmly as she squirms away.

My lips nibble at her neck as Althea keeps squirming.

"Where the fuck do you think you're going?" I whisper. "We're fucking tonight, princess. Right here. Right now."

# Chapter 11
# Crazy, Stupid, Desperate
### Althea

I must be some mixture of crazy, stupid and desperate because the way my body reacts so intensely to Lucky has me teetering on the edge of a completely foolish decision. He felt like a man in my mouth, a real, powerful man an utter slave to his desire for me.

Every movement from my lips drove him wild and when he came...

I thought Lucky might be bitter or even a little sour but his cum in my mouth tasted sweet and I got so wet imagining the dick I tasted between my legs. Ten years is a long damn time to turn down every temptation and every hot make-out session that threatened to turn into something more. It didn't help that my last time was with a monster — the same monster who just came in my mouth.

It definitely didn't help that I never felt a connection with anyone since. Ten years and no connection with a man is hard. But how the hell could I worry about dating with my baby girl?

With Lucky, it's different. We share her. There's a bond

between us I want to deny but that bond is walking around and running around and I've stared lovingly into her face for years. Wanting Lucky feels wrong and dirty, like I'm completely fucked up in the head. But there's a part of me that feels right wanting him, that knows his actions were a mistake and that he wants to make up for it.

He wants to give me the love I should have had ten years ago. I believe it.

"We can't do it right here," I tell him. "I'm too grown not to do it in a bed."

He nods understandingly. He had me last time leaned over a bathroom sink. I was there to perform a service for him. If Lucky wants me, if there's even a shot in hell of something between us, he has to treat me the way I deserved back then and better.

He grins. "I've dreamed of getting your sexy ass in my fucking bed."

There he goes with his rough language again. Before I can protest, Lucky scoops me off the ground like I'm weightless. That hasn't happened in a long time either. Drew tried it in one of his fruitless attempts to romance me, but he only ended up giving me a concussion and costing me $1,300 in medical bills which he never helped with, of course.

Lucky's suave and smooth, his firm grasp pushing me to wrap my thighs instinctively around him. He takes me directly to his bed. From the little I can make of the room, it's clean and luxurious. Lucky might not indulge in cocaine anymore, but that doesn't mean his room is without indulgence. There are large windows, an enormous balcony and the largest bed I've ever seen against one of the crisp ivory walls of his bedroom.

I swear you can even see a lighthouse in the distance out the window. To Lucky, this incredibly luxurious bedroom is just normal. He doesn't stop to gape at the view the way I want to. He kisses my neck and collarbone and runs his fingers over the top of my breasts with a glut of excitement.

"I want to lick every inch of that black pussy," he murmurs, tossing me back onto the bed.

His body presses atop mine and Lucky's lips return to mine as he caresses me with feverish kisses.

"I'll even put my tongue in that sweet black ass," he murmurs. "Fuck, I want to taste every inch of you."

I can feel his hardness jutting from him again. Damn, that didn't take long. He just came in my mouth but he's already stiff and ready to fuck.

He unceremoniously rips my shirt off — physically rips it — and kisses the tops of my breasts, easing my boobs out of my bra so his greedy tongue can run circles over my flesh and then zero in directly on my nipples.

An inadvertent moan escapes my lips when I really mean to be telling Lucky off for so brazenly running his tongue over my nipples. His tongue rolls around in slow circles and my moaning gets louder. I want to push him off but instead of doing that, my hands grab onto his firm back and I pull him closer to me.

"Yes…" I whisper. "That feels so fucking good."

My body is a traitor. A damn traitor. A gush of wetness spreads between my thighs and I don't just want Lucky's tongue on my breasts and I definitely don't want to feel his tongue teasing me to a slow climax again.

I want something more…

It's like Lucky can read every signal I'm sending out. He

spreads kisses over my breasts and quickly moves his lips down to my stomach as he works at peeling away any layers on my lower half. Thankfully, he rips none of my other clothes until he gets to my underwear.

Lucky grunts and pokes his finger at it before completely ripping it off.

"Those were my good drawers…" I murmur, but Lucky doesn't seem to care. He spreads my lower lips apart with his tongue and makes a deep sound in his throat almost like a purr after he tastes me.

"Soaking wet," he grunts. "Good."

"Condom," I say weakly. "We need a condom."

Lucky chuckles and kisses the top of my thigh.

"Why do we need a condom?"

His kiss sends an irresponsible tingle straight through me. Right. Why use a condom? Why not have another kid with a crazy big-dicked mobster? What the hell could go wrong with that? There's just someone trying to kill you from the first damn time you allowed Lucky to have his way with you.

My face tightens and I give Lucky the sternest expression I can muster. This is the worst conversation to have while you're wet with the most tempting hunk of a man in bed right next to you.

But I have my daughter. I have to think about Chiara.

"Haven't we both learned that was a terrible idea?"

Lucky chuckles again and gives me another one of those pussy-throbbing kisses on the top of my thigh. He's trying to get me wetter and hotter on purpose. I know this man and what he wants when he gives in to his baser desires.

I press my feet against his forehead, a ticklish sensation

traveling up my toes as I catch wisps of his blond hair. Lucky pushes his head forward bullishly, ignoring my feet and he runs his tongue in a smooth circle around my clit.

Oh. My. God.

I fucking hate him. Another warm gush erupts between my legs. He removes any sense of decency and control I have. My foot falls away from his forehead, but Lucky doesn't have his way with me yet.

"What's such a terrible idea?" he says. "We're two parents... maybe we want to have another kid."

"Are you out of your fucking mind?"

"I'm 100% more sober than I was the first time we tried this."

"There was no 'we' with making Chiara. That was all you."

Lucky scoffs. "Pretty sure I gave you enough to cover the morning-after pill."

"Don't judge me for what I did with the money, rich boy."

"Rich boy?"

"That's what all you mobsters are," I respond defiantly. "Spoiled rich boys who think it's your right to kill and steal just to keep your hands on your money."

I know I'm talking reckless but the consequences to talking reckless seem far more pleasurable than allowing Lucky's crazy Italian ass to cum inside me.

Unfortunately, my words don't deter him. Lucky wants what he wants. He's too stubborn not to push back against me.

# Chapter 12
# Her Perfect Mouth
### Lucky

I fucking love the mouth on this woman. If she thinks her attitude will stop me from getting what I want, she's sorely mistaken.

"You're right," I respond arrogantly. "We protect what's ours. We protect our money. We protect our families. We protect our women."

Althea scoffs. "That only applies when those women are white. I know Italian boys don't give a fuck about your mistresses."

Her words feel like a stab in the gut. I can't help but think of John and his reaction to Chiara. I can't help but think of what my father's going to say when he finds out. She knows our people keep to ourselves the way her people keep to themselves.

Althea's no idiot. She knows exactly how fucking dangerous it is to be around people like me.

"Not for me," I whisper, my tongue caressing the top of her pretty brown thigh. "And you're not my fucking mistress."

"I'm your nothing," she says.

"Not true," I whisper, kissing the furry top of her mound and then her thigh again. "You're my everything because you gave birth to my kid, and that makes you the second most important person in the fucking universe."

"After Chiara," she says knowingly.

"Yeah," I whisper, giving those voluptuous thighs another much needed kiss. "After our baby girl."

I touched her, I know it, but that doesn't mean I made a dent in Althea's mile high defenses. She needs those defenses because of me so I'm probably going to be the last person on earth she tears them down for.

"I just want it to be planned next time," Althea says. "Don't you get it? I love Chiara, but it was hard having her alone."

"You're not alone, princess."

I kiss her again. She has to know this. I'll never leave her alone again. I might have been a drug-addicted fuck, but I'm not the type of guy who abandons his goddamn kid.

"Don't make promises you can't keep, Lucky."

"I don't," I murmur. "I mean it, Althea."

"What happens when the blackmail stops? What happens when you have to tell your family? Chiara will be in even more danger and another baby will only make this worse."

"Bullshit," I whisper to her, my voice struggling to stay steady because I mean every word of what I'm saying to her. "A baby brought us back together. There's no way in hell another one could tear us apart."

Althea squirms against my body again. Her protests only get me harder and make me want her more. I don't want to resist this powerful urge anymore. Ten years. I spent ten fucking years healing, preparing, waiting for this chick to come into my life again.

I don't want her to get away.

"We can't have a baby," Althea insists.

"Fine," I whisper. "I'll pull out."

"I could still get pregnant from that."

I sigh and run my lips over her neck. No condom. Every nerve in my body tells me I don't need or want a goddamn condom on my dick. I want another kid. I want her and Chiara and me to be a proper family. A kid is definitely going to make that happen.

"Fine," I whisper. "I'll cum inside you then."

"These are the same thing, Lucky!"

"Okay... Here's the deal," I whisper, running my tongue over her nipples to sweeten the pot of this little 'deal.' "Morning-after pill. I'll give you the money. This time, don't blow it on scratch cards or whatever."

"I didn't blow the money on scratch cards, you asshole," Althea says, punctuating her protest with a little moan as my tongue grazes the sweet spot on her nipple. Fuck yeah. I enjoy her like this.

"Do we have a deal?"

She moans again. I love it, but I want more than her moans before I keep going.

"Yes," Althea whispers.

"Good fucking choice, princess."

I kiss my way down her bare chest, on top her mound and then spread her lower lips to tease her pussy with my tongue one last time before entering her. She's so wet that my tongue swirls between her folds and her pussy coats me with a slick helping of her essence. With my tongue and fingers spreading Althea's lower lips apart, I tease her open and use my tongue to push her to the brink of a climax.

"Cum for me, baby," I whisper. "Cum on my face with that delicious black pussy."

I slide a finger inside her to finish the job and Althea cums hard, gushing around my rigid index finger and coating her thighs with more sticky juices. I press her body into the bed with mine, kissing my way back up to her lips until our hips line up.

The wet spot between her legs guides me to the center of her pleasure. Tension wracks through me. I'm not in control here. A deeper, more primal force has ultimate control and I can't ever feel satisfied with just sex. I have to seed her. I have to claim her pussy and put a baby in Althea for my satisfaction, for my assurance that she's mine and she won't take my family away from me.

Using a firm grasp, I guide the head of my cock to Althea's slick entrance. She's so fucking wet that slightly touching my dick to her pussy nearly makes me cum. I ease her lower lips open and Althea's body trembles nervously against me. She has seen how big my dick is and she's struggled to get it down her throat.

I slide the head of my dick between her lips and Althea whimpers. Her body tenses and her pussy feels like a tight rubber band around my dick. Holy shit. I don't remember this. There's no fucking way my brain cells could have processed remembering something this good with this much detail.

Her pussy grips the head of my cock forcefully and I grunt to thrust more inches between her legs. Althea moans loudly but one small push only gets an inch or two deeper between her legs.

"You are so fucking tight," I grunt. "I love that tight black pussy already."

I'm barely halfway inside her and I already want round two and round three tonight. If I can convince Althea not to take the morning-after pill... I'm getting her pregnant tonight. You get your dick halfway into a pussy that good the only thing on your fucking mind is getting that woman pregnant.

My hips push forward and Althea grips my back muscles as my dick moves another couple inches inside her. Her whimpering and hip grinding increase with frequency and she's weak beneath me with her desire for me. She wants me this time. Fuck, I should have never paid for this when I could have had her honestly. I like her. I could have courted her. I could have treated her like a lady and not a whore.

My body tingles as Althea's fingers brush against the hair at the nape of my head and I forcefully thrust the rest of my cock between her pretty, thick brown thighs.

She moans loudly as our bodies finally join. I clutch her close to me as my cock fills her and my need to cum heightens. Fuck, she's tight. It's hard not to cum instantly, she's so beautiful. I kiss her neck and slowly withdraw my hips so I can feel her tightness. Her thighs tighten around my body as she draws me in deeper. My cock throbs between her legs and Althea cries out.

I don't want to rush this. I waited ten years, I want to savor every fucking moment of making love to her. I move my hands between her legs and massage her clit while maintaining an easy rhythm with my hips. Her sensitive clit responds instantly to my touch and Althea's ass lifts off the bed as she moves me deeper inside her.

The walls of her tightness grip my dick harder as the smooth circles of my thumb on her clit push Althea close to the edge of an intense climax. She drags her nails into the muscles on my back. The tiny pinpricks of pain push me to thrust harder. I'm close. I'm getting so close, but I need to make her cum first.

I won't feel a fucking hint of satisfaction until I make Althea's sweet black pussy cum first.

My thumb moves to the more sensitive part of her folds and I tease her to the edge before removing my thumb and thrusting nice and deep between her legs. She moans with each deep stroke and I can feel her body tightening as she gets close.

"Cum for me, Althea," I whisper. "Cum all over my big white cock."

She writhes beneath me as an intense climax overcomes her. Althea's nails dig deep into my back and her hips buck furiously against mine. I fucking love this. I bury my dick into her deeper as she cums.

"I love your tight black pussy. I can't wait to fill you with my cum."

Althea whimpers as another climax ravages her sensibilities. She moans and tugs on my hair as she climaxes. The tug on my hair is the final straw for me. She's too perfect. Too intense. Too fucking hot for me to handle.

"I'm giving you another mixed baby," I grunt as I push deep into Althea a final time and cum inside her. She gasps and wriggles as my dick gushes inside her but she's powerless against my weight and musculature pushing her into the bed.

I have her pinned beneath me accepting my seed, taking my essence between her legs and I don't want her to move. My cock gushes with three full spurts and I feel the pool of my seed at the tip of my dick as the warm white fluid gushes inside Althea and spills out in a trickle around my dick.

Baby. That right there is how we're going to have one. The sight of my seed pushing its way out of Althea gets me hot. I push my hips deep inside her to bury my cock deep between her folds for a few seconds. Nothing escapes. She's mine and she's having this baby. We're going to make everything right in our world with another baby.

Althea wriggles her hips against me, possibly trying to get away, but only successfully drawing me deeper inside her.

"Feels fucking good, doesn't it?" I whisper. She came hard. There's a part of her that likes this, even if her common sense might warn her away from me. She's a woman, an animal just like I am. She has the same urges as I do, as much as she tries to hide them.

Althea nods, like she's nervous about the truth.

"Say it," I whisper. "Say it feels good to have my big white cock knock you up."

# Chapter 13
# Sneaky Choices
## Althea

Lucky's filthy, incredibly skilled mouth makes me gush again. More cum leaks out of my pussy and a blush of nervous warmth floods over me. Lucky kisses me and then eases out of me slowly. He came so hard and there's so much of it inside me that there's no way I can move without making a huge mess.

Apparently, he finds this enjoyable. A grin spreads across Lucky's face and he plants a wet kiss on my lips.

"I fucked it," he whispers. "Now it's mine. Forever."

"You agreed to a morning-after pill," I remind him.

"It's not morning," Lucky answers. "I have until morning to change your mind."

"That's unlikely to happen."

"Not if I keep you in bed all morning."

Now I have to laugh out loud.

"Lucky, I'm a single mom. I haven't stayed in bed all morning in nine years. I haven't stayed in bed all morning since I saw those double pink lines."

He looks wistful for a moment, but just as quickly as I recognize the emotion on his face, it vanishes.

"You stay in bed all morning tomorrow. I'll have Vinnie babysit."

"Do you really think a mobster is the best babysitter for your child?"

Lucky shifts his weight and his large cock presses into my thigh again. It's so hard to contain a rational thought in my head with that big dick pressed against me. A cocky smirk crosses Lucky's annoying ass face once he notices the effect his dick has on me.

"Vinnie has three kids. He's great with kids. Plus, it's better we have him than my brother John."

I roll my eyes. "I have to see my daughter."

"What you have to do is stay in bed with me and spread those legs again. My opinion."

Lucky kisses me on the lips again as I try to push him off me, struggling against his chest. Once my hands come up against that broad, defined muscle, I can't control myself. I drag Lucky close to me and kiss him again. I'm sending him the wrong message and Lucky is taking the damn message.

He pushes his tongue into my mouth and his weight forces me into the bed. Lucky already has my legs spread open lewdly and I feel his dick coming to life again. Seriously? Isn't this man older than me? How can he get hard again so quickly...

Lucky grunts as his hard dick finds my entrance again, and he pushes inside me. Euphoria spreads through me as his dick enters me more easily, sliding in me all the way to the hilt. He feels so fucking big that his dick becomes mind control.

"You fucking like that, don't you?" he murmurs, nibbling my earlobe and thrusting into me deeper. I wrap my thighs around him and squeeze my eyes shut to enjoy his dick sliding into me and drown out every filthy word coming out of Lucky's mouth.

"You like my big white cock between your legs," he growls. "I fucking know it."

His fingers find their way to my clit again meaning I won't stay in control of myself for long. Holy fuck, he has a way of finding my sweet spot. I moan and buck my hips to meet Lucky's hands. I'm close to another orgasm and my body thrashes desperately beneath Lucky's as his dick pushes me over the edge.

As I climax, he slides his dick even deeper and erupts between my legs again. This time, I don't respond the way I should. I don't push him off and demand the morning-after pill. My thighs wrap tightly around Lucky, pulling him deeper inside me. Another thick spurt of his seed coats my inner walls.

The hot liquid makes me squirm and buck my hips beneath him. I want him so fucking bad. I want to touch every inch of him and pull him deeper inside me. There's even a dirty, depraved part of me that wants to beg him for another round, just to make sure we did the job right. This feels too good for me to resist.

Lucky finally wore me down. His tongue on my neck makes me squirm and moan beneath him again. Lucky chuckles and swirls his hips like he's stirring my pussy juices with his dick. I push against his chest weakly. He doesn't buy my resistance. He knows I've already given into him.

"Let's do it," he whispers. "Let's make another fucking baby."

"This is the worst idea you've ever had. Once you sleep off the orgasm, you'll change your mind and get me the morning-after pill yourself."

"No can do, princess. I've got work in the morning."

"How do you plan to get me the pill then?"

"I don't," Lucky whispers, easing his hips forward and pushing his cum deeper inside me. He's determined to get his way with me and I don't want to listen. I don't want to give in to him easily when I don't know how real he is about this whole thing. It's just sex talk — the dirty sex talk I knew he was into.

His words can't mean anything real.

"Lucky, you can't be serious."

"I'm fucking serious. I'm going to work and I'm not changing my mind."

"What work? Since when do you have a job?"

I know it's a low blow but... I have a point. Lucky alleges he owns a security company, but I know that could be mob-speak for anything on the planet.

The shift in his body language tells me everything I need to know. I just gave a piece of myself to Lucky, but there's a piece of himself he's hiding from me. He has secrets big enough to wipe the cocky grin off his face.

"You don't need to worry about that," he says sternly. His furrowed brows don't deter me from pressing him more.

"You fathered my child," I remind him, ignoring the fact that he might father another one. "I care what you do with your free time."

"It's none of your concern."

"Is it dangerous?"

Lucky gives me an aggressive stare, like he can scare me off his line of questioning. He doesn't get it. I left scared behind a decade ago. I want an answer to my damn question.

"It's none of your concern," he repeats.

"Does it involve something you could go to jail for?"

The flicker of anger in Lucky's eyes tells me I've stumbled upon something.

"Please, Althea," he says in a low, deep voice that sounds almost threatening. "You shouldn't worry about what I do."

I might be brave in the face of Lucky's rapidly changing mood but that doesn't mean my body doesn't respond to the recognition of a threat. I'm naked beneath him and utterly at his mercy. This might not be the smartest time to question him or to bring up the rumors I heard all those years I hid Chiara from him.

"I know you did time," I say to Lucky. "And there are worse rumors. That you killed the two Albanians found dead in the Bronx. You have a nickname. I know you're not just a businessman and I want to know the truth."

"I'm an important businessman," he responds coolly, smirking like he's hiding something. I hate his sneaky ass tone.

Does this man think it's the time to be funny? I shove hard against his chest to push Lucky away from me which doesn't work. He's a solid brick of muscle and my tiny fists do nothing to move him. Ugh, I can't stand him.

"What?" he whispers. "Do you have a problem with me providing for you? For our daughter?"

"You don't do whatever you do because of me."

"It's not what you think, Althea. I'm not the bad guy, I swear."

"You aren't denying that you killed anyone. That's not a good sign."

"Fuck, Althea, if the cops had anything on me, they would've hauled me in by now. The mafia's not like what you see in the movies."

"Right."

"I got work tomorrow. That's all there is to it."

Lucky kisses me and then he kisses his way between my legs and eats me out until I cum several more times. If he's trying to distract me, it works like a charm and I fall asleep in his arms until he wakes me up for round three.

Round four happens after another brief nap and in the morning, Lucky refuses to let me out of the room to see Chiara. I can't believe his ass was serious about keeping me here all morning and keeping me away from a morning-after pill.

Asshole...

LUCKY EVENTUALLY FREES me in the morning so I can have breakfast with Chiara, but he's adamant about going to work and even more adamant that I don't leave the house because it's "dangerous" out there. I don't know if I believe him. It's not like I can say anything in front of Chiara, but based on what happened upstairs all morning... I can't rule out Lucky having ulterior motives for keeping me locked in his house.

Maybe he's using this blackmail thing to keep me here as his personal sex slave or something. I don't know. I can't accept that he really wants to be there for us. It's been a decade. He didn't even know about Chiara. How can he possibly care?

Chiara won't stop talking about her "Uncle Lucky" all morning. Nothing I do to distract her works. If I didn't know any better, I would say some deep part of her senses their connection and this is her subconscious way of reaching out to him. Thinking that at all makes me feel guilty. What Lucky and I did all of last night makes me feel worse.

I should have been thinking about my daughter, not the big dick pressed against me and how incredible it would feel to cum on it. I need to pray the hoe spirit away from me expeditiously.

Lucky stops at home for lunch, which he didn't tell me about. I spent all morning with Chiara on the tennis courts simulating lacrosse drills on the half court and then brought her in from the pool. She had lunch before me and went upstairs for a nap before Lucky's arrival. When he walks into the kitchen, he looks like a different man from this morning.

"Where are you going?"

"None of your concern," he mutters gruffly before storming off to his bedroom. None of my concern? Has this man lost his mind?

"Fine. Then I'm going out."

Lucky stops and glowers at me. "Where the fuck do you think you're going?"

"For a walk on your excessive ass property. I'll be fine."

Lucky responds with an irritating grunt and storms off toward the bedroom. The second he leaves the room, I high-tail it towards the door. I don't have time to pack, but I have to get out of here. Vinnie's in the house to babysit Chiara already and I can always text Shana to come over. Lucky says I can have guests, right?

I quickly text Shana and then run outside. The tail lights on Lucky's Escalade blare orange and red. I'm glad he's taking the biggest car in his stable of unnecessarily large toys. I rush over to it, grateful that none of his men are loaded up yet. I probably only have a few minutes to hide and there's no guarantee of success. I climb into the car in the very back and pop the seats up. Yes.

There's enough space underneath the seats in some giant compartment for me to hide in. I overheard Lucky murmuring to John about this feature of the car some time back on the phone. I climb inside and pull the seats down almost all the way. Lucky doesn't take long to return.

My heart pounds outrageously quickly as he closes the doors to the car and pulls out his phone.

"I've got Enrico's address. I'll get down there. If he's meeting with any more than three of them, I'll call for backup."

Work. He's going to meet Enrico for work. I don't know any Enrico, but I may have heard Lucky mention his name a couple times. It's his cousin's name, isn't it? The car makes a soft beeping sound as Lucky reverses it and swings out of his driveway. He's still on the phone, but he must receive instructions from John, because he doesn't say anything for a few minutes, then he responds.

"Sammy's kid might be a fuckup, but if he's helping fuck with the Murrays, he's an idiot."

…

"I know. Yeah, well, the kid's safe. She's with her ma right now."

My heart lurches. Okay, technically Chiara's sleeping upstairs alone, but she's in an isolated mansion in one of the wealthiest neighborhoods in America and she has babysitters and a security team. The biggest danger to her sits in the front seat of this car... I don't think Lucky's headed to any normal ass job and the truth will come out—tonight.

If Lucky won't give me the damn answers I want, I have no problem getting to those answers myself.

"I know I fucked up, John. I'm trying to do the right thing."

Lucky doesn't say anything else after that. He hangs up on his brother and keeps driving for what feels like twenty years considering the messed up angle I have to curl up in to stay in his car. My body is absolutely not built for twisting and turning like this. I need to fart.

I can't, because it would attract Lucky's attention, but I really want to and that makes twisting up like that even more uncomfortable. By the time Lucky stops the car, God shows me a little mercy and the urge to toot dissipates. Lucky hops out of the car. I can't see where he's going yet, but he slides open the backseat of the car. I freeze. Any sudden movements or noises could accidentally alert him to my position.

I squint to get a better view of Lucky and watch him unpacking a long gun out of a case. What the hell is that thing? He peers into the action and sets the gun down before reaching into another case for another similarly sized weapon with a smaller barrel. My heart nearly jumps into my chest.

What the fuck could those guns be for? I can hear the surrounding city, so I know for damn sure he ain't going buck hunting. I run my tongue over my lips and struggle to quiet my breathing. Freaking the fuck out will hurt more than it will help, but what the hell am I looking at?

If Lucky has this many guns in the back of his car, does he have any in his house? My concerns for Chiara's safety sky rocket. I started believing that Lucky was just a businessman. Sure, maybe he punched a guy once or twice, but you don't need two big ass guns like that to rough someone up a little. My stomach swims. What the hell is he doing?

Lucky's phone rings again. He answers.

"I'm a couple blocks away, give me the address."

He checks the action in the second gun and sets it down before glancing over his shoulder nervously.

"28 Bleecker. Got it. We got a crowd on our hands?"

Another pause. I'm worried about throwing up now and I miss the painful bubbling in my gut from before. He's a killer. He's a legitimate killer.

"I'll take the shotgun then. Get Sammy to text him, lure him out. I'll watch what happens. If he's anywhere near one of these Irish fucks, I'll take 'em all out."

He sets down the gun with the skinnier barrel and reaches underneath one of his front seats for a box of ammunition. He slides a few red shells into his pocket and shuts the door. I have to wait a few minutes for him to leave, so I hope I can find him. 28 Bleecker Street. I don't know the place, but how long can it take to find the spot with my phone? After waiting a painful amount of time, I pop open the seat compartment all the way and unravel my body completely from that crunched up position.

I hurriedly unlock my phone and type in directions to Bleecker Street. It's only two blocks away. Straight for one block, and then I turn right. There's an isolated alley behind the building. I bet that's where Lucky ran off with his gun.

I need proof of what he's up to. I get out of the car and hurry over to Bleecker Street, paranoid that Lucky will find me. I have to be sneaky and staying out of sight is pretty hard. The address leads to a little apartment complex with what looks like four units stacked on top of each other. I duck behind a staircase leading out of the brownstone units when I see Lucky ring the doorbell at number 28, not bothering to hide the enormous bulge in his jacket.

There isn't much foot traffic on this street. That's it? He's going to this place with a shotgun and he's just going to ring the doorbell?

The door to the apartment opens and… a black woman answers. What the hell? Lucky's facing her, so I get closer. I sprint to conceal myself behind the next set of staircases ahead of me so I can get a better view of both of them.

The black woman who steps out of the apartment is way shorter than Lucky, full-figured and she has straight black hair that looks freshly done. She's also wearing a large men's white button-down shirt, no pants and Ugg boots. I don't know if she's the person Lucky's searching for.

I can hear him talking to her.

"Enrico in there?"

She nods and I hear her call out to Enrico. A few minutes later, a teenage boy with a shock of messy brown hair and intense blue eyes emerges at the door, putting his arm around the black girl.

"How did you find me here? I was just about to leave," the younger man says to Lucky with a frustrated tone.

"I know," Lucky snaps. "Get to the casino. We need you out of the way tonight."

"You're working tonight?"

"Yes."

They exchange a strange look. Working. I suppose that's what Lucky calls running around with a gun tucked under his jacket so he can kill people. The sick feeling in my stomach hasn't subsided. Chiara needs a father, not a mobster. Lucky quickly says goodbye to Enrico and then turns to walk in my direction. Shit.

I press myself against the stairs and stay silent, hoping he doesn't see me. He doesn't. But now he's going to get to the damn Escalade first unless I go the other direction and run like hell. Running isn't exactly my forte, but the idea of Lucky leaving me behind in God knows what part of the city with nothing but my cell phone scares the crap out of me. I get to the car first and scramble back into my hiding spot with only seconds to spare before Lucky swings the door open to put his guns away, on the phone with John again.

"Cross Enrico off our list. Heard anything about Emilio?"

…

"Got it," Lucky says. "I'll come get you."

That must be John, the alleged mob boss of the Vicari family. The discomfort in my stomach intensifies and I wish I could call Chiara or check in to make sure she's settling in okay with her Uncle Vinnie. No one in that house would dare harm my daughter. She's safe. I need to keep telling myself that.

# Chapter 14
# My Woman
## Lucky

I don't want to pick up John tonight. If John and I aren't the ones running into trouble, we just sent Sammy on his own to deal with our rat, which means we don't have a lot of time. My car smells like Althea's perfume. Or maybe I'm just fucking thinking about her that much. I don't want her to see this side of me. I don't want her to think there's a part of me that enjoys doing this type of work.

I'm going to kill tonight. I'm going to live up to the nickname John gave me when I was nineteen after the "unsolved construction site murders" on the Upper West Side. The Executioner.

I meet John outside his favorite takeout place. He gets into the car and sniffs around.

"Smells like a woman in here. Sure you were working?"

John is one suspicious motherfucker. I can't stand his ass.

"I'm sure. What's the deal with Early?"

"Not him."

"Where the fuck was he, then? Why were you being so weird on the phone?"

137

John grunts and fastens his seatbelt. "Start the car. We gotta go to the laundromat. That's the last I heard from Sammy."

I start the car and head towards the laundromat, waiting for my brother to answer my damn question. What's the big secret?

"I found him with a dick in his mouth," John mutters, so quietly that I almost can't hear him.

"A what?"

"Fuck, don't make me repeat it. The image. I can't get it out of my head."

"A dick in his fucking mouth?"

"Christ, Lucky," John snaps. "Don't say it out loud again. Yes, he had one–you know what, I'm not talking about this. He's not our guy."

"So you walked in on him and the dick was right in there?"

"Can you shut up?" John snarls.

I smirk. This is my only chance to get under my brother's skin and if tonight goes badly, it might be my last chance. Just because you have guns doesn't always mean you win the fight.

"You think it's him then?" I ask my brother. I regret getting serious, but if Sammy's in trouble, I want to know the truth.

"I don't believe on of our own people could do this."

"How the fuck did he know about my kid?"

"Who owned that place?" John asks, ignoring my question. We might never find out how the Irish found out about a kid that I didn't even know about.

I wish I could remember the guy's name. There's only one

name I can remember from that night–the manager, Mikey. Maybe that's where the leak came from. I don't fucking know. It doesn't fucking matter. I missed my daughter's childhood and I can't ever recover from that. All I have left is protecting her–keeping her safe from the horrible shit in my world. I love her.

"Dunno," I mutter. "Doesn't matter. I love them, John. They're my family."

"What is she, a waitress?"

"No. She owns a hair salon. She's been at my place and… I don't want to lose her. I really don't want to lose her, John."

"What, like a mistress? You can put her up in an apartment if you need to."

"That's not what I mean. I want her to stay with me."

"Lucky…"

"I fucking mean it, John. I swear, it's not a mind game, she isn't fucking with me. She's done a great job with our kid. She never asked for a fucking dime. She's never asked me for shit, John. She's a good woman."

"Good women are rare," John says, which is as close to agreement as I can expect from my older brother. I don't blame him. We're getting closer to the laundromat which means getting closer to the colossal bullshit we need to deal with.

"Yeah. You're right."

"Don't fuck it up if it works. But this is our life, Lucky. The life fucks up everybody who touches it."

"Not our kids. If we do this right, we don't have to screw up our kids."

I drive only a few minutes longer before we get to the laundromat parking. John grunts and points at Sammy's car.

Fuck. Sammy wouldn't leave his car like this. John and I get out of the car quickly and check our firearms. I still have the sawed-off pump-action shotgun and John probably has his revolver. Or two stashed on his body.

We hop out of the car. The laundromat door is wide open and there ain't nobody around. John and I nod at each other. There could be someone in there with a firearm, so we can't just walk through the door. John and I take either side of the door. He runs in first and screams something. Yup, we've got company.

"Put the gun down," John yells. I enter the laundromat and point the gun straight at Emilio Zagarella. Sammy's on the ground. He doesn't look like anyone shot him, but he looks like Emilio kicked the shit out of him. He mustn't have been here alone if he knocked Sammy unconscious and on his ass.

Emilio swings around and points the gun at John. Huge fucking mistake. John shoots the kid in the foot. Emilio screams. I don't take any pleasure in this. With a shot to the foot, the kid could pass out, but chances are he won't and we'll get plenty of fucking opportunity to question him. John expects me to do that part. He picks the casing up off the ground as Emilio stumbles backward and then slumps onto his ass against the back wall of the laundromat.

The loud noises from the two running dryers hopefully silenced the gunshot. Doesn't matter, anyway. Everyone in the city knows this is mob territory and when you hear gunshots, you close your fucking mouth and you don't say a word. Nobody likes a rat. A Vicari ought to know that.

"Emilio, listen. You have fifteen minutes before you bleed out. If you want me to take you to the hospital, you listen carefully and you answer me honestly, do you understand?"

Emilio whimpers and then yowls. They always do this.

"Emilio, I need you to listen. What do the Murrays want? Why are they coming to our city and why the fuck are you helping them?"

John rolls his eyes as Emilio yelps like a coyote again.

"I'll search the area for signs of other men," John says as he grabs Emilio's weapon from him. Emilio reaches for John's sleeve, desperately clutching onto him.

"Please, John. Please, have mercy. It's not your fault. I didn't mean to fuck with your family…" Emilio groans. He's a Zagarella. He shouldn't see our families as separate. They're our cousins, our people. Emilio is a lost fucking cause. Sammy's still passed out on the floor and I'm fucking glad he didn't hear this shit.

Sammy doesn't have the fucking sanity to stand here and listen to this shit. Our families have stood together for a long fucking time.

John shakes Emilio off. "Shut the fuck up and answer my brother. I don't have time for this."

John leaves the laundromat with Emilio's weapon. We don't have to worry about working out in the open like this. We have the city's silence. We keep order in these streets and in exchange, the people here keep quiet. It's a simple arrangement.

"What do they want?"

"They want revenge," Emilio says to him with a strained, desperate voice. He groans again. Pain. He deserves this pain. When you betray our family, you fuck with your life.

"On us? What the fuck did we ever do to a Murray?" I

question him, searching Emilio's face for signs of deception and steeling myself to what I know we'll have to do tonight. For us to do our job, Emilio will have to become less than nothing to us — this man who was once family.

I can feel my emotions changing. It's almost like my blood really runs cold. Emilio coughs and chokes nervously on his next words.

"Not on you. On your father. The boss," Emilio groans.

"My father hasn't been in Long Island in months."

"Exactly. They're testing John, poking at old wounds... it doesn't matter. Fuck, Lucky, I know what you have to do. Just fucking do it."

"Not until I get more," I tell him. John doesn't want to see this shit and he shouldn't have to deal with this. If our father were here, he wouldn't deal with bullshit on the ground like this.

"I don't know more. It doesn't matter, anyway. I shamed my family."

"Why?"

"Why do any of us do anything? I had to help someone I cared about."

"You kicked your cousin's ass."

Apparently he knocked Sammy out cold because the motherfucker hasn't moved a muscle since John and I walked in here.

"I didn't do that," Emilio says, grunting and barely able to compose himself. "But you're in the wrong place, Lucky. Hurry and kill me because you've got more important places to be and more important people to track down. Closer people."

"Like where?" I scoff, pulling out a shell from my pocket

and opening the action on my gun. Emilio closes his eyes and shudders. He knows what's coming, and he's handling it better than most. He betrayed our family. I don't know why or how the fuck he strayed this far, but it isn't my job to sort that out. It's my job to finish this.

"Your daughter. She's alone. They went to find her. John won't find anyone here because they left for Westhampton. They want her."

"My daughter's safe with her mother. They won't get anywhere near her."

"No," Emilio insists. "She's alone. I can promise you that. Finish the fucking job, Lucky. Just do it."

"Is there anyone else in our family helping you?"

Emilio chuckles and shakes his head. "My foot hurts. My foot fucking hurts."

The smell of sweat and adrenaline in the room almost makes it difficult to keep my finger near the trigger.

"Answer me."

"I can't, Lucky. I've said all I can. I have my loyalties too."

"You chose the wrong family, Emilio. I will pray for you."

"Pray for me now."

He closes his eyes and starts praying. He knew what he risked coming here. I don't know why Sammy's second cousin betrayed our family, but he made his choice and it's time for me to do my duty. John will hear the gunshots and return soon so we can finish this up. We'll send people here to clean the place and make sure nobody around talks. We won't have to work hard for that.

Everybody knows the mob handles business.

I hold the sawed-off at my hip and shoot. It's close range —way too fucking close. The mess sprays all over the room.

Not John's favorite kind of work. My stomach lurches. I hate this part of the job. Emilio emits a final, shuddering gasp and then his lungs and heart and every part of him stops working. There's blood everywhere, and it soaks through his hair and his close. He'll be a sloppy mess stuck to the floor if John doesn't get back here soon.

I hear a strange sound and glance over my shoulder. There's no one outside, no one in the laundromat. Still, I can't help the feeling that someone's watching. It's a predator's instincts. John comes back into the laundromat after a few minutes, nearly scaring the crap out of me, even if I still have ammunition in my gun. I unload the gun once he comes in. John glances at Emilio's body, a grim but emotionless expression on his face.

"Got anything to wrap him up?"

"I've got a whole kit in the car."

"I'll grab it."

John leaves and I begin the work of moving Emilio's body. There's so much blood and fuck, the kid is heavy. He spent hours in the gym working out with Sammy, the same man lying on the ground next to him. John returns with my kit and glances at Sammy on the ground.

"He's still out like a light?"

"Sleeping like a fucking baby."

"Gunshots didn't wake him up?"

John heads over to Sammy and gives him a sharp slap on the face. Nothing. John checks his pulse.

"Fuck, he got hit bad. His head's swollen," John comments. "I'll call Geno to deal with him. He's heading back to Boston soon to do some recon for us, so he has time to handle this shit and skip town."

"Do you trust him?"

"Yeah," John replies. "For now."

"Enrico's hiding a girl. Did you know about that?"

"Didn't care."

"She's black."

John gives me a strange look followed by a smirk. "Since when do you care about that?"

"I don't," I reply. "Thought you might care."

"I don't," John replies. "When dad comes back, you two will have to answer to him."

We get to work on moving Emilio's body. It's tough work getting him in the tarp and getting him to the car. We have to wait until it's dark for that. I'm just glad Althea and Chiara are safe and very fucking far away from this mess. This is the dark side of my work, the part that brings me the most shame, but it's what I must do to keep my family safe.

I have to be the man my family needs me to be—the Executioner. I lost the capacity for guilt years ago. Emilio knew our family code the way the Pope knows the Bible. He chose his own death. Once John and I have him in the back of the car, Early and Enrico get there to get Sammy to the doctor. We can't take him to a hospital, but we have a cousin in Westhampton who handles shit like this when we need it done.

"When he wakes up, have him call me," John commands them as he gets into my car. The smell of Althea's perfume is so fucking strong as we drive out to our spot on Sammy's construction site near Pier 25 on the Hudson. John doesn't speak for most of the drive. Killing fucks him up and I know he wants to stop. He was only here tonight because he's family. Matters like this are too petty for him.

**145**

When we get close to the construction site, John sighs.

"We have a long fucking night ahead. What did the bastard say?"

"Said my kid was alone and people were coming for her."

"But the kid isn't alone," John says. "You're sure she's safe with her mother."

"Absolutely," I reply confidently. "Chiara's safe."

"Once we finish the job, we'll double check. She's your kid. We gotta be sure."

This is the closest to acceptance I can accept from John.

"GOT IT."

WE GET out of the car and get Emilio sorted out for his river burial. Cutting a man to pieces ain't exactly light work. After we get the last piece of Emilio tossed into the river and we're both covered in sweat, John takes a pack of cigarettes out of his pants pocket.

"Want one?"

Fuck yes. This is the only time I smoke. Nicotine makes handling killing more tolerable. It's the only thing that works.

John lights mine first and then lights mine. He stops suddenly after a couple puffs.

"Do you hear that?"

"Hear what?"

John's voice drops to a low whisper. "There's someone out here. Someone near the car."

"Revolver," I whisper. "We'll sneak up on them."

There's enough adrenaline in my body already that there's no noticeable shift in my demeanor as I approach the car. John reaches for a flashlight in his pocket and lights up at the Escalade. The person watching us shrieks. *Holy shit.*

"ALTHEA? What the hell are you doing here?" I growl, my cigarette falling from my lips and burning out instantly on the ground.

# Chapter 15
# My Big Screw Up
### Althea

John Vicari lowers his gun. He terrifies me. My gaze shifts quickly to Lucky. The man I betrayed. I've watched him do the most horrible things in the world and now he's giving me the most terrifying look and I know what he's going to do. I watched him kill one man—what would it mean for him to kill me? He could kill me like it was nothing.

I scream so loudly that my lungs and stomach vibrate. I turn on my heels and run. I have what seems like a half mile of construction to cross, but I race as fast as I can. Both men are chasing me and of course, Lucky catches me. I shriek as he wraps his arms around me and try to fight for my life.

"I won't let you kill me!" I scream at him, kicking Lucky in the stomach as hard as humanly possible. He grunts, but he doesn't let go of me. It's Lucky, of course he doesn't let go of me. I've been stuck in his grasp before and tonight, I know exactly how dangerous he is.

"We can't worry about that right now," Lucky roars.

"Because you're here which means Chiara's in danger. Stop fucking fighting!"

I want to listen to him, but there's too much adrenaline rushing through me for me to stay in control. I bite down hard on Lucky's arm and he screams loudly, letting go of me. John thwarts my second attempt to run away. He wraps his arms around me and practically tosses me back to Lucky, who holds me against him and attempts a different strategy.

"I need you to calm down. I need you to stay still and calm down or this will never end."

"I didn't leave her alone," I plead. "I swear."

"Who is with her?"

"Shana. You said I could have guests, I invited her over."

My heart rate hasn't slowed in the slightest. Lucky puts his hand on me and growls. "You are fucking infuriating."

"Don't kill me," I breathe. "Please, think of Chiara."

Lucky puts me down, still holding me, but allowing me to stand on my feet. John glares at both of us impatiently.

"I won't kill you." He sounds disgusted with me, but I know what I saw. I want to retch, but I can't bring myself to show more weakness than before.

John chimes in angrily. "We need to get the fuck out of here. I'll handle this bullshit later. We need to check on your kid."

"She's with Shana, I swear. And Vinnie. She's fine."

John gives his brother an uncomfortable look. He seems reluctant to speak up, most likely because of my presence. I've never been this close to Lucky's older brother before, but he's even taller than Lucky with a more severe face and untamed facial hair.

"I haven't heard from Early or Enrico. We don't know

where Sammy is and we don't know what the fuck is going on. We need to get out of here."

"Althea, come," Lucky says firmly. My stomach lurches as I approach him. I watched him shoot a man without his expression changing in the slightest. Killing was far too easy for him and now that I've seen what he's hiding, my fear of Lucky only escalated.

It doesn't help that right now he's filthy and stinks of dirt, blood and a grimy mixture of fresh water and chemicals from the Hudson River.

"Call Shana right now," Lucky says. "John? I'm ready."

I call Shana as Lucky leads me back towards the Escalade. John gets into the driver's seat this time after Lucky tosses him the keys. Lucky sits in the back seat next to me, glancing over every few seconds with a worried expression on his face. I've never seen him like this.

"Chiara's fine."

His body stiffens. "If nothing else, tonight should have given you a glimpse into the fact that everything is certainly not fine."

"I watched you get rid of the problem," I say to him with an icy voice. The thought of pissing him off when he's like this scares me. I know how easily Lucky can kill me, but I can't hold back.

"You think you understand this, but you don't," Lucky says sharply. "Let's hope my daughter's safe so I don't have to send both of you away."

"Are you pissed at me?"

"Obviously," Lucky huffs. "What possessed you to leave our child alone and follow me?"

"This wouldn't have been a problem if you told me what the hell you were doing."

"Do you think I want to announce to the mother of my child that I might have to kill someone?" He growls. His face tightens and his jaw clenches. *Fuck*, Lucky is good looking, but he's also dangerous. My heart can't stop racing and his scowl won't dissipate. *His outrage terrifies me, but I have to talk to him.*

"You claim to care about me, you tell me the truth."

John clears his throat. Apparently we're getting too personal. I try calling Shana but she doesn't pick up. It's late now and probably after Chiara's bedtime. Knowing Shana, she fell asleep watching America's Next Top Model reruns with Chiara curled up in bed. She's a great babysitter because she always allows Chiara the tiniest acts of rebellion like that.

I fold my arms and lean back until we approach Lucky's house. I know there's a problem the second John pulls into the excessively large driveway. Too many cars. Too many doors open. My daughter. I leap out of the Escalade before John stops the car. Lucky screams at me, but he can't stop me.

I hear him calling my name as I burst through the front door of his house, screaming my daughter and Shana's name. I race into the kitchen. There are three bullet casings on the floor. I shriek. John and Lucky enter the house behind me but I take off again towards the living room.

"SHANA!" I shriek. My best friends limbs are splayed in every direction and there was definitely a struggle in the living room. *No. This can't be happening.*

John commands his brother sternly. "Fan out, search the entire house. I think we know what happened here."

I don't know what happened here, and this isn't what I want to hear. I race over to Shana, screaming her name and trying to get her to wake up. My fingers find her pulse. At first, I think I can't feel anything and I get more frantic, but then I feel gentle beats as I press my fingers to Shana's thin wrists. Lucky's behind me.

"She alive?"

"Yes," I choke out.

"Althea, they most likely took our daughter. Do you understand?"

I can't look at him. I keep shaking Shana as tears stream down my face. I can't formulate a response and I definitely can't look Lucky in the eye. This is my fault. This is my fucking fault.

My chest heaves, and Lucky puts a protective hand on my shoulder.

"YOU DIDN'T DO THIS," He says. "You fucked up, but you didn't do this. Get your friend awake and I promise, I'll get our daughter back."

"You said you could keep her safe," I whisper back to him. I regret trusting him. I regret trusting myself. I regret letting my guard down for one fucking second with my baby girl. Discovering the truth wasn't doing the right thing. Now, I know her father's a monster, but I need to trust that monster if I want her back. I need to believe he's the good guy.

I finally turn away from Shana and get to my feet. I can't

stop myself from shaking, but I find the courage to speak my mind.

"What's going to happen to her? Who are these bad people who want to screw with you, Lucky?"

"I didn't choose this," Lucky says. "These people hate our family because of what we have. They went after her because of her connection to me. I know I failed you, Althea."

"You didn't. I just… I need you to find her."

"Do you trust me to find her?"

"Yes."

The words come so immediately that I'm surprised. Shana groans and her body shudders on the couch, briefly taking my attention away from Lucky. When I turn away from him, he quickly grabs my hand and forcefully pulls me against him. My hands press firmly against Lucky's chest and he kisses me as Shana groans again. Sensing I'm about to pull away from him, Lucky places his hands on my cheeks and firmly holds me in place.

Fuck, he's a good kisser. Lucky's lips communicate everything. His apology, his promise, his determination to save our daughter. I kiss him back and when he pulls away, he presses his forehead to mine.

"John's right, we need to search the house. After that, you and Shana will move to a safe house until we find her."

"A safe house? How long do you think this is going to take?"

Lucky can't meet my eye, which makes me worry.

"How long will these people have my daughter?" I try not to shout, but my voice trembles and the rush of emotions through me drives me crazy. I'm not stupid enough to suggest the police this time. Lucky can't exactly confess to where he was and I can't exactly confess to following him or mention a word of what I saw.

I witnessed firsthand how the Italian mob handles rats.

"Your friend is waking up," Lucky says. "Get her awake. I'll get John."

I rush over to Shana and call her name. She says mine and attempts to sit up. Shana gets too dizzy to sit up straight and falls over again. Shit. At least she's waking up. I glance over my shoulder, but Lucky's gone after John. I'm sick to my stomach. I would give everything to hold Chiara again.

Everything.

Shana adjusts better to the Tennessee farm house than I do. There hasn't been a single day since Chiara's birth that my life hasn't been all about taking care of her. Lucky has one of his cousins managing my salon–a precocious Italian girl who apparently feels extremely comfortable with our city's black community. Shana didn't have any photo-shoots or auditions scheduled anyway and she feels extremely comfortable with our "country vacation" at Lucky's expense.

It's definitely country as hell out here. At least we're miles away from anyone in this sleepy old town. The first week, I couldn't get out of bed. I couldn't stand the mornings without the sound of Chiara's voice. I even missed Lucky— his warmth, his kisses, the side to him I denied I was falling in love with. Three weeks. How was three weeks enough? It's like we exploded when we touched each other again. Maybe something special happened ten years ago. Maybe I was too shocked and scared to accept that our physical connection was more than either of us could handle. How fucked up it is to fall for the guy who paid to sleep with you?

It's foolish. But I might be a fool for Lucky Vicari, as much as it pains me to admit. I miss him too much and it's impossible to get him out of my head with a permanent reminder of him running around. It's impossible for my daughter not to remind me of her father. I just learned to live with the reminder of the man I thought I would never see again.

Shana tries to take my mind off things a few times a day, even if she's still healing from her head injury and missing Chiara almost as much as I do. When she isn't numbing out with her new favorite reality television show, *Fuckboy Island*, she takes me out onto the balcony with some of the sweet tea she learned how to make from the *Food Network*.

It's a little too sweet. Shana joins me on the porch, making me close my novel – the one book Lucky has at this place. He swears he never read the erotic novel, but there are several heavily underlined passages. Hm.

"I brought you sweet tea," Shana chimes in a fake Southern accent. We don't leave the house at all. Lucky has a trusted Italian relative – one of his Corradini cousins – bringing us groceries and everything we need, especially an abundance of sweet tea ingredients. I don't have a clue where Shana's getting this accent from.

I sit up on the porch swing, making room for my best friend to sit down. She hands me my glass of tea and plops down, dramatically crossing her skinny legs.

"Do you think today will be the day he finds her?"

This is our daily game. Shana knows thinking about actually finding Chiara is the only thing that can drag me out of my miserable funk.

"Will he ever find her? Maybe she's already dead and Lucky's too scared to call me and admit it."

"Doesn't he call you every night?"

My cheeks get warm. Yes, he does. Some of those phone calls get a little... heavy. Shana smirks which makes me worry that the walls to this safe house are far too thin. I clear my throat and focus on the subject at hand.

"Yes, but that's not the point. This is huge to him. I think he really loves her."

"He really loves you too, obviously," Shana scoffs. I shake my head. I don't know what the hell she's talking about. Lucky enjoys having sex, which doesn't make him unique to any other man. But he doesn't love me. I squeeze my thighs shut guiltily. That didn't stop me from allowing him to cum inside me. It's way too late for a morning-after pill to take care of this, so I'm taking an enormous risk.

"That man doesn't love me, Shana. You don't know what he did to me."

"I can guess," Shana says. "You told me about the man who fathered your child and I'm sure Lucky was that devil just like you said. But this guy... He's fighting for you. Maybe he changed."

I scoff and take a huge swig of sweet tea. Shana's recipe has grown on me. "Men don't change," I answer her cynically.

Shana rolls her eyes. "Whatever. He might be an asshole but he's fine as hell and he's putting you up in this big house for free."

"I don't need a man to keep me. I have the salon. I have my daughter…"

Except… I don't. I stare out over the fields fighting back the tears that have flowed freely every day of our separation. The only reason I don't leave and look for her myself is because I've seen the consequences of not trusting Lucky to handle his business alone. I've tried not to "go there" but it's nearly impossible not to blame myself.

Who else is there to blame? I'm her mother. She must have been so scared. She's probably still terrified. Chiara's a fighter, I know that, but what if that works against her? My soft crying turns into full-blown sobbing and Shana throws her arms around me, setting the tea on the floor for a minute.

"Shhhh," she whispers. "Everything will be okay. Chiara will come back. Lucky will bring her back."

"She doesn't even know he's her father," I whisper, suddenly filled with regret for never allowing my daughter to know the truth about her father. I want to believe she'll get back into my arms safely, but what if she doesn't? I would have denied her the one chance to know her dad — the dad who would burn the world apart to save her.

"Do you want him to know?"

Shana's always careful not to force my hand. She isn't shy about sharing her opinions with me, but my best friend believes my choices are mine and mine alone. I appreciate that about her. She tucks some of her hair behind her ears and considers me inquisitively.

"What I want is too terrifying for me to admit to myself."

"Which is?"

"I want what Lucky wants," I whisper. "I want us to be a family."

The tears come after that because I don't have my family. I have nothing without Chiara and if we weren't hundreds of miles away from Long Island, that very evening I would have considered risking it all to go look for her.

Shana gives me nothing but understanding.

"Tell him," she says. "I've seen what he's done for you, Althea. He cares about you. If you just tell him what you want... what's the worst that could happen?"

"He could abandon us."

"That won't happen," Shana says. "He'll bring Chiara back and everything will work out just fine. You'll see."

I really want to believe her so I wipe my tears away and change the subject to something with a higher chance of holding my waterworks at bay. Shana enjoys talking about college football too, so we share our theories about the up-and-coming McGraw College team from some small town in the middle of nowhere.

Shana makes us second and third glasses of sweet tea and by the time the sun crests over the horizon, I'm ready for bed. I either sleep all the time or I can't sleep. There's no in between. The insomnia makes me feel crazy, but I consider it my punishment for losing my daughter. I would deserve so much worse than insomnia if anything happened to her.

"I'll wake you up if I hear your phone," Shana says after walking me to my bedroom. I don't think I can stay awake in time for Lucky's call. I'm too exhausted and sad to wait up. I nod appreciatively and thank Shana for her sweet tea and her company. She heads to her bedroom, most likely to stalk some of those college football players we talked about on the internet.

I crawl into my bed and fall into a painful sleep.

THE KNOCK at the door feels like a bad dream. It feels like it's in my bedroom. In my head. But it's just the front door to our safe house. I leap out of bed and grab the revolver that Lucky quickly briefed me on how to use. I've never practiced before and I don't even want to shoot the gun, so I don't bother grabbing ammo before I rush to the front door.

Shana must have heard the noise too because she tiptoes behind me armed with a wooden accent chair from her bedroom. It's probably a better weapon than an unarmed revolver.

"Doesn't this old place have a doorbell?" she hisses.

"Maybe it's a neighbor?"

BY THE TIME we get to the front door, we realize that our late night visitor isn't a neighbor at all...

## Chapter 16
# Goodbye
### Lucky

I hold my sleeping daughter in my arms, pleased that she didn't have to witness me ending the lives of the men who held her captive. John accompanies me to Tennessee because we're family and what we have to do after returning my daughter to safety brings neither of us any pleasure. Sammy's still out of it and we haven't broken the news to him but... this will rock our family.

The culprit, the true rat, was nowhere near my daughter when I found her. My little spitfire spent less than four days with her captors before escaping. Unfortunately, her trouble didn't end with escape. She wandered the streets for five days surviving before they caught her again. She spent over three weeks with them before I found her.

I failed her. I failed my family and I can't ever forgive myself for what I've done. John disagrees with my solution to the problem. He's too soft on me because I'm younger. If our father were here instead of traveling, I know what he would tell me to do. They're not just in danger because of who I am. They're in danger because of who they are.

## Goodbye

My daughter can't spend another minute of her life in danger. She sleeps easily against my chest, completely ignorant to my identity. I honor Althea's wishes and even as I hold her, I can't bring myself to tell my baby girl how much I love her, how I would die for her. I can't ever tell her how I killed for her but one day, perhaps she'll wonder and a part of her will know that her father would burn the entire world to keep her safe.

Chiara makes a soft whimpering noise as she rearranges her tiny body against my chest. Even John cracks a smile which quickly wavers.

"Are you sure you want to do this?" John asks. I don't want him questioning me right now. This is the best course of action to keep them safe. Clearly, New York is out of the question. There aren't enough people on the ground to keep my daughter out of harm's way and Althea has her own ways of getting into trouble that I ought to curb.

Nah, I have to stick to my guns. I can't have John of all people getting me sentimental. Shit ain't right with the world if John's getting sentimental.

"I'll talk to her tonight. I'll make her listen."

"Make her?" John snorts. "Good luck with that."

Maybe he understands women better than he lets on. John knocks loudly on Althea's door as I hold Chiara against my chest. There ain't a single part of me that wants to let my daughter go, but I have to if I'm gonna kill the motherfuckers who kidnapped her. They must've had help and they must've been our people. Part of me regrets killing that motherfucker before getting the names.

"Can't believe the kid slept the whole night," he mutters,

which is John-speak for him leaving me to sort out my shit how I see fit.

"She's an angel," I murmur, running my hands through Chiara's soft brown curls and feeling my heart break. Chiara stirs on John's second loud knock on the door.

"I told you to fix the fucking doorbell out here," John complains. I don't bother apologizing. Althea and Shana answer the door after "subtly" peeking out the window. Althea reacts with a shriek and grabs Chiara from my arms before saying a word. I don't blame her. Chiara stirs once she makes contact with her mother, muttering in a disbelieving whimper.

"Mommy? It's my mommy..."

Chiara sounds sleepy still, but she wakes up fast as Althea squeezes her and spins her around promising loudly to never let her go. John observes everything quietly as Shana gives both of us a suspicious once over.

"Couldn't you have given us any warning?" Althea's friend complains. "She's been worried sick. We thought you were axe murderers."

John gives her a warm look. He's not here to be a monster or a boss. He's here for family.

"I didn't want us to waste any time. We took my dad's private jet and got here as fast as we could. I just wanted Chiara and her mom to be together."

Chiara clings to her mother tightly and I can't stop watching them together, feeling like an outsider, feeling guilty about what I came here to do.

"You'd better come in then," Shana says. "I'm sure you have a lot to tell us."

"Not much," John says. He doesn't intend of giving the

gory details of our recapture to Althea or Shana. That certainly wouldn't improve my favor and it doesn't matter, anyway.

We still have one person to track down who could ruin everything and still harm my daughter. We still have work to do that will pull me away from the people that I love. It's not that what I have to do doesn't hurt like hell. It hurts, but I have no choice. It hurts but I have to do anything possible to keep my girls safe, even if it means losing the woman I love.

ALTHEA PUTS Chiara to bed after about an hour. Shana makes espresso for everyone, which John seems impressed by. Nothing impresses John, so noticing his calm demeanor, I relax and by extension, everyone else relaxes more. Nobody enjoys when the boss is tense.

Chiara's tired from the flight and exhausted from what she went through. Now that she's safe, Althea and I have a lot to discuss. Our pending conversation weighs on me so I dread the inevitable moment when Shana suggests that she and John leave us both alone for the night.

Althea and I say goodbye to John at the door. He's taking Shana to a hotel for a night as a thank you gift for looking after Althea. I don't have to warn John about Shana — he's sworn off women for quite some time.

Once Althea shuts the door, she presses her back against it and gives me a long, hard look. I want to touch and hold her so fucking badly after all the time we've spent apart. It's been miserable being away from her, not knowing what was happening to both her or Chiara.

"What happened?" Althea asks. "I want the real story, not just the bullshit you had to say in front of John."

I understand why she asks, but I still have a code of honor to uphold.

"I'm loyal to my family. There are certain things I can't talk about."

"We're talking about my daughter. I need to know the truth about what happened to her."

"Someone in our family helped kidnap her. They knew she was my daughter and harming her would only lead to disaster, but that didn't matter. Chiara ran for her life."

Her face falls. "What?!"

"She got away and survived on her own for five days before they found her again. Still, they didn't mistreat her badly. They left her alone, fed her and clothed her, but she was still terrified and didn't know what would happen?"

"No one touched her?"

The pain in Althea's voice twists my heart and threatens to pull it right out. I want to put my arms around her. Why stop myself? I rush towards Althea and pull her close, wrapping my arms around her and holding her like I don't want to let her go. I would do anything to avoid having to let her go. She's everything to me.

"No," I whisper, kissing the top of Althea's head. "I got her back, and she's safe."

"Thank you," Althea whispers. "I appreciate you getting her back."

I close my eyes and feel Althea's warmth towards me. I want to kiss her and hold her here, but I can't right now, not before we talk about the important issue between us tonight.

Althea pulls away from me, her instincts as sharp as always.

"Something's wrong," she says. "You should be happy to be here, but you're not."

She can tell from the way I'm holding her. Fuck. I hate feeling so exposed and I especially hate having my feelings surge to the top in a bubbling mess when I have to do what's right.

"You have to leave New York City with Chiara," I say flatly. "But you can't stay here either."

Althea jumps away from me, which is a reaction I should have expected from her.

"I can't just leave New York. Chiara's on a lacrosse team. I own a hair salon. What about my girls?"

"I'll assign one of my cousins to work with your girls until we find a buyer for your business. I'll get you the money safely so you don't have to worry or work. We may not be together but I'll always look after you."

She flips from confusion to outrage in a flash. Althea's hand comes swinging towards my face before I catch it. She yanks her arms away once she realizes that hitting me won't work and settles for a scowl.

"What's the problem?"

"I don't need you looking after me or my daughter and I don't want to leave New York."

"Someone kidnapped our daughter, Althea. From my home. My home should have been safe. Too many people got hurt for this. I can't have it happen again."

"Shana's fine and so is Vinnie! Even Chiara's fine. It worked out."

"Can't you see how serious this is?"

She makes this more difficult the less agreeable she is. Doesn't Althea realize that I desperately wish she could stay in Westhampton with me? I already have plans to remove the tennis courts and build a private playing field for my daughter. The last thing I want is to send them away from me when they belong right by my side.

"Of course," Althea says, frustrated. "That's why I didn't tell you about her because I didn't want my daughter getting anywhere near the fucking mob."

"It's too late for that."

"Whose fault is that?" she snaps back. I know I deserve this, but that doesn't make it hurt any less. I don't want to send my daughter away.

"Chiara's future is on the line," I remind her. "It doesn't matter whose fault all of this is. We need to keep her safe."

I know Althea doesn't want to be away from me. She can't hide her feelings as well as she thinks. This will hurt her — I know it. But I can't let her see the way it will rip me apart. Our father taught us the power of always staying strong for your family. That's what I should be for her — strength.

"How is taking her away from everything she's ever known keeping her safe?" Althea protests, because she protests fucking everything. Her fire drew me to her. The moment she walked into that cramped restroom, I wanted her. Buying her body was foolish. I should have stopped right there and changed everything about who I was...

I suppose some changes take time. But for what? I will have lost her in the end. My chest tightens. I can't show any of this hurt on my face. Without my determination, I can't convince her. I can't keep her safe.

"She'll be alive. And if we're lucky, this will all be over

soon," I respond sternly. I know how cold and unfeeling I sound in contrast to Althea's pleading. Her voice shows me how much she cares, but my voice betrays nothing.

"You can't predict when this ends," Althea states, although it's more of a question.

Now's the time for stern honesty. "No. I can't."

I move closer to her again. Althea might be furious but it's been far too long since I've seen her and all I fucking want is to be close to her again and to hold her and to thank her for waiting for me. I want to whisper sweet words into her ears and make love to her until I forget all the fucked up shit I had to do to protect her.

Althea lets me touch her hair, which I tuck behind her ears. She has cute ears and a cute round face. I missed that face. My fingers linger on her cheek and a surge of desire shoots straight through me.

"Are you going to make me leave?"

"John will talk to Shana tonight and make her a similar offer. She gets to live with you, we cover all her expenses. All you two must do is keep my daughter safe."

"What about us?" Althea asks. My chest tightens. She knows me so fucking well that what I have to do hurts even more. I move my hand from her cheek to her shoulder.

"I love you, Althea."

"Answer my question," she says sternly. I can't deflect or run away from this anymore. The moment I dreaded for so long has finally come.

"We can't be together. It's too dangerous for you and Chiara. I love you both too much and I can't risk losing my daughter."

Althea's eyes well. I've never seen her express this much

emotion and I'm sure she considers it a point of pride that she's kept herself this walled away from me so far. It breaks my fucking heart to watch her eyes well with tears and know that I can't do anything but what I promised her.

I have to break her heart.

"You're going to banish us."

"I'm going to go to great lengths to keep you safe. You'll have a big house, a new business if you want... I just want you out of trouble and away from New York. The mob won't think to look in Tennessee. Maybe Jersey, maybe Delaware, but they'll never come down here."

"You decided all this before talking to me."

"I had to arrange your safety. Your protection is my responsibility."

"What if I don't want to leave?"

Her gaze flickers defiantly to mine.

"You must."

"For Chiara?" She says, her expression softening as her will weakens. She doesn't want this either, but this is one thing we shockingly have in common. Even if I just met my daughter, we will both put Chiara first, even over our love.

"It's not because I don't love you."

"I thought you wanted more," Althea said. "I would have never let myself have feelings for you if I thought—

Her tears break and I can't help myself. I grab her cheeks and kiss her. She doesn't stop crying. Tears stream down her face and I kiss her, holding her until the tears meet my thumbs. I use my fingers to wipe her tears away as I keep kissing and kissing the precious mother of my child.

I got my daughter back, but I failed to make the city safe

and until that happens, we can't be together. I can't risk a fucking thing happening to them.

When I pull away from her, Althea shudders and sniffles.

"I'm fine. I'm fine," she insists in a soft voice that definitely doesn't sound fine.

"I missed you," I whisper, running my fingers over her cheeks and then using my thumb to touch her soft lips. "I want to say goodbye."

"I don't," she says. "I want us to stay here. I want this to be our life."

There's a part of me that wants that too. But I'll never be able to stay here with my family while there's a war brewing in New York, traitors in my family that I have left to punish, and John. My brother needs support through all of this until our father returns. I have to do all of this to keep Chiara safe... I can't be with them too.

"I'll think of you every day."

Althea shakes her head and kisses me. No. She doesn't want this and there's a huge part of me that wants to resist it. I have my duty to her. Damn my feelings and damn hers. Love won't keep our daughter out of the hands of the Irish or Italian mob.

"No," she whispers, grabbing my cheeks. "No."

"We don't have a choice, Althea," I murmur, my hands moving purposefully to her hips. I missed her. I hated what I had to do to get our daughter back, but I loved working in service of her and our family. Her soft hips sink into my palms and my cock stiffens instantly. I need her upstairs.

"Don't make me do this alone."

"You won't be alone," I whisper pushing hair out of her face. My heart hurts for what I have to do, but I can't avoid

**169**

my duty. "I'll take care of you wherever you are and I'll be there for Chiara financially..."

"It's not the same," Althea whispers, running her thumbs over my lower lips. "You know it won't be the same."

"I'll leave you something to remember me by," I tell her, my lips moving to her pretty neck. This is where she smells the best. The second I press my nose into her neck, my desire for her mounts. I need Althea in my bed tonight. Badly.

"Stop," she whispers. "Don't go."

I kiss her again, parting her lips slowly and running my fingers through her hair. Tasting her is incredible. Her lips part and my tongue slips into her mouth. Althea kisses me back slowly and my hands move to her shirt. I lift the shirt off her and as it drops to the ground, Althea wriggles in my grasp.

My hands touch every inch of her. As my fingers brush over her nipples, Althea makes a soft whimpering sound that turns my cock into a steel rod.

"Fuck, woman. You're soft."

She makes a whimpering noise and I pull her closer. "Get your ass upstairs."

"To my bedroom?"

"Go wherever you want me to fuck you, princess."

Althea slips away from me and hurries up the stairs. I love seeing her eager for me. I need her. I follow her slowly, stripping my shirt off and leaving it on the stairs. My chest pulses with anticipation. I need her. I catch her halfway up the stairs and grab Althea, lifting her off the ground.

Her thighs wrap around me, and as her hips grind into me, my cock stiffens. My hands grasp Althea's ass and she pushes her body against mine. I push back, holding her against a wall and Althea's toes run over the backs of my thighs. I want her.

"Let's do it here," I growl. "Let me fuck you against the wall."

"You crazy," Althea murmurs, her fingers running through my hair again. "One crazy motherfucker."

"Yes," I whisper. "Let me get your pants off."

Althea squirms to stop me from trying to get into her pants in the hallway, but nothing could stop me from getting into those pants. A loud ripping sound makes Althea's body tense, but I don't care. I want to get in those pants.

"Lucky, are you crazy?" She whispers. "You can't…"

The fabric comes away from Althea's flesh and she squirms as my fingers slide along her thighs beneath the place where her fabric fell away. My hands rub her thighs and I push until I reach the apex of her thighs. Althea gasps as my fingers slide over her underwear.

"You're so fucking wet," I grunt. "Let me get in there."

I push her panties aside and run my finger over her slit. Fuck, that's incredible. Althea moans as my index finger slides past her entrance and I press into her. Her pussy tightens around my finger and I move out of her slowly. Althea moans as I rub my fingers against her inner walls.

If I can't fuck her out here, I can at least make her cum. I use my hips to hold her against the wall and slide my fingers into her deeper. Althea moans again as I touch her sweet spot and I keep rubbing the most sensitive parts of her. Althea pushes her hips forward and my fingers go deeper.

"Cum for me, princess."

Althea whimpers and pushes her hips forward. That's all it takes before she cums. I nibble on her ears and lick her

**171**

neck as she finishes, drawing her towards me and pushing my fingers deeper as she cums.

"Fuck, I love your pussy."

"Lucky…"

"Yes," I whisper. "I'm very fucking lucky."

I take my hand away from her pussy and lick every drop of her juices off my fingers. She makes little a squirming movement against me which nearly makes me cum in my pants. I grab her ass with my licked-clean hands and drag her to her bedroom. We don't make it through the bedroom door. I press Althea against the door and it doesn't budge.

"We can fuck here," I whisper. "We're basically in the bedroom."

"We're not," she says, kicking me with her heels. "Open the door…"

I struggle with the handle, but I don't want to make it to the bed. I want her now. After a few minutes, I muscle the door open, but I don't get Althea in bed. I drop to the ground with her and as Althea squeals, I mount her and spread her legs apart.

"I know we shouldn't," I whisper. "But I want you so fucking bad."

# Chapter 17
# **Banished**
## Althea

Lucky has me pinned to the ground and powerless in his grasp. I can feel his big hard dick against my thigh and I know I don't have an ounce of control over what's happening. He wants me tonight and Lucky always gets what he wants. He grabs my hands and pins them over my head before he runs his tongue slowly along my neck and earlobes.

"I'll fucking miss you, princess."

His gruff voice gets me even wetter. I struggled to stifle my moans in the hallway but in the safe house bedroom, I don't have to worry. Lucky's tongue feels fucking amazing on my neck. I press against his grasp on my wrists to see if Lucky has any intentions of setting me free. He doesn't.

Lucky's grasp tightens as I fight him.

"Stop," he whispers. "I fucking need you one last time."

He rips the rest of my pants off and then my underwear. I don't bother protesting. Lucky pushes his pants down and takes his cock out. Without wasting a second, he presses the oozes head of his dick against my entrance. He's so hard and huge. Lucky's dick presses against me, attempting to push through but my tightness resists him. I move my hips up and Lucky pushes in again.

This time, he gets the head of his dick between my legs and pushes hard. I moan as he gets the head inside me. My nails dig into Lucky's muscles which tense immediately from contact. He moves his hips to push the rest of his dick inside me. His cock pins me to the floor and I grunt as he keeps me there, entirely submissive to him and spread for him on my bedroom floor.

"I missed this," he growls. "I missed you every fucking night."

I moan as Lucky moves his hips, and pleasure surges through every inch of me. Losing control to him is so fucking easy. A gush of juices between my legs makes it easier for Lucky to get deeper inside me. The deeper he thrusts his big dick inside me, the closer I get to an orgasm.

"Give me more," I whisper. "More."

Lucky drives his hips into me and pushes me over the edge. An intense climax takes over every part of my body. I want more of Lucky. I grab him deeper, digging my heels into his muscular ass and pulling him close.

"I love you."

Lucky growls and kisses my neck. "I love you too."

He releases my hands and moves his hands to my neck instead. He doesn't close his hands around my neck, he just holds me in place with his hips and his hands.

"You will always be mine," he whispers. "Even if I never see you again, you'll be mine. I will always take care of you."

Lucky moves his dick inside me, stirring me to moan loudly again. Every time that dick moves inside me, a shudder of pleasure moves through me. I know I'm going to cum again. I pull my heels against Lucky's ass again, drawing him deeper.

"More…"

Lucky chuckles and pulls his dick out of me. This is the opposite of giving me more and he knows it. He runs his thumb over my lower lip. The smell of my pussy lingers on his fingers. "Turn around," Lucky says. "I want to feel you beneath me."

Lucky pulls away from me and flips me over, giving me little chance for disobedience. He runs his hand over my ass and grabs a little too hard. I whimper and Lucky mistakes my painful whimper for one of pleasure. He bends over and gives my ass a soft kiss.

"I'll miss every inch of this pretty black ass," he growls.

I expect Lucky to slide his dick into me unceremoniously, but I feel a soft wet tongue spreading my ass cheeks apart. I squeal and wriggle my hips aggressively because what the fuck is he doing back there. My movement causes Lucky to hold my hips more forcefully so I can't move. I just have to lie still and feel his warm wet tongue spreading my ass apart and diving between my folds.

I cry out as Lucky's tongue dives into an unexpected place.

"Lucky!" I gasp. "You can't put your tongue back there."

Unperturbed by my complaint, Lucky's tongue slides into my back door. I cry out and push my hips back against him, inadvertently driving his tongue deeper into me. Lucky interprets my loud moans in response to his invasive touch as me prompting him to go deeper. He pushes his tongue further into my ass and teases my pussy with his fingers.

I moan even louder and Lucky removes his tongue, sliding it over the full length of my wetness. He pushes his tongue against my clit, rubbing it in slow circles to push me close to the edge again. As I wriggle against Lucky's grasp, he gets more possessive and he won't let go of me until he makes me cum several times. Holy shit.

Before I can recover from Lucky's tongue, I feel a soft nudge against my entrance. I gasp for breath and Lucky thrusts his entire dick inside me. My ass throbs as Lucky buries himself inside me. I can't stop myself from screaming. It's pain. It's pleasure. It's loving him, losing him and everything else. Our bodies meld together on my bedroom floor and sweat works up between us.

Lucky licks the sweat off my neck as he drives his cock deeper inside me.

"I'll miss this tight black pussy," Lucky growls, his kisses turning into possessive bites as he eases his hips into me from behind. I used to hate when he talked like that. The closer we get, the more I love the dirty things that come out of Lucky's mouth and how my Italian mobster speaks straight from the heart whenever a feeling or thought pops into his head.

"Shut up," I whisper, pushing my hips against him and taking Lucky's dick deeper inside me. I don't want to talk tonight. I just want to feel Lucky's body against mine. Lucky grunts and thrusts into me deeper, moving his hand in front of me to stroke my clit as he takes me from behind.

With each thrust he gets more possessive and pushes into me harder and deeper. I can't hold myself back from climaxing anymore and I cum hard all over Lucky's cock. He pulls out of me and drags it to the bed. We hardly make it to the bed before we do it again. He gets on top of me and makes love to me in bed three times before he gets up for a glass of water and insists on a shower. We take a shower together which leads to making love beneath the stream of water.

Lucky grabs me by the hair and takes me from behind in the shower with soap suds covering every inch of our bodies.

When he finishes that time, we get out of the shower together and Lucky lavishes me with affection. He dries me off and rubs lotion into every inch of my skin, kissing me on every spot of flesh he covers. My skin feels alive. Lucky chuckles and runs his hands over my naked flesh.

"It's almost morning," he says, drawing me to him and kissing my forehead. "I have to leave you soon."

"You don't have to." He has to know I don't want him to leave. This time I'm not the one pushing him away.

"I do."

"Are you sure you're not scared?"

"Of what?" Lucky growls.

"Of us being together. Of having something real."

Lucky's gaze snaps to mine as I slide on a bathrobe.

"I want to be with you, princess. But not if it hurts you or our daughter. I wasn't a man for all those years, but I'll be a man now."

He means it. I know he means it. Lucky takes my hand and puts it on his chest.

"I'll think about you every day."

"What about the future? Won't the city ever be safe again?"

"I couldn't ever risk losing you. I'd rather you have

another man in your bed and have you safe halfway across the country."

"I don't want another man in my bed."

I mean that. I haven't had a man in ten years since Lucky and I know I could go a lifetime alone. I would rather be alone than have anything less than this — the weird magic between me and Lucky Vicari.

"Good," Lucky says, and I don't know if he's joking. "Because then I might have to kill him."

"Do you really think Shana will move to Nashville with me?"

"She will," Lucky says. "You will be safe. I promise."

He wraps his arms around me. I'll miss his hugs. Lucky presses his nose into my neck. He hugs me even tighter.

"Hug Chiara every day for me when I'm gone."

I hate that he has to say that. I grab onto him and pull him close to me again. I don't want to talk about him leaving and I don't want to talk like we're running out of time, even if we are.

Lucky and I climb into bed again and I don't want to admit to myself that it's the last time I'll have this. I curl up in his arms and press my head on Lucky's tattooed chest. Those muscles... I'll miss those muscles. But I'll miss so much more than that.

I'll miss my monster.

SHANA RETURNS in the morning after Lucky leaves. We wake Chiara up and leave because we already wasted enough time and Lucky wants us to be safe. I have to explain to Chiara that we're moving to Nashville and why she has to come with us. I don't think she understands, but she's definitely happy to be with me. She doesn't leave my side and having Chiara at least distracts from the fact that I don't have Lucky by my side.

We get to my new place in Nashville in the middle of the afternoon. Nashville is hot as hell and I already miss New York City. They call this a city? It's sweltering and different from New York. I'm way too quiet on the journey towards our new neighborhood, so Shana takes up talking to Chiara who views this as one big adventure thanks to Shana.

Shana keeps Chiara chatting as we unlock the house for the first time and she handles everything when I freak out at the place Lucky got us. He has to be joking. How much is he spending on this? Shana holds Chiara's hand, so she doesn't get lost exploring the new house. Lucky told me a small family home. He didn't tell me he bought a freaking mansion.

Chiara and Shana's voices echo throughout the house and I pull myself together to be more positive for my daughter. The movers get there shortly after we do and we end that first night in the house eating pizza together on the living room floor. Chiara falls asleep in my lap and I take her to bed. After that first night, I don't want her sleeping alone anymore and I think Chiara agrees.

Our first week in Nashville is pure craziness. Lucky doesn't call. I think it's too painful for him and I don't blame him. It's too painful for me to even think about hearing his voice. The worst part is Chiara. She keeps asking for Lucky and I don't know what to tell her. I wanted to tell her the truth, but now it seems wrong. Shana doesn't have any advice for me, but I'm not in the position to press her too much for advice considering how much she's giving up for me.

"I'm not giving up a career for nothing. Your man is paying me $10,000 a month to stay here looking after you. Do you know how small my paychecks are?" Shana insists.

I insist Lucky isn't my man, but Shana refuses to think anything but the best of him. I'd rather not talk about Lucky at all. Even if it will always be impossible and always has been from the first day I met him — I need to forget Lucky Vicari.

# Chapter 18
# Changed Heart
## Lucky

I'll never forget her. My phone rings several times again in the morning. I'm sick of John calling to check on me. I'm sick of everyone. I know Althea and my daughter are safe, but my heart aches without them. I'm completely empty without my daughter and Althea... I still smell her on my clothes. I can still call the scent of her skin to mind with just closing my eyes.

I need new ink. My phone rings again and I pick up.

"What do you want?"

"Still in bed, loser?" he taunts me. I hate him right now.

"Shut the fuck up."

If John doesn't have a reason for calling, I'm hanging up. I groan and roll over before my brother makes his purpose known.

"Let's go out," John says. He never says that. What the fuck does he want.

"I'm fine."

"You haven't left the house in two weeks."

"Give me an address so I can blow a motherfucker up and I'll leave the fucking house."

John sighs. "You never handled breakups well."

I hate when John tries to act like my big brother. I prefer when the roles are clear, when he's just my boss so I can steel myself against him and blame him for all the shit I've had to do. It's hard for us to be in the life together and keep our relationship strong.

"I'm fine," I mutter. Nothing means anything. I won't get out of bed for John to torture me with wise quotes or whatever the fuck he plans on doing.

"Get your ass out of bed and head to the range. Twenty minutes. I'll see you there."

"Is that an order?"

"Yes, you lazy asshole, it's a fucking order. Vinnie got to my place with sixteen boxes of ammo we can blow."

"Sixteen boxes. Fuck."

"Ass out of bed. Now."

JOHN WAVES at me across the parking lot with three gun cases balances precariously in his hands.

"I brought the AR-15," he says excitedly. "Did Sammy tell you he added a new silencer?"

"He did not."

"Cheer up, motherfucker. Shoot your feelings. That always works."

I take a case from John, his standard .22 judging by the weight. He carries the bigger guns into the range and we get everything set up including John's homemade targets. I don't want to be in this fucking place at first, but I can't help loving it once I get a few shots off.

I hit dead center, which brings a smile to my face. John pats me on the back as he stands the unloaded .22 against the wall.

"Fucking great," John says. "Better?"

"Yes. Shooting a target completely healed the wound left by my missing daughter," I grumble. John says the dumbest fucking things sometimes.

"You are such a fucking dick," John says.

Is this John's idea of making me feel better?

"Why are you making yourself miserable? I didn't ask you to send the kid away or her mom. You think this is the best choice for them, you have to live with it, Lucky. I don't need any over emotional bullshit right now."

"I'm not overemotional."

If my brother wants, we can take this shit outside. I've been nothing but loyal to him. I took my trouble out of state and I've waited patiently for his orders about who I need to kill next.

"We still have no idea where Enrico is. Early's gone. I'm in deep shit if we can't find him. Dad thinks he's the problem."

"Dad spoke to you?"

John nods, but he isn't smiling. The thought of our father returning to Long Island wouldn't put a smile on anyone's fucking face.

"He wants to come back and set shit straight with the Murrays but he needs me to handle this first."

"Fuck."

"Yeah, fuck. Sammy can't get a hold of Enrico and he still

has headaches from the attacks. We have a lot of bullshit ahead of us."

I run my hand over my overgrown facial hair.

"It's better for my family to stay far away from all of this."

"Imagine if dad said that about us. We wouldn't be the men we are today."

I wonder if my brother thinks we're good men, or if it even fucking matters. I've done dirty shit, but I'm not the only one. I've only killed to protect people I love and to protect the system that keeps us safe. Without the mafia, Italians would have been the shit beneath American boots when we first got here. The family protects us. The family keeps our traditions alive and our people prosperous. I serve a more noble cause than right and wrong. We serve the fucking future.

"Althea and Chiara are safer away from us. If you've been talking to dad, you've told him they're... you know..."

John gives me a cynical smile.

"What?" I ask after an uncomfortably long haughty look from my brother.

"You think you're the first Italian guy to chase a chick like her? We try to follow our rules, but we're just guys. We can't help ourselves. We're like dogs."

"I guess."

"If you want to be with her, don't let dad stop you. I sure fucking wouldn't."

My brother's lying, but I appreciate the sentiment behind the lie. If he meant what he said, he wouldn't have spent the past decade refusing to get close to anybody. He's hiding himself away from a real relationship or family just as much as I am.

"I want to be with her," I admit to him out loud for the first time. "But I know it's fucking selfish. I hurt her. I caused our kid to get hurt. I have to be stronger than this."

"Consider this, idiot," John says impatiently. "You have to feel like that. Being a fucking dad is about feeling like a failure every fucking day."

"You're the expert now?"

"Nah, Sammy got drunk last weekend and told me this shit. Does it sound like good advice?"

"It sounds like drunk bullshit," I tell him. "But it's better than nothing."

"Go after her," John says. "Get her back. If you need more security, we'll downgrade at the casino. When you have to go after Enrico, I'll look out for her. After all, the kid's my niece and we haven't even properly met yet."

I'm skeptical about having John anywhere near a child, especially one of mine. He isn't exactly dad material, and he knows it. He's the one person in our family even more fucked up than I am.

"You wanna meet my kid?"

"She old enough to go shooting?"

"Althea won't let you take her fucking daughter shooting, are you crazy?"

John shrugs. "It's important for a girl to learn considering who her father is."

"A monster?"

John chuckles. "Calm the fuck down and stop being a girl. We aren't monsters. We're protectors. Big fucking difference. She needs to learn from you how to take care of herself. Fuck knows you can't rely on anyone else."

"Yeah."

"It's your choice," John says, emptying out another box of ammo. "Tell me what you want and I'll make it happen."

"What about Enrico?"

"That's still on you. When I find him, I'll expect you to handle it."

"Got it."

John loads the gun. We get our safety gear on and he lands three rounds dead center. It's time for the AR-15. Fuck, that'll be great to get my hands on.

I CAN'T GO DOWN THERE without telling her. It ain't fair to her. The second I get home from the range, I call her from bed. She doesn't know it's me because I have to be discreet and use private methods our family perfected to keep my phone number anonymous.

"Who the hell is this?" she answers nervously. "How did you get this number?"

Only one person has her phone number — Shana. She has an emergency line up to John programmed into the phone, but that's about it. There shouldn't be any phone calls and Althea knows it.

"It's me."

"Who? State your full name and prove who the hell you are, or I swear I'll get my baby daddy to—

I interrupt her before she can continue what I'm sure would have been a detailed threat.

"It's Lucky Vicari, Chiara's dad. The guy who can't stop thinking about all the ways we made love the last time we saw each other."

She's quiet for a few beats and then she whispers, "Fuck you."

Yeah. That's what I deserve.

"I deserve that."

"What the fuck do you want?"

She's trying to hide the emotion in her voice, but she can't hide from me. Maybe she could at first and maybe I didn't want to see her emotions. I want to see her now. Understanding her has become the most important fucking thing in the world to me aside from protecting her.

"How are you? How's Chiara?"

"Answer my question, Lucky," she responds sharply, her voice trembling with rage. I deserve that. I dumped her. But I'm going to fix this. I just need her to give me a chance.

"I want to know how you're doing because I miss you and you're my family."

"I thought communication would put us in danger."

"I'm coming for you, princess," I tell her. "No more fucking danger. I want to be with you."

She doesn't respond for far too long. My nerves are fucked to hell by the time Althea sighs on the other end of the line.

"What the fuck are you talking about?"

"I made a mistake."

"Okay."

She's still tense. It's Althea. She wants me to work for her heart because she's put in so much effort into healing it. Only a worthy man deserves her love after the shit she's been through. I get it.

"I love you and I should have never tried to send you away. Yes, it's fucking dangerous up here and I don't have a right to put you in danger. But I don't have a right to take you away from what you want. So if you want to be with me… I'll be there tomorrow morning."

Althea inhales loudly. I can't tell what she's thinking. I can't look into her eyes and see her, and that hurts so fucking bad. It's pure anguish.

"What about Chiara?"

"You haven't told her yet."

It's a statement, not a question. Althea has always been firm about her stance on revealing myself to Chiara. I haven't proven that I'll be there for her forever. That'll fucking change.

"When I see you tomorrow, I'll tell her myself. I'll explain the whole fucking story."

"Um… please do not tell our daughter you paid me five thousand dollars to have sex with you in an Italian restaurant. That doesn't reflect well on either of us."

I smile a little.

"I'm sure there's a way to make it appropriate for kids."

"I'm skeptical."

"What if I tell her I was destined to be with you and we made her by pure cosmic accident because that's what was meant to fucking happen? You and me. Forever. Bound by a little girl."

"You still used the f-word in your kid appropriate story," Althea protests. "Still skeptical."

"I'll tell her I left you, then. I'll tell her that I failed as a father, but I want to work hard the rest of my life to make it up to both of you. That's the truth."

"The rest of your life?"

"Yeah," I whisper to Althea. "I want forever, princess."

"What if I want to stay in Tennessee?"

"Doesn't fucking matter. I'm coming for you and I'm coming for Chiara. I'm done being a fucking coward, okay? I love you."

"I love you too," she whispers. I'm a monster for leaving her.

Fuck, I miss her so bad. She doesn't know how much it kills me to be away from her right now. Every minute I'm away from her hurts like hell.

"Are you alone?"

"Shana and Chiara are practicing lacrosse outside. It's safe, I think."

"Good," I whisper. I'm happy my daughter's safe.

"What are you wearing?" I ask Althea. "I'm sure it's real hot down there."

"It is," she says. "I'm just wearing a big t-shirt."

My dick stiffens instantly in my pants. Why am I such a horny motherfucker?

"Just a big t-shirt?" I ask her.

"Yeah," Althea says. "And some panties."

"No bra?"

"No bra."

Now my dick wants to hop on a plane and get down to fucking Tennessee. This is pure fucking torture. I need to touch myself.

"I wish I was there to take those panties off right now," I mutter into the phone. My desire for her is too desperate for me to ignore. My hands are in my pants and I'm stroking my cock with slow movements, imagining Althea's body right here – naked.

"What else would you do if you were here?" Althea asks.

I could get into all types of fucking trouble if I had her in my bed. Every stroke from my palm drives me fucking wild. I need her.

"I'd spread your lips apart and taste you," I tell her. "I'd put my tongue on your sweet little clit and lick every inch of your lips until you screamed."

"Fuck…" Althea whispers. Shit. She's touching herself too. I've never done this before, but I need her too fucking badly to stop myself.

"Touch yourself, princess," I murmur. "Spread your pussy lips and fuck yourself for me."

"Lucky…"

"Yeah… that's right," I whisper. "If I were with you, I would put my dick in you right now after getting you nice and wet. I would lick your pussy until you screamed and then bury my dick deep in your sweet black pussy…"

Fuck, I'm gettting close. Just talking about her pussy and putting my dick in her gets my cock insanely fucking hard. How the fuck can I hold myself back? I grunt in response to Althea's whimpering on the other end of the line.

"Cum for me, princess. Make yourself cum for me…"

"Yes…" she whispers. "Yes…"

"Rub your pussy until you cum… do it…"

I hear a little moan from Althea's end of the line and I push myself over the edge once I suspect she's in the throes of a climax.

"Fuck…"

I cum hard. Really fucking hard.

"I miss you," Althea whispers.

"I'LL BE THERE SOON, princess. I promise."

.    .    .

I COULDN'T HAVE RUSHED myself to the airport faster. I tell John what I'm doing and pack my shit to head down to Tennessee. I'll get a car once we go down there and by then, John will have a couple people he can send to help move us back to New York.

It's not just seeing Althea I look forward to. I fell in love with our daughter during the short time I knew her and now I can't imagine a world without her in it. I miss Chiara's laugh, the way she twirled her lacrosse stick, and how her voice carried through the house with so much fucking innocence.

John's right. If I want to have a family, I have to stop being a fucking coward. If I'm the man I need to be, I can keep my family safe. I can't run away behind booze or drugs or sex anymore. I have to face the facts of who I am – Lucky Vicari, son to the Vicari family boss, the Long Island executioner. I can still be the man I need to be for my daughter.

Without their light in my life, I can't stop myself from being a monster.

DESPITE MY BEST efforts to get to Tennessee quickly, it's 2 a.m. before I get to the house. I can't tell if there's anyone home. There's one light on downstairs and I can't make out anything else from outside. I pay my cab driver and watch him drive off. It's strange being down here with no weapons on family business. I have a pistol stashed secretly in a safe in the house (which thankfully, Althea doesn't know about) but aside from that, I'm unarmed.

# Lucky

I walk up to the front door. Althea should be expecting me, so I knock instead of ringing the doorbell. I assume that light on in the living room is her, but when I knock on the door, I hear footsteps that sound too light to be Althea's. The door swings open slowly and Shana's teary face greets me in the doorway.

"Hey," I whisper. "I got here as fast as I could."

Shana steps outside and shuts the door behind her. What the hell is going on? Is something wrong?

"She's gone," Shana chokes out. "I haven't told Chiara yet. I just got her to bed. I don't know what the hell happened, Lucky but Althea's gone and I don't know who took her or how this happened."

"What do you mean, gone? I was just on the fucking phone with her this morning."

I don't like the sound of this, but Shana doesn't sound like she has more information.

"She goes for a walk every afternoon. I tried to get her to stay in just for tonight, but she swore she needed to clear her head. I would have gone out to look but I was too scared to leave Chiara alone."

"What about the emergency phone?"

"She took it with her."

Thank fucking God.

. . .

"GOOD. It has a tracker. Don't worry, Shana. I'll come in and see Chiara and we'll go out and look for her. Is she worried?"

"I calmed her down for the night, but she's sharp. She'll figure out something is wrong pretty quick."

"Let's head inside."

"Do you think one of your people got her?" Shana asks. She gives me a piercing, knowing look. I don't know what Althea told her – probably not everything – but Althea told her something.

Before I can respond, Shana blurts out, "It's not what you think. She didn't tell me anything. I'm not an idiot. I figured it out."

"There's no way anyone could have known she was down here. If it's one of my people, we have big fucking problems in New York."

"Do you think she wandered off?"

"You tell me. Maybe I scared her and she ran away."

Shana shakes her head. "She wouldn't leave Chiara. No matter how she felt about you, she loves Chiara more than life itself. She would never leave her behind."

"Is there anyone else from your life who could have traced her down here?"

"Her mama knew," Shana says. "That's all I can think of."

"I strongly doubt her elderly mother kidnapped her," I mutter, muddling through the problem in my head. "But it's a lead. I'll get my brother to send me the data from the GPS on her phone."

Shana opens the front door and I step into the house I thought I would never see again after the day I closed on it. It's the perfect farmhouse safe house with vintage wooden details everywhere and antique farm decor. Shana and Althea have made the place their home with additional details and fresh flowers. It hurts to walk in here and know my family lives here without me – that my daughter still doesn't consider me family.

That will change after tonight. I promised Althea I would get to the point and tell my daughter the truth. Shana leads me to her bedroom and Chiara sits straight up. At first, she rubs her eyes with confusion on her face, then she smiles once she sees me.

"Uncle Lucky." Chiara stretches out her arms and I hurry for her. I grab her and wrap my daughter in my arms. I never want to let go of her. I'll never let go of her again – not for long. This time, everything will be different. I'll be the father I should have been in the first fucking place. I'll be the guy she needs me to be.

"Hey, Chiara. I missed you so much."

"Missed you too, Uncle Lucky."

I spin her around and set my beautiful daughter on the ground. Her hair floats in a halo around her head with soft, wild curls. Her brown eyes gaze up at me with love and hope. We have a connection. She's my little girl – my feisty, wild-haired, biracial Italian girl with mean stick skills.

Shana stands in the doorway watching us. I want time alone with my daughter, but I appreciate Shana doing what Chiara would have wanted – looking after her daughter. I crouch down to Chiara's level and give her a big look so she knows what I'm about to say is really important.

"Hey kid, we gotta talk."

"It's late," Chiara says. "Does my mom know you're here past my bedtime?"

"Nah. I snuck in."

Shana quickly interrupts, "Don't listen to him, I let him in."

Chiara giggles and presses her fingers to her lips. She'll keep my secret.

"What do you want to talk about," Chiara says. "Can we go to the kitchen and have some milk Aunty Shana?"

"Sure, let me get y'all some milk."

Shana walks out the door and I follow her and Chiara to the kitchen table where Shana sits us down and heads to the kitchen to pour us glasses of milk. I don't drink milk, I'm a grown ass man, but tonight, for my daughter, I'm drinking a glass of fucking milk.

"Hey, kid. I missed you a lot."

"You already said that," Chiara says nervously, twirling her finger around her hair. "Is mom home yet?"

Fuck, she's so worried about her mom. I am too, but I have to do this first.

"Not yet. But you don't have to worry because I'm here and I'm not your uncle, kid."

"Okay… I know that."

"I'm your father."

It sounds blunt and like the moment ends too quickly. Chiara presses her palms to the table and opens her eyes dramatically.

"Are you kidding me?"

Okay, that's not the response I expected, but it's Chiara, so I never know what to expect. She's pure fucking Vicari like that.

"Nope. Dead serious. I'm your dad."

Shana approaches the table with the milk and sets glasses

down in front of us. Shana doesn't consume things like milk. She sits at the table with a glass of water.

"Now?" she says. "You're doing this now."

"I promised Althea."

Shana nods and sips her water. Chiara glances at her and then at me.

"Did you know about this?" Chiara asks Shana, who shrugs.

This isn't Shana's burden to bear. This was a secret Althea chose to keep and we both respected her decision. I don't need to drag her into this.

"Your mom and I had a complicated past," I tell my daughter. "I should have been there for you and I wasn't. But I'm here now and I'm your father."

My throat tightens. Saying this feels freeing and terrifying. I love my daughter, but I don't know how she'll react and I've built up to this moment for weeks, desperately wanting to tell her every moment we were together.

"You were my mom's boyfriend?!" Chiara says, shrieking and looking a little grossed out.

"Something like that," Shana says.

"Something special happened between us," I explain to my daughter. "We didn't realize we were meant to be together."

Chiara raises an eyebrow. "So you've been my dad this entire time?"

Now she reminds me of Althea and it's a painful reminder that every minute I spend here is a minute I lose that I could be looking for her. I need to do this for my daughter. She's my blood and she needs to know the truth.

"Yes. Your mom wanted to make sure I was for real before we told you."

"Are you for real?" Chiara asks, throwing up that sassy eyebrow again and shaking a mass of curls out of her face. If she's still tired, she doesn't act like it at all.

"I'm for real. I'm here. I'm your dad and… I'm taking you back to New York."

Shana raises her eyebrows, but thankfully, she doesn't comment. Chiara bites her lip and then looks away from me. My daughter's brows knit together. She doesn't cry, but the most heartbreaking words come from her mouth.

"I always wanted to know who my dad was."

Fuck. I took that from her. Even if I say I would have stepped up, if I hadn't hurt Althea, she would have never kept my daughter from me. This is my responsibility.

"I'm sorry, kid. I should have been there."

I set down my milk and get up from the table. I have to hold her. I stretch my arms out.

"I owe you a big fucking hug."

"And probably a lot of child support," Chiara says earnestly. She sets her milk down and rushes to embrace me. I hold my daughter close, trying not to fucking cry and failing. I don't want her to see my tears, so I just hold her tight until I can pull myself together and show her that strength and give her the protection she never got from me throughout her childhood.

"I'm heading out to find your mom."

"Did something bad happen?"

Chiara pulls away from me and gives me a serious look like she means business. It's crazy how much she looks like her mom when she does that. It's like I wasn't even in the fucking picture and she's a clone of her mother's jawline and facial expressions. I love my kid and I love her mother too. I need us to be a family – John's right.

I'm a Long Island Italian and at the end of the day, the only thing that makes 'our thing' worth it is a fucking family to come home to.

"I don't know, but it's my job to keep you both safe and I won't let myself screw up again. I'm bringing your mom home and then we're going to be a real family. Understood?"

"Capisce," Chiara responds unprompted. A gentle smirk crosses my daughter's face. I wish I could stay here with her all night, but there's no way in hell I'm leaving Althea out there on her own.

"I have to leave you with your aunt tonight, but I'll be back, okay?"

"Okay."

"Cool."

"Do I have to call you dad now?"

Fuck. I never thought of that. I start stammering, when Shana chimes in. "Why don't you see how you feel after a while okay? Don't rush into anything. This is all big news."

"Yeah," Chiara says. "Huge."

"Come here, baby," Shana calls to her. Chiara walks over to her and sits on Shana's lap, staring at me inquisitively. I like that I can see the light in her eyes and sense that her precious mind is always whirring and thinking about the world. My daughter is fucking smart and I love it.

Shana holds Chiara tightly with a strong, protective grasp. I'm confident my daughter will be safe with her for at least the rest of the night. I hope I don't have to disappear any longer than that.

"Is this related to your line of work?" Shana asks. The question is subtle enough not to raise any alarm bells with my daughter, which I appreciate.

"I don't know."

I don't want to say more in front of my kid. She deserves her childhood and her innocence preserved.

"Don't be gone long," Shana says.

"I WON'T," I tell her. "Wherever the fuck my girl is, I'll find her. I promise."

# Chapter 19
# This Is How I Die
## Althea

What scares me the most is knowing the man who burst out of the woods and dragged me into his car isn't white. If he was white, I could blame it on the Long Island mob or one of their enemies – maybe even the Irish guys from Boston I would hear Lucky muttering about on the phone all the time. I know what a brother sounds like and the guy who dragged me out of the woods was definitely black.

It's a random attack—at least as far as I know, because I don't know a single soul down here except for Shana. I haven't seen the guy's face, but I know he's a man and he's using some type of weird voice disguise machine. I can tell he's black, but other than that, there's no grounding familiarity that could give me any clues about the person who grabbed me.

My body aches like hell from fighting back. He didn't expect me to fight back and I can tell because he beat my ass to shit once I started, like he never considered I might push back against literal capture and out of sheer surprise, he fought me.

Fighting didn't help my situation. He had a mask on, so I didn't get any details about him and he was covered from head to toe. I barely got any idea of his height because it all happened so fast. Motherfucker put me in the trunk of his car... It's hot down here. Tennessee is hot as fuck and you think it would cool down at night but it's just a hot muggy ass mess. The grossest sweat you can imagine glues my thighs and ass cheeks together. Breathing is nearly impossible.

When the trunk opens, I want to escape, but that motherfucker tied me up. I can't see shit when he opens the trunk. We must have been driving for hours, but I can't tell if we were driving in circles or straight up the highway. I'm tired, fucking thirsty and I'm just happy this psycho didn't get their hands on my daughter.

"Who are you?" I croak out.

I hear his distorted voice. "Cellphone."

"I don't have one," I lie to him. I do what any smart woman does when she realizes shit's getting real—she puts her phone in her bra. Duh. It's not like I can use my phone since my hands are tied up, but at least the dumbass forgot to pat me down. Maybe he isn't a career criminal.

He moves to close the trunk, and I want to beg him to keep it open. My desire for dignity in this highly undignified position wins out, but my perception was completely wrong. He isn't closing the trunk, just reaching for something. My heart rate increases when the syringe comes towards my thigh and the last thing I remember is a tiny pinch on my right thigh.

.  .  .

# Althea

Fuck.

When I wake up, I'm in a house. This motherfucker must be strong to have dragged me into a house, but maybe not considering my body feels freshly bruised like someone dragged me across the ground or something. There are scrapes all over my shoulders and thighs.

The only person on my mind is Chiara. I hope Shana keeps her safe and more importantly – I hope Shana can reach out to Lucky without my cellphone. He's coming anyway. I know I can trust him – but that doesn't mean I sit on my ass waiting to get saved. Nope. This motherfucker thinks he can mess with me and he can, for now, but everyone has weaknesses.

Even this stranger who might not be a stranger.

This motherfucker tied me to a bed, but I'm not blindfolded and even if I'm on a bed, I'm fully clothed, which is hardly a victory, but I have to take every opportunity at optimism afforded me considering my situation. I wait awake for what feels like several hours before the door to the bedroom opens. I still can't see his face because of how he tied me up. Whoever did this must have planned it.

"Hello, Althea. You might wonder why I brought you here."

I'm not playing this sicko's game. If he wants to talk, he can talk. My only job right now is getting enough information so that I can find something that I can use to assist in my escape. Responding to this asshole isn't part of my plan.

He continues with no response which doesn't surprise me and it doesn't matter. The more he talks, the more I can learn. Keep talking asshole. Every second he wastes gives Lucky a chance to get closer. He has to know I'm gone by now, right?

"We need to talk about your daughter, Chiara Little."

My heart sinks into my stomach. I'm glad this sicko didn't get his hands on her. I don't respond because there's nothing I have to say to this creep about my daughter. I try to fight against the binds on my hands as subtly as possible, but they don't budge and I can't even wriggle my wrists around a little. I'm entirely trapped and there's enough adrenaline coursing through me that if I weren't bound to the bed, I would scratch and screaming for my life in here.

"I need you to answer me, Althea."

I don't respond and to my surprise, I regret it. I can't see anything, so I don't see him coming towards me with a small taser. He presses it to my back and I yelp loudly as an electric charge surges through me with enough strength to force my teeth to chatter and my muscles to all tense into one miserable ball of pain. Tears prickle my eyes against my will from the shock as I keep spasming on the bed, oxygen struggling to get into my lungs.

Fuck. Holy fuck. This guy is crazy. Holy fuck.

I struggle to catch my breath, but I can't allow myself to give in to any weakness.

"I'll ask you again about your daughter. Who is her father?"

What the fuck? Didn't Lucky's blackmailer choose him for being Chiara's father? Isn't this the forbidden knowledge that forced us into hiding and out of New York? Whoever this is might not be a mobster, but they still know about Chiara.

"Tell me who the hell you are and maybe I'll answer."

"Isn't it obvious, Althea?"

Obvious? What the hell is– Holy shit.

"Drew?!"

"Hello, baby mama."

Oh, fuck no.

Fuck NO.

I thrash in bed harder and Drew brings the taser down on the base of my spine. Excruciating pain forces me to spasm and throb in the bed and foam escapes my lips as I choke and gasp for breath again. If he keeps this up, I'll die here.

As I lie there in a whimpering mess, Drew drops the voice disguise bullshit. I don't know if it's a device or what, but his familiar, annoying ass voice returns and I'm in pure hell.

"Did you really think I would let you run away to Tennessee with my kid?"

"She's not your kid, Drew. It's been ten years and I keep telling you the same thing—what the hell is wrong with you?"

"Don't lie to me, Althea. That baby is mine and you know it."

"Are you dumb? Seriously, Drew? Are you dumb?"

I'm in no position to talk to him like this, but I can't help myself. I expect him to tase me again, but he doesn't because he's still fixated on his monumentally stupid mission to prove that a black man could have fathered a biracial child with a black woman.

"It all hit me when you ran away to Tennessee. I stopped by your mama's house to see my daughter and she tells me you take my kid away? What the hell is wrong with you bitches?"

"Chiara is not your daughter, you idiot."

"Why won't you admit the truth? Why you keep fucking lying?"

"BECAUSE I'M NOT!" I scream. That takes all the energy out of my completely fucked up body and my head slams into the pillow. Tears pierce the corners of my eyes again as I anticipate more of Drew's ruthless treatment.

"Fine. If you say she's not mine, we can always have another kid."

That's the point when my heart stops. I know I'm completely vulnerable with no way out. Drew might not be as large as Lucky, but he's big enough to subdue me and he has me entirely under his control. He tied me to a bed facing away from the door and facing away from him and it suddenly occurred to me that Drew had these intentions all along.

"How the hell did you find me?"

"Your mom is old, Althea. She doesn't have a passcode on her phone. I read your conversations. You can't get away from me. We've known each other our whole lives and you are mine…"

"We barely talk, Drew!"

"We'll have plenty to talk about after tonight."

My stomach sinks again. I don't want this to happen. My body belongs to me. Only me. After the incident with Lucky, I promised I would never have another man between my legs that I didn't enthusiastically want. Drew wants to force me. He wants to rape me. He's known me my entire life and he's never taken "no" for an answer.

I regret dating him. I regret ever even meeting him, but it's too late for that. His so-called love for me and Chiara has morphed into this dark, overwhelming thing, pushing him well over the edge. It's horrific to watch, but it's even more horrific to experience. I can't let the horror overwhelm me. I have to survive.

"What's going to happen tonight?"

Sound calm, Althea. All you need to do is to sound calm.

"We're making a baby, girl. After tonight, we're going back to Brooklyn and you're done fucking around, okay?"

"Drew. We haven't dated in a decade."

I have to fight my urge to fight him. If I fight him, I'll never win. Hell, I've already lost. I don't want to lose even more.

"Can you stop fucking arguing? It's been a decade and we're still in each other's lives. That means something, Althea. We're practically family."

It hurts to do this. It hurts to be here, but I have to convince him to let me go.

"Okay," I tell him, trying not to sound as physically disgusted as I am. "I'll fuck you, but you have to untie me. I want…"

Oh God. I try not to to throw up, but I have to get the words out. I have to make him believe it.

"I want to look at you while we make a baby."

. . .

BILE RISES in my throat and I have to choke it back down with a painful, acidic gulp.

DREW MOVES around the room so I can finally look at him. My stomach tightens in a knot. Drew looks worse than when I last saw him and he hardly looks like himself. If I didn't know better, I would guess he was on something — a drug aside from entitlement that is.

He gives me a triumphant smile that gets me even sicker. This loser really thinks he's won something, huh? I have to play along until he unties me.

"Is that so?" He says. "Look at me now, baby. Accept what happened between us and accept it's going to happen again."

"I still don't understand why you're doing this."

"Love," Drew says. "Love, baby. That's all."

I don't think Drew would understand what love is if it smacked him into next week Tuesday. Unrequited obsession isn't love. Delusions aren't love. Believing that you own another person isn't love either.

"Get these ropes off, then. Let's make some love."

My stomach lurches. This feels like I'm betraying Lucky, even if I haven't done anything except try to survive. Drew settles his attitude and approaches me to undo my binds. He works with a pocket knife and he refuses to look me in the eye. His hands shake as he works one of the binds. Drugs? Or is it scaring the crap out of him that after all this time, he finally went this far...

It's hard not to throw my fist straight into Lucky's face

when he gets my first hand untied. My wrists hurt like hell, so it's probably best for me to wait for the blood to flow back into my hands first. Drew moves over to the other side of me and undoes my other hand. Now, I have to convince him to let his guard down even more.

Drew might be entitled and he might be completely convinced that he's Chiara's father, but he doesn't know the shit I've been through the past ten years as a single mom. He doesn't know how strong I am knowing that Lucky Vicari is 100% behind me.

He licks his lips as I sit up on the bed and catch my breath, trying to move onto the next phase of my plan without making my excitement that Drew's stupid ass untied me extremely obvious. Drew considers this a victory judging by the smile on his stupid ass face. I meet his face with a genuine smile. I'm not smiling for the reason Drew thinks I am, but he doesn't have to know that.

"You finally coming around to the truth?" Drew asks hopefully.

"You've gone so far to prove your love to me," I respond calmly. "I'm starting to see how much I mean to you."

"Finally," Drew says, sighing with relief and broadening his smile. "You've been driving me crazy, baby girl. Crazy."

"That's what love does," I reply stiffly. "It drives you crazy."

Crazy enough to do what the fuck I have to do so I can get out of here. Lucky will have to understand. He has his guns and I have weapons of my own which are a bit more subtle.

"So are you going to admit it? I think you should tell me the truth before we make love."

"I'll tell you the truth. But it's been years since I've seen you Drew. I want to see you naked before we do this."

Drew's grin nearly breaks his damn jaw. I wish I could crack a fucking hole in this man's face. Patience.

"Do you think I'm stupid?"

"Huh?"

"You don't have any feelings for me, do you?" Drew says.

"What the hell are you talking about?"

"You don't want me," Drew says, his voice changing in that scary ass way that tells me he's done listening to me and maybe he never planned on listening in the first place.

"What? What are you talking about?"

"You think I'm stupid, huh?"

He reaches into his pants and I see that I'm in big fucking trouble. It doesn't matter that Drew freed me. He has a way of keeping me in line and he knew that the entire time. He reaches into his back pocket and pulls out a small ass revolver. I'm fucked if he has ammo in that thing and do I want to take chances with this motherfucker?

I glance at the door. Maybe I fucking do. Drew doesn't notice me looking at the door, thank goodness, because he's fiddling with his gun, trying to turn the safety off and exhibiting no control of the muzzle. I can't even flinch as he waves the damn thing around because I don't want him to sense any of my plans or fears in the situation.

"I shouldn't have tried to screw you over," I tell him.

Drew nods and holds the gun at me.

"Turn around and take your damn clothes off," Drew says. "I'm tired of playing these fucking games with you."

"I'm tired of playing games too, Drew. But most importantly, I'm tired of losing."

My crazy ass leaps out of the gun. Drew fires the gun. It clicks. That motherfucker doesn't have any bullets in the gun. I get to the door before he knows what hit him. He thought his stupid ass unloaded gun could scare me too much to try to save myself? Drew must be in love with the old me because the new me is much different.

I burst out of the room and race toward the first door that looks like an exit. This place looks like a damned AirBnB. Knowing Drew, it probably is. I have to run down a flight of stairs to get to the street. By the time I hit the bottom of the stairs, I can hear Drew coming after me.

"Get back here!" He yells. "I swear I'm coming after you, bitch!"

Drew leaps over the railing with the same athleticism he had in high school. Unlike my ex, I've slowed down over the years. Single motherhood and putting on more than a few pounds didn't exactly turn me into a marathoner.

I push myself to run faster, but Drew's closing in on me. I can feel him getting close enough to grab me. There are cars in the street, but none of them are stopping and there's no way I can get away from Drew unless I do something crazy. Unless I do something that could kill me. I glance at the oncoming traffic.

Drew attempts to grab my forearm but I'm so sweaty that his grasp slips off me. I shriek and push him off as hard as I can. There are still cars coming, but I have a better chance with the oncoming cars than Drew and his stupid revolver. I take my chances and I run into the street.

· · ·

## This Is How I Die

Bright lights hurtle towards me and in the split second of consciousness I have left, I wonder if all of this was a huge mistake.

## Chapter 20
# Getting My Girl Back
### Lucky

I slam down on the brakes. It's her. It's fucking her. John's on the other end of the line and I hang up the second I nearly miss hitting Althea, who collapses in the middle of the road without me touching her.

I leap out of the car and rush over to her, glancing around to see if there's anyone else around. A guy in a Jeep Cherokee zooms past, slamming on his fucking horn because I'm parked in the middle of the street.

I race to Althea and lift her off the ground. She groans as she regains consciousness. I didn't hit her, she just fainted. It happens with too much adrenaline sometimes — fucking awful when you need to kill the guy later.

Hoisting Althea over my shoulders is easy, getting her into the car is hard because she attempts to unravel herself from me, but can barely hold herself up. She keeps babbling and trying to tell me something, but I need to get her safe first and then I need to find the motherfucker who took her and put a bullet in his goddamned head.

Once she's in the car, I turn it on and look over at her. She's gaining her consciousness, but still a little groggy.

"Am I dead?" She asks in a hoarse voice.

"You're in my car and I'm here. I got you."

"Go get him. Don't stay here," Althea groans. "His house has the green roof."

"Who?"

"My ex."

Althea groans and rubs her forehead. "I'm getting it together."

"I don't need you to get it together. Tell me what weapons he has. I need details, Althea."

"He's tall. Black. He has a little revolver and he looks out of it. I think that place is a rental."

"What car does he have?"

"I can't remember. I didn't see it. Did you see him drive off?"

"I don't know," she says. "I'm sorry."

It doesn't matter. She's given me enough. Unless he took a car, this bastard couldn't have gone too far.

"Buckle up," I tell her. "We'll get further if we follow him in the car."

"Don't you want to check the house?"

"If he saw me, he didn't run into the house."

"He doesn't even know who you are."

"He'll find out," I grunt. I never heard a damned thing about Althea's ex and I wonder what exactly gives the man the idea that Althea is unclaimed. "Did he hurt you badly?"

"I'm fine."

"You don't look fucking fine."

"I don't want you to do anything crazy."

"Too fucking bad," I grunt. There's no way this stupid motherfucker is getting out of this alive. You don't touch my woman or hurt my family and get away with it. That's not the way the fucking world works.

I turn the car on and turn the lights off. We have to move as quietly as possible and there are enough cars parked on the street out here that we can get away with moving through the streets unnoticed. Althea won't take her eyes off me, but she won't speak. She looks like this guy fucked her up — so now I'll fuck his ass up all the way back to Long Island.

"There the motherfucker is," I murmur, pointing a way up and pulling the car off to the side behind a navy blue Chevy Impala. I turn the car off. Tall black male with a hoodie up glancing around furtively? He's not too far from where I found Althea. It must be the guy. She nods and gives me a concerned look after that.

It's him and Althea knows he's in trouble.

"Wait here," I tell her.

"Where are we?" She whispers.

"Doesn't matter. Wait here."

I give her a serious look and Althea nods. Her fire isn't gone, but it's certainly dimmed. She's scared out of her fucking mind. I lean over and give her a kiss. It's all I can afford to give her without potentially losing sight of Drew. That kiss gives me life. I press my tongue into her mouth and confirm with my body that I'm loyal to her and only her.

I fucking love her.

When our lips part, I open the car door and run towards Drew with my sawed off at my side. He doesn't know what hit him. I smack into him, the way I used to when I played football in high school. A good old tackle brings the mother-fucker's ass to the ground. I beat his fucking face with my fist. He yells and after a few more hits, he stops yelling.

I get his ass back to the car and toss him in the back. Althea glances back and she stifles what I suspect would have been a scream. She turns to face the windshield, gripping the front seat of the car. He's unconscious and a bit bloody, but that doesn't matter.

"Althea, calm down. Everything will be fine from now on. I'm right here and nothing will happen to you anymore. I swear."

"I can't look at him," she whispers. "Is he going to wake up?"

"I don't know."

"He's dead?"

I grimace. "No."

It'll take a lot more work than a few blows to the face to kill the motherfucker. I don't mind doing the work, but I don't want Althea to see this knowing how she feels about me and what I do. She still refuses to glance behind her, even as I start the car and think of my daughter – how this moth-erfucker hurt her mother and how he'll pay for how he hurt my daughter by proxy.

"What are you going to do to him?" Althea asks nervously. I swear she can read my fucking mind. None of her protests matter. I knew what I would do to this sicko the minute I left Althea's place.

"Let's just say they'll need to clean the fuck outta this rental."

"What about the police?" Althea whispers. It didn't take her much to get tentative about the cops, but she isn't wrong to worry. We ain't exactly in New York and redneck cops could be a problem – a risk I'm willing to take. Our family stretches down the East Coast, into the Midwest and across America. Italians look out for each other wherever we are. I have to trust that'll be the case here.

"Let me worry about the police. Try to get some sleep."

"You're about to kill someone," Althea hisses. "It's not exactly a lullaby."

"Do you want me to take you to Chiara first?"

I mean what I ask, but Althea must know that we're several hours away from her daughter and if I take her to Chiara first, that makes Drew in the backseat even more of a wildcard than before.

"No. That doesn't make sense, does it?"

"You don't have to be a part of this."

"I'm already a part of this," Althea snaps. "I was a part of this from the night we met at Il Pappa's and I'll be a part of this forever."

She sounds angry, but also resigned. This isn't how I want her to feel. I want my love to be the thing that brings us together. I want her to see how much I give a fuck out of her and how far out of my way I'll go to keep her safe. I love her dearly.

"I love you," I grunt. "I don't do this for pleasure."

"I know it's useless," Althea pleads. "But you don't have to kill him."

My grasp on the steering wheel tightens to the point where my knuckles turn white. I clench my jaw to stop myself from saying something insensitive to Althea. I love this chick and I know she's been through hell, but I can't let her heart of gold save a monster.

"What did he do to you?" I ask calmly. Give me a fucking reason to spare him, princess. If you want him spared... I need a damned reason.

"If I tell you, you'll kill him."

"Exactly," I grunt. "That's the point. Loving you. Keeping you safe."

"I don't need my ex dead."

"Then what do you propose, princess? How the fuck do you want the executioner to get rid of the man who touched his girl?"

I drive thirty minutes back towards our place. The sun is almost up already. I don't think Althea's slept a fucking wink, which I hate. We still have Drew passed out in the back seat and I don't know what to do with him.

"Scare him," Althea says. "He's a coward. Sneak him back to the house, we can get him past Chiara and you can have a little chat with him in the basement—mob style."

"Usually when we go into basements, talking isn't part of the equation."

"Change for me, then. Just this once."

"Do you love him?"

I know it makes me sound like a stupid, insecure fuck, but I have to know. I have to know if she's saving him out of love or if Althea's just a good fucking person.

"No," she says quickly. "We haven't been together in years. His obsession with me and Chiara has been a damned nightmare. But I couldn't live with myself if he died. I just couldn't."

I get the implication behind it. She wants to know how the fuck I can live with myself after the shit she's seen me do and she hasn't even seen all the shit I've done.

"Loving you is the only thing that makes this shit worth living through," I tell her. "Before you, I used drugs to cope. I did horrible shit. I believed there wasn't anything good and pure in the world. You changed that. Our daughter changed it."

"Then do something merciful," Althea says. "Scare the crap out of him and drop him off naked by the side of the road… then we can be with our family without this stain. Please, Lucky."

"Do you trust me, princess?"

"OF COURSE. Of course I trust you."

"Good," Lucky whispers. "Fucking good."

# Chapter 21
# It's John.
## Althea

Shana and I take Chiara for a long drive in a new rental car – not the one Lucky caked in Drew's blood – while Lucky has a "conversation" with my ex in the basement. I gave Lucky permission to rough him up, but he swore on Jesus Christ's name that he wouldn't kill my ex. I believe him, but that doesn't make the anxious wait for Lucky's return any less painful.

Chiara asks lots of questions about him in the car. Lucky told her the truth, and she's accepting it far better than I imagined. I thought she would be angry with me for not telling her, but apparently Shana explained it all at a kid-appropriate level. That worked out great for me except now Shana thinks she has the hang of this "mom thing" and she can't stop talking about how badly she wants a baby once we get Chiara to a restaurant and distract her with these kiddie coloring pages.

I don't know if Shana is exactly mom material, but hey, who am I to impede her new dream?

Shana orders a milkshake, which is rare for her since she's

always watching her figure. I shamelessly order breakfast, because it's almost sunrise and my body craves delicious pancakes coated in blueberry compote and real maple syrup. Man, the cooking down here is elite. Chiara stumbles through her order but eventually settles on Texas toast, bacon and eggs.

Chiara puts her headphones on and starts coloring and singing along to her kid music while we wait for the food. Shana calls her name to make sure the headphones are sufficiently drowning out our conversation. My daughter is absolutely hooked on her coloring page and can't be bothered with our conversation at all. She seems to handle this well, although she's glued to me and keeps glancing over at me anxiously every few seconds.

The kid is pretty damn tough and I can tell she'll be back to her old self soon. And as for Lucky...

Shana shrugs and then leans in, trying to whisper so Chiara can't hear what she's saying.

"Is Lucky gonna whack him?"

I can't believe she's asking this in the middle of a diner.

"I don't know, Shana," I whisper. "And keep your voice down."

"Are y'all together?" she hisses, glancing nervously at Chiara.

"I don't know."

"He told her the truth," Shana says. "He took responsibility, and he acted like a man. How the hell is he the same guy who did... you know... who hurt you."

"I don't know, Shana. I ask myself the same damn question every day. I don't know if I'm meant to end up with him."

# It's John.

Shana's eyes bug out, so her brown irises get tiny.

"Are you out of your damn mind?"

"Why would I be out of my mind? He has my ex-boyfriend tied up in a basement and he's doing God knows what to him. He's not exactly husband material."

"Exactly!" Shana nearly shrieks, grabbing onto my forearm and digging her fingernails in forcefully. "He's beyond husband material. He's better. He's a crazy asshole with a big dick, lots of money and he fathered a child with you. Honey, you secured the bag."

"Can we maybe leave his dick out of the conversation?"

Shana rolls her eyes. "Chiara's headphones are bullet-proof. Trust me."

Chiara hasn't looked up once. She colored her mermaid with dark brown skin and purple hair with pink and green streaks in the purple. Athletic and creative. That's my baby girl. I want the best for her and I can't be selfish. It's not just my heart I'm putting out there – it's hers.

"I love him, Shana. I love him harder than I ever loved someone, but I can't choose him if he's a danger to our daughter."

"He would go to the ends of the earth for her, Althea. I looked into his eyes. I saw it."

"So you're clairvoyant now?"

"Girl, I've always been clairvoyant," Shana says and I don't think she's joking. Our server finally returns with our food and Chiara takes her headphones off so it's officially time for us to stop our grown up conversation.

Instead of freaking out externally to Shana, I'm freaking out externally within. After taking the biggest bite of bacon ever, my daughter seals the deal for me.

. . .

"I wish Lucky were here... Sorry... I mean dad. I wish dad were here."

My little girl means it. She scoops eggs onto her Texas toast and takes a big bite. Once she swallows, Chiara has a gleam in her eyes.

"So mom... I hear you have a secret romance."

"I do not have a secret romance. Who told you that?"

I'm ready to give Shana a big kick under the table, but she shrugs and gives me a look like she didn't say anything. Chiara laughs mischievously.

"I can't reveal my sources but now I know it's true..."

"Child, eat your toast and stop bugging me about romance..."

"Mom and dad sitting in a tree K-I-S-S-I-N-G..."

"Chiara... I mean it."

Chiara giggles and winks at me as she takes a bite of her toast. "What's dad doing, anyway? He should be here tasting this awesome toast."

"He's taking a business call," Shana says. "When we head back to pack our things, you'll see him. I promise."

That's it. I can't be selfish or afraid anymore. I know the right choice I have to make for Chiara. I finish my breakfast and take a few sips of Shana's milkshake. Once she's done with her milkshake, Shana eats some of the leftover bread crust from Chiara's plate and we sit together having a very exhausted girls' morning until Lucky calls us.

. . .

## It's John.

HE FINISHED HIS WORK, and it's time for us to go home.
Safe.

I GUIDE the movers up to Chiara's bedroom with the last
box of her things. I made Lucky promise that no matter what
happened, he wouldn't make us move again for at least
another year. He questions whether I'll be okay living in
Westhampton but... I could get used to this luxury. Lucky's
cousin will keep running my business for a few more months
while I get Chiara settled into her new fancy school with a
much better lacrosse team.

I don't know how the hell Lucky pulled it off, but he got
Chiara enrolled in a private school and used old footage from
her last lacrosse game to guarantee her a spot on the team.

"Every kid that played lacrosse at that school went to Yale
or Harvard," Lucky announced to me excitedly.

Once the last box lands on the floor of Chiara's room, I
call her upstairs to help with the unpacking. Just because
Lucky hires people to do every last thing for him doesn't
mean we have to live the same way. I want Chiara to learn
that she has to do things for herself. She has to become a
survivor, especially considering who her father is.

Chiara bounds upstairs to the bedroom, but she doesn't
show up alone. Lucky has his cellphone out and he's calling
to her, "What about a Golden Retriever, huh? Would you like
a Golden Retriever?"

"What are you two talking about?"

I get off Chiara's bed and dodge two boxes in the way
before I head to the door to see what Lucky's showing our
daughter on his cellphone.

"Puppies!" Chiara shrieks. "Daddy's getting me a puppy for Christmas."

"Is that what's happening?"

This is the first I'm hearing of any puppy and considering Lucky spends most of his time at the casino, I wonder who he thinks will walk this puppy and pick up its doodoo. I have my hand on my hips when Lucky turns the cell phone towards me.

*Oh my God.* The cuteness. I can't help the squeal that erupts from my lips. I cover my mouth and remember that I'm the adult here. Lucky might want to spoil his daughter out of guilt but there's no way I'm falling for those adorable eyes or that cute little face...

"Isn't she perfect?" Lucky asks. "She'll be ready right in time for Christmas and I'll have time to get the best trainers and we can have Vinnie come in a couple times a week to walk her."

"She can play lacrosse with me," Chiara says excitedly. "I'll teach her tricks like jump and sit and everything. Mom, you can't say no. Please. Pleaaaaaaaaaaaase."

Lucky will learn his lesson one day when Chiara turns her begging tricks on him too. I can't resist my daughter's brown eyes any more than I can resist the puppy. Lucky turns on the most smoldering gaze I've ever seen, rendering me utterly useless against their manipulations.

"Hm. I guess a puppy might be a good idea. We can spend more time together as a family."

Lucky's shoulders relax and he wipes his forehead dramatically. "I didn't know what I would have to do later to convince you."

**It's John.**

He winks at me and I roll my eyes. Lucky puts his phone in his pocket and glances at the boxes in Chiara's bedroom.

"Okay, let's get started kid. Go on, boss me around."

Chiara loves the idea of bossing Lucky around and she starts with her bookshelf and stuffed animal corner, which Lucky has already expanded significantly. We put together her bedroom all night and I don't even have to convince Chiara to go to bed on time because she is 100% ready to fall asleep in her new queen-sized bed, courtesy of Lucky needing to spoil his daughter to make up for all the time he missed.

Once Chiara's fast asleep, Lucky asks if I have the energy to unpack my clothes in our bedroom. I don't.

"What about unpacking the pool room?"

"What's there to unpack in the pool room?"

"NOTHING," Lucky says. "I have something to show you down there. That's all."

"Is it Drew's body?"

Lucky wrinkles his nose. "No. Althea, why the fuck would you say that?"

"Sorry."

"Drew's fine. Well, he'll be fine after a couple months in the hospital and a few more in crutches. This isn't about my bullshit. It's about us."

"Now I'm scared."

Lucky leans over and kisses my forehead. He looks so fucking good in that white t-shirt and jeans, plus he smells like a dream. His large biceps close around me and I want to kiss Lucky right where we stand in our house. Lucky clears his throat and sighs.

"Come with me before I do very dirty things to you, princess."

I used to hate when he called me that. Now his words send a surge of desire straight through to the apex of my thighs.

Lucky drags me to the pool room downstairs. He keeps the indoor pool heated, and the room decorated with enormous ferns. The man has taste, I'll grant him that. Tonight as we step into the pool room – it's different. There are little orange fairy lights everywhere illuminating the pool and shimmering off the surface. Then there's a little table with a giant gift box on it and a card – and two chairs.

Lucky has a tiny speaker system in the pool room and there's romantic jazz music playing from it. When the hell did he pull this together?

"What's this for?"

Lucky wraps his arms around me from behind and leans over, kissing my cheek. He's so warm and I'm so fucking happy that I'm here with him and not sleeping in bed alone. I let him hold me and it feels good to allow myself to be held.

"It's a surprise for you. A gift and a dance. But… I want you to open the gift first."

"What's in it?"

"Surprise, princess. Surprise."

He lets me wriggle out of his grasp and saunter towards the gift box. It's too big to be a wedding ring. Lucky stands behind me, observing carefully as I pick up the card first.

"Which should I open first, the card or the gift?" I ask him without turning to him.

"Gift," he says confidently, so I choose the gift. I'm tempted to shake it, but I'm too self-conscious because the box is velvet and already feels more expensive than any gift I've received before. I lift the lid and move the white tissue paper aside to reveal Lucky's present.

OH MY GOODNESS. He didn't.

"I THOUGHT I owed it to you," Lucky says. I still can't bring myself to turn around and face him. He bought the restaurant where we met – Il Pappa's. There's the deed right there. I thumb through it and Lucky encourages me to keep turning the page.

That's not it. I run my index finger beneath the address several times.

"Is that my old place?"

"If things don't work out between us, I want you and Chiara to always have somewhere to go. I'm in it for the long haul, princess. For forever."

I turn around to thank Lucky, wrap him in a hug and then kiss him until he turns red, but when I turn around, Lucky's not standing up. He's on his knees and holding a light blue box.

"Lucky…"

"Hold on," he says. "Before you get started, let me speak."

"Okay. Fine."

Holding my tongue has never been easy, but tonight, I want to hear every word Lucky Vicari has to say to me – for once.

"I'm sorry I was such a dog when we met. I'm sorry I put

you in the position where you had to give me a second chance. You're a fucking angel, Althea. Pardon my language. I swear the second I touched you... I saw the bad shit in my life for what it was. It was like... finally seeing sunlight."

I've never heard Lucky get this poetic. There's a part of me that wants to jump into the pool to avoid the awkwardness of having someone lavish you with attention when you were firmly convinced that you would never find love.

"You are giving me the chance of a lifetime. Most guys like me don't get a second chance. I want to prove I'm down with you forever, princess. So would you do a guy from Long Island the honor of being his lawfully wedded wife and mother of his child?"

Lucky opens the ring box and I nearly drop to the floor. I'm not one for too much fantasizing, but I know expensive rings and I've seen a few on social media. This is one of those rings. I know the diamonds are real because of the blue box but what I really didn't expect was how huge they would look. The center diamond on the band is around the size of my thumbnail and surrounded by small pavé stones. The band has pavé diamonds too and before I can even say yes, Lucky takes my hand.

I'm nodding frantically, but too giddy with excitement and surprise to actually form a complete sentence. I'm too happy to even care how silly and awkward I am nodding like a crazy person while Lucky slips a ring on my finger.

"Yes!" I gasp once he has the ring all the way on my finger and I finally regain some semblance of control over my senses.

Lucky gets off his knees and wraps me in a big hug. I hold

him tightly, careful not to lose hold of the deeds, and he spins me around in a circle. I love him.

"I love you," Lucky whispers. "I love you the way no one can ever fucking understand."

I kiss him after he says this, tangling my fingers in his brown hair and enjoying the way his lips feel against mine in a way that feels finally free. I kiss him hard and I don't want to stop. We're in the pool room. It's dark. It's special. We're engaged… I want to make love to Lucky here.

BUT WE CAN'T – because Lucky's in the mafia. What does that mean? His phone always rings at exactly the wrong time, like when I have my tongue in his mouth and I'm getting ready to straddle him and drag his naked behind into our heated pool.

He glances at his phone, desperate to ignore it, but he says two words that neither of us can ignore.

"It's John."

FUCK.

# Chapter 22
# The Kill Order
## Lucky

"**S**omeone had better be dying," I growl into the phone. "Or better yet, already dead."

"I found Enrico. I need backup."

"WHAT? What do you mean, backup? Now?"

"No. Not now. Two in the morning. I don't want to move until it's quieter. Understood?"

"Where is he?"

"Upper West Side. Can you get there in time?"

"Yes. Definitely."

"How are your girls?"

I glance at Althea. She looks fucking gorgeous with that ring on her finger and she'll look even better once I'm done with her tonight and she's coated in thick spurts of my seed. I haven't given up my mission to impregnate her.

"They're great. Big news. I'll tell you later. Listen, bro... I gotta go."

"What? I'm not done."

"Two in the morning, Upper West Side. West 94th?"

"Yeah. That's the spot," John mutters, not bothering to hide his flicker of frustration. I agree to meet him again and then hang up. Althea gives me the most broken-hearted look.

"Are you leaving?" she asks softly.

The way she's looking at me could break me in half. I hate that I have to leave her like this. A part of me will always hate what I have to do to protect my family, but my duty to her is the strongest feeling of all.

"No," I tell her. "John got Enrico, but I won't meet up with him until later. Tonight is about us."

"Until?" she asks frantically. By now, she understands the intricacies of the life and the way it can chew you up at random.

"Two in the morning."

"Are you going to… you know…"

I shake my head. "Don't worry about that, princess. Worry about the time we have left."

I wrap my arms around her and pull her close to me. Our queens don't have to worry. We do the dirty work out there in the streets and her job is right here – our home. Stay close, let me spoil you, let me protect you and please princess, be an excellent mother to my kids.

Althea kisses me back, and my hands wander straight to her perfect ass. I love that ass. I don't plan on leaving here tonight without getting another taste of that ass and pressing my tongue between her forbidden folds until Althea begs me to stop.

When I squeeze her ass and pull her closer, Althea rakes her fingers through my hair and the sensation of her fingertips against my head gets me hard as a fucking rock. I can't wait to be inside her.

I kiss her neck, and as she moans, my hand wanders underneath her shirt.

"I want you so fucking bad," I whisper.

Her hands roam to my bicep, and her fingers draw swirls over the outlines of my tattoos. She loves messing with my ink and teasing my skin with her fingers. Her gentlest touch drives me fucking wild and after tonight, I'll have her forever. She said yes.

"Good," Althea whispers. "I want to spend all night soaking wet."

I glance at the pool and smirk along with Althea. Fuck yes. I want her in the pool so I can take her from every angle and get closer to making a baby with the beautiful woman I fell for ten fucking years ago.

"Get your clothes off," I murmur back between planting kisses on Althea's neck. "Tonight I'm gonna fuck you in the pool until we make another kid."

Althea quickly drops the rest of her clothes and steps carefully down the ladder into the pool. I strip off articles of clothing one by one as I follow her, watching her beautiful brown-skinned ass jiggle every step of the way. One look at Althea's naked body gets me rock hard. I can't wait to be inside her.

The second our bodies submerge in the warm water, I pull Althea against me and press her against the pool wall. She's finally mine and I'll have her here forever. She's the woman I want to come home to. I want her in my bed every fucking night.

As I kiss Althea, I spread her legs apart and stiffen as her warm thick thighs wrap around me. She's so fucking beautiful. Althea tilts her head back and my lips find my favorite spot on her neck. She moans and edges her hips forward as I kiss that sensitive spot on her neck. I'm too impatient to wait for her tonight.

I press the head of my cock against her entrance. She greedily slides her hips forward before I can thrust into her. My cock head welcomes the warmth as I enter her tightness. Althea moans and I grunt furiously as I bury my entire length inside her. She's so fucking tight tonight. Holy shit.

Althea whimpers, and her stomach moves nervously as she gasps for breath.

"You're so fucking big," she gasps. "Oh my God. You're so big."

I grunt and move deeper inside her. Althea's hips clench around me, tightening her grip on my dick. Holy fuck, I want to cum, but I need to watch Althea finish on my dick before I finish. She responds to my slow thrusts between her legs and kisses on the neck so I hold her tightly against me and fuck her nice and slow. As she gets closer to her climax, my fingers slide between Althea's legs and I slowly rub her clit as I thrust into her.

With a deep shuddering gasp followed by a loud moan, Althea climaxes all over my dick and I can't control my orgasm as she finishes. My cock stiffens and explodes outside of my control. I empty myself between Althea's legs, slowly withdrawing as I hold her body against mine.

"I love you," I growl as I move away from her. I'll have energy for a second and third round but now I just want to kiss her as my seed seeps deeper inside her. I clutch Althea close again and kiss her until I've lost myself.

"I love you too," she whispers. "You're the best surprise I've ever had."

"Surprise?"

"You're proof that people can change," she whispers. "You might have been a monster once, Lucky Vicari... but deep down, I know you're a good man and you're a good father to Chiara. I want to marry you. But promise me one thing..."

"What?"

I'll promise her anything.

"Don't get yourself killed out there. Whatever John called you to do, promise me you won't get killed."

I smile.

"They don't call me Lucky for nothing," I whisper. "I'll be safe, princess."

"Good," she says. "We need you. Chiara and I need you."

"I know, princess. I know."

I HATE that I have to leave her, but we spent all night tangled in each other's arms and John needs me. Hours of making love energizes me rather than tiring me out. Althea makes me promise to call her the second I can. She's right to worry. Any night could be my last and it's not typical of John to call me to the Upper West Side.

For all I know, I just made Althea a promise that I couldn't keep. What the fuck could be going on near Columbia University? It's just a bunch of rich kids and Harlem gangs our family knows to stay the fuck away from. Trust John. He's your brother. He's not going to kill you.

'The life' can make you paranoid, uncertain and you can feel real fucking unstable if you let it get to you. I have my strength at home – my daughter and my girl. With them, I pull myself together and stop my car a few blocks away from where John told me to meet him. I have a Glock 49, which John hates, but it's much easier to get rid of in Manhattan than a bigger weapon.

I smell tobacco before I see John, which doesn't put me at ease because he only smokes on nights when he's planning to do a job. He's standing in for our father, which technically makes him the boss. He steps out of the shadows once I get closer. This street is kinda loud for a meetup.

"What the fuck is going on here?" I ask John as I step closer to him.

"Cigarette?"

"I should pass."

"Smoke the fucking cigarette."

The boss tells you to smoke a cigarette, you smoke the fucking cigarette. John hands me one of his Camel menthols. What the fuck is wrong with him tonight? He hands me a cigarette and lights me up. I don't ask any questions, I wait for him to talk.

"Fucking college kids everywhere," he says. "We have to hang out here until they all head home."

"Okay."

John gives me an irritated look like he expected me to fail some test of obedience that I suddenly passed.

"Dad called with the orders. This wasn't my choice. I wanted to do something diplomatic, send the fucking kid to stay with Giovanni Doukas, who owes us one by the way. Not to mention Loukas Pagonis whose fuckin' daughter nearly burned down one of our clubs last year. One of them could have stepped up."

I nod in agreement.

"We're killing Enrico tonight."

"Sammy's kid?"

"Yeah."

"Does Sammy know?"

"No," John says. "And dad wanted me to do this alone."

"FUCK, JOHN."

"I know. We have to do it, Lucky. We have to kill our nephew."

"What the fuck is he doing on the Upper West Side?"

"What the fuck do you think?" John snaps. "He's doing a college student."

THE REALITY of what we're about to do hits me like a bus. Dad wants us to kill our own nephew. He knows how close we are to Sammy. He knows what a loss like this will do to Sammy. Our cousin ain't a fucking dummy. He'll know we did this.

"Give me another fucking cigarette."

"Finally," John grumbles. "You're catching on."

"Are we gonna do it?"

"YEAH," John says. "We're gonna kill the fucking kid. And then we're gonna burn in hell for the rest of our days."

"Fuck."

"Yeah," John whispers, puffing on his cigarette. "Fuck."

**THE BEGINNING...**

Click here to order John's story
Book #2 Long Island Mafia Romance
smarturl.it/longislandmafia2

**Sign up to get a text message notification when my next book drops:** https://slkt.io/gxzM

# About Jamila Jasper

*The hotter and darker the romance, the better.*

That's the Jamila Jasper promise.

If you enjoy sizzling multicultural romance stories that dare to *go there* you'll enjoy any Jamila Jasper title you pick up.

Open-minded readers who appreciate **shamelessly sexy romance novels** featuring black women of all shapes and sizes paired with smokin' hot white men are welcome.

Sign up for her e-mail list here to receive one of these **FREE hot stories**, exclusive offers and an update of Jamila's publication schedule: bit.ly/jamilajasperromance

**Get text message updates on new books:** https://slkt. io/gxzM

# A Preview 💙

*Sample these chapters from my Amalfi Coast Brotherhood Italian mafia romance series while you wait for the next mafia romance series.*

*If you enjoy dark & twisted mafia romance stories, you can binge the entire completed series on your eReader.*

*Enjoy the free chapters.*

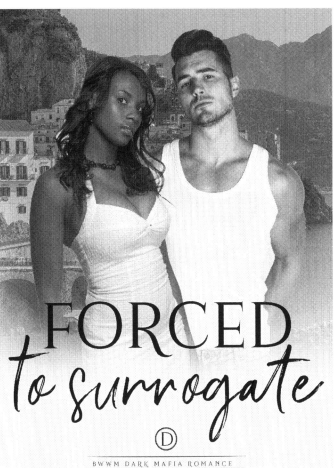

# FORCED
## to surrogate

BWWM DARK MAFIA ROMANCE

*the amalfi coast mafia brotherhood #1*

# JAMILA JASPER

# Description

**The last thing Jodi remembered was a shot of tequila.**
Next thing she knows,
Italian sociopath Van Doukas has her chained in his
basement...
And he's claiming she agreed to become the mother of his
child.

There's a detailed contract and everything... with her
signature.
Jodi will do whatever it takes to get away from him...
But she doesn't count on the 6'7" Italian Stallion being skilled
with his tongue and excellent in bed.

# Series Titles

*Forced To Surrogate*
*Forced To Marry*
*Forced To Submit*

# Content Awareness

# Chapter 1
# Produce A Pure Italian Heir
### Van Doukas

There aren't enough cigarettes in the world for meetings with my father. The boss. Tonight, I meet with him to discuss something 'very important'. He calls everything 'very important', but tonight, I know exactly what he wants from me.

He wants me to kill again, this time for my foolish sister, who can't seem to keep herself out of trouble. Everyone in the family heard about what happened to Ana by now. That idiot Jew was foolish enough to put his hands on her with witnesses and expect nothing to happen? That's not how the Doukas family works, which he'll soon learn.

You mess with the Doukas family, we retaliate. If the Jew had any wits about him, he would disappear from the Amalfi Coast and head for the mountains or Sicily, or somewhere we don't have ears. He could go to Albania like Matteo. Maybe then we wouldn't find him. But fuck, I don't want to carry out another hit. Why can't that lazy fuck Enzo do it? Or better yet, Eddie. I carried out my first hit when I was two

249

years younger than him. We spoil the new generation and wonder why our family falls apart.

None of this would be my responsibility if Matteo would get over himself and come down off his fucking mountain.

I stop my motorcycle and approach my father's front door. The all white old European style mansion sits on an excessive and opulent lot on the coast, right above the cliffs with a long path to the beach, a 'fuck you' to the tax collectors and the government who want to stop us from doing business.

Most of my siblings still live here, but I prefer keeping myself far away from papa and his... associates.

I can hear the party from the entrance. Seriously? On a fucking Tuesday afternoon? I assumed he called this meeting because he was working for once. He's intertwined in a different business based on the noise filtering outside. Please, Lord, let me not walk in on my father having sex with a model... *again*.

I open the front door to our old family home without knocking and immediately regret it when a completely naked foreign woman runs giggling toward the door, too high and drunk to feel self-conscious, exposing her completely nude body to a stranger. At least I didn't find her twisted in bed with papa, although this isn't much better.

"Oh! Good afternoon, sir!" she teases me in crude Italian, spinning around to show off her assets. *Whore. Foreigner. Her tricks possess little interest to me.* My brothers Lorenzo and Matteo would sway more easily.

"Where's my father?"

She giggles and spins around again. Fucking hell, I wish the ground would swallow me up. My father's prostitutes do not interest me.

"Your papa?" she says, standing to face me with her legs slightly apart, daring me to ogle more of her body. I have no interest in whores and I want her to answer my fucking question.

Before I can answer, another one of my father's toys saunters into the foyer, naked. This one is young—she looks eighteen just about—far too young for my father. I grimace and keep my gaze firmly fixed away from the nude females. Just because the men in my family are bastards doesn't mean I have to follow suit.

If we don't conduct ourselves with respect, how can we expect the respect of the Amalfi Coast?

"Yes. My father. Sal," I grunt, failing to hide the irritation in my voice.

The woman ignores my irritated tone with her response.

"Oh, he's in the back with Boyka. I can take you there after we take you to bed upstairs."

How much is he paying these women? We're still struggling to get Jalousie off the ground and he spends all his money on Slavic hookers.

"Not interested. I have a meeting with him."

"Are you sure?"

I don't dignify them with a response. I walk past the girls, keeping my eyes away from their bodies. Where the hell is my father? I pass the long hallway with the family portraits and follow the loud music and the louder giggling from near the pool. The familiar sound of pool jets betrays papa's location.

He's in the fucking hot tub again, I know it. He spends all fucking day in the hot tub, dishing out orders and expecting work to happen without him lifting a fucking finger. It's a fucking miracle anything gets done around here.

My father chuckles loudly, and I brace myself before approaching him. He's the boss and you don't question the boss, even if he's your father and even if he cares more about partying and women than our family — than our future.

When I enter the back patio, the pungent smell of tobacco and marijuana surrounds me. Judging by the bottles of vodka on the ground, the piles of cigarette butts and the other piles of detritus, they've been at this fucking party since last night.

Fuck. I put the cigarette tucked behind my ear into my mouth and approach my father's outdoor speakers, unplugging them and stopping the little dance party happening around his hot tub. Three women, each wearing next to nothing with their tits out belly dance for him while he chuckles loudly, his fat stomach causing waves in the hot tub. When the music stops, they stop too and look up at me indignantly.

They don't have to ask who I am. The ones who don't know Van Doukas can tell that I'm related to Sal. I have my father's eyes, but thankfully, I don't have his overweight body or his bald head. The girls make booing sounds at me, but I brush them off.

"I'm here for our meeting," I say sternly to papa.

He chuckles and nods. "Yes. The meeting. I almost forgot."

Almost? He doesn't look like he's fucking prepared for a meeting.

Papa dismisses the girls, except for one — Boyka. She slides into the hot tub next to him, twirling his thick plumes of chest hair around her fingers and sliding his freshly cut cigar between his lips. Nauseating. Papa coughs after a puff and taps the cigar over the edge of the hot tub.

"You're early."

"I'm twenty minutes late."

"Oh?"

"Papa, you said it was important. Shouldn't we conduct this business alone?"

None of the girls are dumb enough to rat on Salvatore Doukas, but unlike my father, I don't see the sense in taking risks.

Boyka's hand moves down my father's chest and I don't want to imagine what sorry shriveled part of him she touches next. I just want my orders so I can get the fuck out of this bachelor pad.

"I'm getting old, Van," he says. "I'm getting old."

He didn't call me down here to bitch about his old age. I furiously puff on my cigarette, waiting for him to get to the fucking point. Papa grunts as Boyka touches something... sensitive. Cristo...

Watching my father grunt through a hand job might be the only thing worse than watching him stick it to a woman.

"Do you mind postponing your fucking hand job until later?"

Boyka's hand rises guiltily from the water and I choke down bile. She really was touching the old fuck. I shouldn't swear at him or set him off. Papa might seem old, but he can have me killed. Any of my brothers would do it if he gave the command. Tread carefully, Van.

"Maybe I should leave," Boyka says, giving me a flirty glance as she plays with her tiny pink nipples.

"Yes," I snap. "Please get the fuck out of here."

Papa scowls. "Be respectful, Van. Boyka is a very dear—"

"I said please."

Papa smirks. "Boyka, return in thirty minutes. If we're not done…"

"We'll be done," I interrupt, glowering at my father. I don't have all afternoon for his games when I have the club to attend to.

Boyka reluctantly leaves.

"Are the women in this house allergic to fucking clothes?"

"None of them are allergic to fucking anything."

I'm not doing this with the old man today.

"Why did you call me here?"

I start another cigarette. I keep swearing I won't touch another, then I spend five minutes around papa and change my mind.

He leans back in the hot tub, displacing several pints of water over the edge.

"I'm tired, Van," he groans, leaning back and rubbing his forehead.

"From working?"

My father doesn't pick up on the sarcasm. He hardly leaves his fucking hot tub anymore, and he hasn't done anything even remotely resembling working at either of the nightclubs, restaurants, apartment complexes or construction sites around town.

If it wasn't for me and Enzo, he wouldn't have the fucking time to boink Boyka or whatever the fuck he does with all these young Slavic women.

I still have to tread carefully around him. He's still my father, my boss, and I must obey him.

"Yes," he says, coughing. "From working. I need someone to take my place and lead the family soon. I want to retire, Van. You and I both know I need a break."

He spends every fucking day on vacation while his sons and nephews run his businesses. Vacation? We're the ones who need a fucking vacation.

"Perhaps you should contact Matteo about that."

My older brother spent his entire life preparing to be the boss. It's not my fault he fucked off, leaving his worthless children with us, I might add. I'm already halfway through my fucking cigarette and he hasn't closed in on the point.

Papa scoffs. "Matteo hasn't left Albania in four years. He left his children, his business, his fucking money, and he's not coming back. Give up on him."

"You're the one who trained him for the role. Send Enzo after him. Better yet, send his fucking son."

I don't want to go into the mountains to bring my jackass older brother back and I don't want to have this conversation with my father.

"Why don't you go to Albania?"

"Every time I'm in the same room as Matteo, he tries to kill me," I remind papa. I love Matteo, but he isn't exactly easy to get along with.

I'm surprised a woman tolerated him long enough to allow him to give her Eddie.

"Fair. But I need a replacement, Van. I don't want to be the boss anymore. I can't take the stress much longer."

Stress? What stress? Does my father seriously think sitting in his fucking hot tub banging whores counts as a job?

"Have you considered the role?" He asks before I can spew something disrespectful in my father's direction.

"Why would I want to be the boss of this fucking family? It's filled with degenerates, fuck-ups, people who need more violence to be kept in line. I kill enough as it is. You don't want me to be the boss and nobody in this fucking family wants me as the boss."

"People respect you, Van."

"People fear me. There's a difference."

Papa nods. "Exactly. Personally, I think you would make a good boss."

"I disagree."

But I don't completely. Yes, the job would be horrific and I'd have even more blood on my hands than I do now by the end. I could bring honor back to our family, clean the streets of our scum, stop the Jews from fucking with our shit... but I can't. Not with Matteo gone. Even in the fucking Albanian countryside, he would find out what I did and Matteo would kill me.

"No," Papa replies calmly. "You don't. But I agree with your assessment that you're not quite ready."

"I never said that. I said I didn't want the job."

Nobody smart wants my father's job. He spent twenty years walking around with a target on his back before he built up enough trust, enough loyalty, enough captains in the streets of Italy to ensure his safety. I don't want to lose my freedom.

"You didn't have to say anything. I know my son."

"Hm."

Arguing with my father is entirely senseless.

"You need an heir, Van."

"What?"

"I will give you the leadership of this family without the ritual, without the sacrifice and without the financial investment required. All I want is an heir."

"Why don't I go up to fucking Albania, then? Because I can't produce a child out of thin air."

Papa chuckles. "Don't you have women? If you want a woman... I filled this house with them. I have very young ones too. Eighteen. Nineteen. They make good mothers."

"I am not interested in fucking teenagers."

"Then find a whore like that old Greek Pagonis fuck. I don't care how you get the heir. You can prove how serious you are by giving me a child. I'll be generous. I'll give you a year."

"I don't want this role," I snap. "So the likelihood I'll produce an heir is slim."

Papa laughs, which only infuriates me further. There's nothing funny about bringing a child into the world.

"You can't lie to me, Van. You were always the most ambitious child. Maybe it's because you were smack in the middle and we didn't pay any attention to you. Who fucking knows?"

My father spent little time raising any of us, except for Enzo, and look how that fucking turned out.

"Thank you for the psychoanalysis."

Every time I visit my father, my desire for alcohol increases exponentially, along with my cravings for nicotine. He brings the worst out of everyone, especially me.

"No problem," he says, again ignoring my sarcasm.

"What happens if I don't produce an heir? Eh? You still need someone to take your place."

"I make this offer to Lorenzo if you don't produce what I want."

"What?" I would have at least expected him to mention one of our cousins, one of the very obedient captains from the northern coast, or even fucking Eddie, Matteo's 18-year-old son, would be better than my irresponsible fuck of a brother. That old fuck really knows me well because he just said the only thing that could get me to reconsider his stupid fucking offer.

"You heard me."

"Lorenzo would ruin this family. For fun."

"I know. And it would become your responsibility to save it. You would have to act as the boss to save Lorenzo from himself. You might as well earn the position."

Fuck this old man...

"I don't want a family life, papa. I don't want the fucking wife or the fucking family. I want this life. It's what I'm good at. Business. Killing. More killing. That's who you taught me to be."

I'm not a man who can picture himself kicking around a football with my children or taking them to the beach. I'm not built for seducing women for more than a night and dealing with the danger of introducing them to my life or worse, hiding it the way papa did with our mother.

He can pretend it's not his fault what happened to her, but we all know the truth. No woman deserves our life. I can't afford to react. He loves when he can draw a reaction out of me.

Papa continues, as if my reaction is irrelevant. "Part of this life means having a family. I can't expect my other children to carry on my bloodline."

"Matteo has a son. You have a fucking bloodline. Why don't you make him the fucking boss?"

"Eddie? Eddie will not survive long the way he lives."

"That's a way to talk about your grandson, eh?"

"Have another cigarette, Van."

I'm already on my fucking third. But I'm not in a position to turn down his offer, considering the shit he wants me to deal with right now. An heir? I thought he wanted me to kill someone. Producing an heir in a year… It's just fucking impossible. I stick the cigarette in my mouth and light it.

"You can't let the family fall apart. We aren't the only people who would suffer. What would happen to our people, good Italian people, when the only people around they can get money from are the fucking Jews, who hate our guts?" He says.

I can't let his guilt trip work on me.

"I want an heir."

"Hm."

"Consider what you would sacrifice by turning down my offer, Van. It's not just about the family. It's power. You act like you're a fucking saint, but you are my son. You enjoy power. You're just too much of a stuck up cunt to let yourself enjoy it."

"Thanks papa."

"You're welcome. Now, onto the matter of the Jew."

Fuck. I hoped my father would only piss me off one way today, but if we're discussing the matter of the Jew, I won't leave here tonight without an assignment. Someone else could easily do this job, but he wants me to kill. Because I'm good at it.

"I suppose none of my other brothers have the free time to do this?"

"I don't care. I need you to do it. The cunt offended this family."

"Perhaps we waste too much time retaliating for every offense. Ana told you to drop it."

I'm taking a risk just questioning his order, but he's pissed me off so much that I stopped caring.

"Decision making isn't women's work. It's our work. The man signed his own death warrant. I want it done soon. Call me when you finish the job."

"Hm."

"If you don't like the way I run this family, Van, you know what to do. I want to retire. Make an old man happy."

Drugs and whores are the only things that make my father happy.

"An heir," I scoff. "You want me to have a fucking bastard child to continue your bloodline? A bastard won't have any loyalty to his family. Children have a mother and a father, a mother they spend all their time with. If I fuck some poor woman, you won't have an heir. You'll have a problem on your hands."

"Then get creative. If you need to get the baby and kill the mother, do what you must."

What's happening to this family? When did we lose our way and talking about murdering women for our own ends? Papa… This life changed him. It was slow, but it changed him completely. Too bad there's no getting out.

"Thank you for the advice."

"You're welcome. Now get Boyka back in here and get the fuck out. I need relief."

"Good evening, papa."

I drop my cigarette on the ground without bothering to step on it. Maybe my father's right — it's time for him to retire. But how the fuck will I get an heir? I need help.

There's one person I can call on for assistance in these matters. I don't like involving the Greeks in Italian business, but... they're our cousins. She answers after a few rings and it sounds like she's at a nightclub. She has an inordinate amount of time for parties...

"Ciao?"

I can barely hear her over the sound of the music.

"Miss Pagonis. It's Van."

She giggles. "Duh. What's happening? You finally have work for me?"

"How soon can you come back to Italy?"

## Chapter 2
# Single AF On The Amalfi Coast
### Jodi Rose

I'm the last single woman in my family.

Three months in Italy, and I haven't had so much as a kiss, but my younger cousin Raven gets married to her college boyfriend and he looks like a dream. I drop a congratulatory comment on her photo, but my heart sinks.

*You ugly, Jodi. Get used to it and stop chasing all these men out of your league. Settle with Kyle. He's the best you can do.* Maybe mama was right. I'm not the marrying kind, anyway. I spent all my dating years focused on school and look at where that got me...

"Edo!"

The bartender gives me a sympathetic look. Ugh. Edo is so hot. Too bad all the hot guys are gay, especially in Italy, apparently.

"What happened?"

"Look at this."

I show him my phone and Edo cracks a smile. "Beautiful! Is she your sister?"

"No, my cousin. She's getting married and here I am... single... again."

And I'm running away from my problems with a one-way ticket to Italy. When my family finds out I'm not coming back, they're going to lose their minds. Everyone already thinks I'm crazy for leaving Kyle...

"Fuck your ex, Jodi. Seriously, fuck him," Edo says with all the passion of a best friend, even if we barely know each other.

I have major regrets about getting drunk my first night here and spilling all the drama about my ex-boyfriend to a bartender, but at least it made us fast friends. Although I'm not sure if Edo just likes the fact that Americans tip, unlike our Italian friends. He always has a way of scamming some extra euros out of me. At least he's a damn good listener.

I groan and dramatically lean against the bar as I make a proclamation that I wholeheartedly believe.

"I'm never going to get with another guy again. This is it. I'm dying alone."

I've read the statistics. Or at least I've read what women on Lipstick Alley say about the statistics. I'm a thick, well-educated black woman who is tired of the dusties and has real ass standards — according to the internet, I'm dying alone.

Edo grins and shakes his head. Since he learned I was American, he's done everything in my power to take me under his wing since I got here. I just hate getting too far out of my comfort zone, so I've ditched all his invitations to visit the local clubs in favor of spending my nights drinking cocktails alone and checking social media. I'm in Italy. I should have daily adventures and bread. I can't forget the delicious ass bread.

"You will not die alone," Edo says. "At least not without trying… my latest cocktail creation."

Edo does a dramatic dance before revealing some clear beverage that looks like some horrible mix of vodka, vermouth and orange juice.

Good. I want to get completely fucked up.

"That looks… clear."

"You'll love it, I promise."

"Will drinking really make the pain go away?" I muse, twirling the glass around so the little orange peel swirls inside it. Kyle. Why do you always miss the ones who fuck you up the most?

Hopefully, this drink will get my ain't shit ex off my mind, but let's be real. What I really need is a summer romance. Ha. Like that's going to happen in a country where half the people think I'm a prostitute because of my skin color.

"Yes. It will. Absolutely." Edo replies with a wink.

"Cheers." I swirl the drink around despite Edo's repeated claims I ruin his creations by doing that. I pour it down my throat and taste a pleasant citrus flavor before a powerful vodka burn. It takes everything in my power to get the rest of the drink down my throat. Whew! That was a damn burn.

"What the hell did you put in that?"

Edo winks, but offers no response. Tricky ass Italian.

"My shift ends in ten," he says. "I'll take you out tonight to Jalousie. No getting out of it this time to watch *Empire* in your apartment."

How the fuck does this skinny ass white boy know me so well already? I shake my head, prepared to reject his offer to take me to the club, but Edo won't let it go. He wriggles his brows suggestively.

He loves regaling me with stories about all the shenanigans that go down at the Amalfi Coast nightclubs. I'm not really a nightclub girl. Small bars like this one fit me better, but didn't I come to Italy to have fun? Meet someone? I should put in some effort.

The only men who give me any attention are the creeps on the beach who say so much nasty shit to me in Italian that I'm glad I don't understand.

Maybe I'll meet better men at the club, especially a club with a fancy ass French name like this one. Jalousie. Wait… Edo's mentioned Jalousie to me before in the past.

"Ain't that the club with the mafia shootout you told me about?"

I don't believe half the shit that comes out of Edo's mouth, but he loves regaling me with stories about the real Italian mafia, which he claims is apparently far worse than any mafia in Long Island or Staten Island. How could anyone who lives in one of the most beautiful parts of the world hurt and kill other people? I think he likes telling tall tales to impress tourists.

I get people on Staten Island killing each other, but the Amalfi Coast? Hell fucking no. The sea is perfectly blue, the air smells fresh constantly, and it's plain peaceful out here. Italians have a rich culture, amazing food, better wine and the guys here are hot.

Not every guy, but when you walk down the streets here, you definitely encounter more than a few hotties. They all dress like supermodels, too. I've never seen so many regular ass people sporting Gucci and Fendi.

"Yes," Edo says. "But you're here for 9 more months, right? Have a fling. Don't tell him your real name... and disappear. You can find a hot and incredibly rich man to spoil you during your trip."

"Wait... is this a gay club or my type of club?"

Edo chuckles. "The guys are hot. I didn't say they were gay. You haven't earned your way into going to a gay club with me yet."

"Wow, Edo. I thought we had something going here."

Edo shrugs. "My private life is my private life. That's how it is in Italy. Your private life, on the other hand, is my playground. I'll introduce you to people. I know people who frequent Jalousie."

"Hot guys?"

"Eh..."

"Hot straight guys?" I correct myself before he answers. I don't want Edo tricking me into going out for nothing.

"Not exactly... I have a girl friend in town who goes all the time — Cassia Pagonis."

He says the name like I'm supposed to know who the fuck that is.

"Who the fuck is that?"

Edo chuckles. "A very fun girl with very hot brothers."

I perk up a little until Edo tells me they're all married. Great.

"Great. They're married..."

Before Edo can reassure me (again) more customers wander into the bar and Edo scurries to the other end of the bar to take orders.

I gaze into my phone again, looking at pictures from Raven's wedding. My cousin looks gorgeous, but I can't help a twisted pang of envy. I know it's wrong but… will that ever happen for me?

My homegirls from college keep sending me articles about the sorry state of marriage for black women. Alyssa says that we need to divest completely from marriage and just have fun.

My idea of fun isn't keeping a collection of all "my dicks" in a private folder on my phone. I want the real fucking thing! Even if the world loves reminding me that 'the real thing' only happens for white women or black women with the lightest dusting of melanin… I want to believe in love.

I scroll past Raven's pictures and my feed is all babies, new puppies, new jobs, new houses, new apartments, new husbands… new everything. Before Italy, I was just doing the same old shit. I wanted to shake things up. I don't know why my life hasn't transformed entirely. I'm in the prettiest place on earth — the Amalfi Coast.

Edo's shift ends, and he calls my name from the other end of the bar, beckoning me over to the cash register.

"Any tip for me today?"

"I saw you slip that five euro note out of my wallet. I think we're good."

Edo shrugs. "Sorry, this job doesn't pay well."

"I get it. I'll pay for our drinks tonight. Happy?"

"Incredibly."

I shouldn't be offering to pay for anyone's drinks, honestly, but I tell myself that I'll worry about all the damn money I'm spending once I get back to America. I have nine months of freedom and then I can worry about these damn bills and loans and everything else.

Edo drags me off my stool, and we step outside into the

cobblestone street. I'll never get over how beautifully blue everything is here. The streets smell like the ocean, pastries, wine and cigarettes, of course. People sell jewelry and fruits on the streets and the Italian accents are… gorgeous. My Italian's still crap, despite Edo's best efforts to teach me a few phrases.

At least I don't have to hear all the street harassment thrown my way, which is plentiful. Edo replies defensively to a grey-haired man who calls something lewd in my direction and grabs me tighter. "Fuck these guys," he says. "You aren't that fat."

I swear, I'll never get used to how fucking blunt they are. But I appreciate Edo doing his best to defend me. We can hear the music from Jalousie echoing down the street before we get close.

"Isn't it early for the club?"

"Why are you so fucking American?" Edo asks, linking arms with me. "Relax."

"EDOARDO!" A shrill voice with a strange accent calls from across the street. I know Italian accents by now, at least how people from the Coast sound when speaking English, and this girl sounds different.

"That's Cass," Edo says to me, a smile breaking out across his handsome face. "Chin up. She'll love you."

Edo waves to the girl across the street and she struts over to us, sticking her hand out to stop the cars making their way down the cobblestone streets. They don't even honk as she passes.

The first thing I notice about her is how striking she is. She's tall, with curly dark brown hair pinned up out of her face and flowing down her back. She's wearing crazy high heels, like all the European girls do, a short leather skirt and a tight black leather crop top.

With her dark red lipstick, she looks like a film noir femme fatale... and she stares like one.

"Edo... is this your American friend?"

She turns to me and smiles. Shit, her accent might be strong, but her English is perfect. Cass's hair falls over her shoulders, her curls carrying a soft eucalyptus scent.

"Jodi Rose," I say, happy to have some female company around here, not like there's anything wrong with Edo. "Nice to meet you."

She takes my hand, three silver Cartier bracelets sliding down her wrist. Wow. Her bracelets aren't the only expensive item of clothing she has.

"Cass Pagonis. I'm sure Edo has told you all sorts of horrible stories about me."

"I did not!"

Edo definitely did. But Cass doesn't seem like a crazy party girl. She rolls her eyes and brushes him off.

"I'm here on the Coast working for my cousin's family," Cass says. "I'm from Thessaloniki. My idiot brothers want me back next week, unfortunately. But I could use a night out before I go."

Edo claps his hands. "Yay! Party time. Too bad Jalousie only caters to the most chauvinistic mafia pigs you can imagine."

"I thought you said they were hotties?!"

"They are," Edo says. "But they might be assholes."

Now he tells me. Edo would have said anything to get me out of my damn apartment. I hope I don't regret it.

"Watch it," Cass cautions, an impish smile on her face. "Those chauvinistic mafia pigs are my cousins and brothers."

Edo shrugs. "Fine. Fine. But I need dick too. Gay rights."

Cass swats his shoulder.

"Edo, why don't you let me take her for the night? There's no one at Jalousie for you, and you can go meet up with Klaus or... that other one."

Edo suddenly straightens his back and reminds both of us that just because he's gay doesn't mean he's given up on old world chivalry.

"I can't send Jodi off with a stranger," he says.

I appreciate the sentiment, but I don't know if Edo would do much damage against... any man who weighed more than his slight 108 lb frame.

"I'm fine," I tell him. "Seriously."

"I'm armed anyway," Cass says. I think she's joking, but neither of them laughs. Is she serious? She doesn't look armed, and she looks more like a model than someone who knows how to use a weapon.

I could use a female friend in my life over here. I've got plenty of female friends back home, but they all want to talk about Kyle and my "healing journey". They don't want to hear that I'm still lost after all these months.

Edo shrugs. "If you insist."

"I insist," I tell him. "You've done enough taking care of me. Plus, I'll get to know my new friend... Cass."

"Exactly," Cass says. "Jodi... I think we can become wonderful friends. We can swap stories about Edo."

"There are no stories about Edo," he chimes in. "Because Edo is an incredible friend and a better bartender."

"Shoo," Cass says. "I can handle things from here."

Edo doesn't quite walk off, but he checks his phone and begins texting furiously to plan his next move.

"It's the last time they have DJ Fat Camel playing here. We'll dance, drink and later, I'll take you home, yes?"

"That sounds good to me."

"Well, you have my number if Cass abandons you on the top of a Ferris wheel," Edo says as he swipes four times quickly across his screen and then shoves his phone into his pocket.

Cass rolls her eyes. "I have done nothing of the sort. Get out of here, you big drama queen."

"Ciao!"

Cass and I say "Ciao!"

Edo walks down the cobblestone streets and lights a cigarette before disappearing around the corner. Cass breathes a sigh of relief and turns to me.

"I just think you're perfect," she says.

Weird comment to make, but I mumble a gracious thank you, assuming something got lost in translation.

"Do you have friends with you?" Cass asks, taking out a hand mirror and fixing her bright red lipstick.

"No. I'm here solo tripping. Had a quarter life crisis and… here I am."

"Do you like Italy?" she asks genuinely. Her eyes are so intense.

"It's beautiful."

"Not as pretty as Greece," Cass says. "But I agree. Shall we go in?"

"We should head to the back of the line," I say, my stomach knotting as I see the line stretched around the block. I hope we can even get into the club.

Cass grins, unperturbed by the growing line outside Jalousie.

"My cousin owns the place. Come on, we go in through the back."

Before I can protest, she takes my hand and we walk around a back alley that smells like trash, vomit and again — cigarettes. Cass drags me over to a door and surveys me once before touching the handle.

"Very proper outfit. Excellent. Let's go. Ready to dance?"

I nod, even if I'm nervous. Sure, I'm trying to have an adventure tonight, but I just met this chick. How do I know she isn't crazy? Well, she has Edo's backing, so at least she'll be a good time. Edo definitely knows how to have fun if his clubbing stories are even 55% true.

Cass punches in a six-digit code and the back door to the club opens. I can smell the club before I hear the music and Cass drags me in through the back before I can second guess myself. What am I really doing? I don't know this chick at all and I agreed to go clubbing with her? Is Edo's word really enough?

Once we're in the back door, a man appears. He's tall, with dark brown slicked back hair, tattoos all over his arms and grey eyes. He has broad shoulders, but is otherwise lean and very muscular. He's handsome, but it's too bad he smokes. I can smell the cigarettes from a distance.

"Cass? What the fuck are you doing here?" he asks, seeming genuinely upset.

"Shut the fuck up, Enzo," Cass snaps, her expression changing suddenly into a disapproving scowl. "I have business here."

The man smirks. He's around Cass' height, but he looks… greasy.

"Is that her?"

"Mind your fucking business."

Cass pushes him hard so we can get past him. The grey-eyed man's eyes land on me and he runs his hand over his jawline before snickering.

"He's going to kill you."

"Shut up," Cass snarls. Enzo laughs and raises his hands in defeat.

"Enjoy your night," he says to me in a sing-song voice. For the first time, I feel real hesitation. But Cass grabs my hand and drags me inside of the club.

Cass drags me all the way to the tables and chairs surrounding the dance floor, chatting excitedly and peppering me with questions about America. I struggle to understand her accent at first, but then I get into the rhythm of her voice and it's easier for us to communicate.

I have to listen in so hard that I barely scan the room we enter. At least the nightclub has a nice interior, and it doesn't seem like any ghetto shit might pop off. Another Edo exaggeration, it seems. I relax as Cass sets me up at a small, two-person table.

"I'll get you a drink. Wait here. If anyone comes to talk to you, tell them you are with Cass Pagonis. That will shut them up."

Before I can protest, or offer to come with her, Cass disappears. Shit. I guess I have to wait here. I already have five texts from Edo about the hotties he met at the club a few doors over. Damn, he moves quick. I've been here for weeks already and I still haven't met a heterosexual male who hasn't been an incredibly old and excessively horny man offering for me to be his 'African prostitute' — offers I have obviously declined.

Cass returns quickly, before I have any time to worry with two shots, each one with some blue flavoring at the bottom.

"Okay, Jodi. This is to a long and beautiful friendship between us, starting with one crazy night, yeah?"

I nod. "Hell yeah. I've never done anything like this before."

I blurt out the last part nervously, but Cass has a way of soothing me. She just smiles and nods. "Don't be scared! I'm a good Greek girl. Now come on... we'll take the shots together."

She counts us down.

"1... 2... 3..."

I take the shot — and it's the last thing I remember about that night.

# Chapter 3
## Not An Italian Woman
### Van

"**W**hat the fuck? Cass!"

"I did what you asked. I have a girl in the back of the Escalade. I did an excellent job. She took the pills very well."

I slam the door shut. Cass must have given this girl elephant tranquilizers because she doesn't even fucking flinch.

"I gave you a list of characteristics, you Greek bitch."

"Careful, Van. Gal's in a boat a few miles off the coast. Don't make me call him on you."

"I said blonde. I said twenty-one. I said 5'4" tall, and I said thin. Does the woman in the back of this fucking Escalade look anything like I told you?"

My voice trembles with rage and that irritating Greek cousin of mine just smiles and fishes a hand-rolled, loose cigarette from her skirt pocket.

"Do you have a lighter?"

"You sound bored. Don't you understand I could shoot

275

you dead and drop your fucking body in the sea for this?" I growl.

Cass snickers. "You could try. Now, do you have a fucking lighter or not?"

I slam the lighter into my bratty cousin's outstretched palm. She lights her cigarette, that impish smile across her fucking face. Never trust a Greek bearing gifts. Why the fuck didn't I remember that before calling her? I only called the little brat because she likes money enough to keep my secret.

"What were you thinking?"

"Men don't know what they want," she says. "That's what I was thinking.'

"No! I know exactly what I want. I wanted a small, blond woman who belongs in the life, not a foreigner... not an African."

"Ignorant cunt," Cass snaps, slamming the heel of her boots into my calf. "She's African American. They're very cultured."

I want to break her in half. If she didn't have three of the most annoying brothers, perhaps I would.

"I don't want her."

"Too bad. She's what you get."

That little shit... Cass nonchalantly smokes. Doesn't she have a child now? That poor baker's son must be at home caring for her brat while she fucks with my life across the sea. If she didn't have a child, I would have at least attempted to smother her by now.

Instead, I'll give my bratty Greek cousin another chance to do the fucking job right.

"Go out again and find exactly what I asked for."

"You idiot. I drugged her and set her up for this. If she

wakes up, she could go to the police, and this happens in your new nightclub? I'll be in Greece and your stupid club will be bankrupt. Does that sound wise?"

"Fuck, Cass. How could you fucking do this to me?"

"I didn't know you were so racist, Van."

"It's not racist. Fuck. I don't expect you to understand."

"Do you know any other words besides fuck? I'm leaving. I did what I came here to do. Sandros is waiting for me on the boat."

"I'm never hiring you again."

"You always say that. Why don't you trust me, cousin?"

"Because you're an evil Greek bitch. That's why."

Cass laughs like I paid her a compliment.

"That's going to be my next tattoo. Her name is Jodi, by the way. She seems very nice. I think she has a good curvy shape too. But what do I know? Ciao, Van."

She leans forward and kisses me on the cheek, leaving the red print of her lipstick behind. I rub my forehead as she walks off. Fuck. I've made a huge mistake and now I have a drugged woman in the back of my fucking car.

I call Enzo. Because he's the brother you call when you have a drugged woman in the back of your car and you need to go kill a Jew.

"What do you want?"

"Meet me at the beach."

"What part?" Enzo huffs. He wants to know if this is for a murder or a party. He'll know by my answer.

"Southern shore. I have a problem."

"Killing David tonight?"

My jawline clenches. "Yes. But I have another problem. I can't do this alone."

"Can't you get Eddie to do it?"

"No. I need you…"

Enzo can be a lazy fuck sometimes.

"See you in ten."

"Be there in seven."

Fuck. I get into the car and glance behind me at the woman laid across the leather seats of my Escalade. Jodi. I've never seen a woman like her in my life. She's confusing, and she's definitely not what I wanted. I need a woman I can produce an heir with—a surrogate to give me a child and then disappear. What the hell was Cass thinking disobeying me?

She's more proof we need to tighten the hold on our family. Nobody respects the Doukas name anymore.

She's still asleep when I get to the beach. I peer into the back seat at her chest rising and falling. At least she isn't dead. I don't have the stomach to dispose of two bodies tonight. Enzo rolls his car next to mine, rolling down the window and expelling an enormous cloud of marijuana smoke.

"You showed up high?"

"Relax. I also brought Eddie."

"Ciao, Uncle Van."

"Why the fuck did you bring Eddie?"

"Didn't you bring someone?" Enzo smirks, which means he probably noticed Cass at the club earlier and pieced everything together. She's still in the back of the Escalade and I don't need my fucking brother or my idiot nephew involved with this.

The last thing I need is Enzo dragging out my personal business for his habitual mockery.

"Shut up. Where's David tonight?"

"Gambling. As usual. Does Ana know we're doing this?"

My brother irks me sometimes. "Do you think Ana fucking knows?"

"Why so upset, brother? Working with the Greek cunt didn't work out? Who could have predicted that…"

"Shut up, Enzo."

Eddie glances up from his phone for the first time.

"Either of you have a cigarette?"

"You're too young to smoke," Enzo says.

"Fuck off. You're only three years older than me," Eddie protests, throwing a powerful punch on Enzo's shoulder. My brother doesn't flinch.

"Doesn't matter. He's your superior. You listen to him," I growl. If papa had taught them discipline from the beginning, neither of them would be like this. Now it's my responsibility whenever we go out to remind these fucks what *cosa nostra* is really all about. Our way of life is falling apart.

Eddie shrugs, and Enzo hands our nephew a cigarette, giving me a knowing look. After what we do tonight, he'll need more than a cigarette. We both remember our first kill and it wasn't pretty.

After two puffs, Eddie grins. "Are we working or what? I have more cunts to catch tonight."

"Quiet, Eddie," Enzo grumbles, tapping away on his phone. "Okay. I've got him. He's five blocks away."

I wonder what weapons my brother and nephew brought tonight. We'll need more than my pistol.

"Who is he drinking with tonight?" I grunt. How many motherfuckers will we have to take out?

Enzo shakes his head. "You won't like this."

"Five other men from his family. We can't be sure he'll leave the place alone."

"We need someone to lure him out," Eddie suggests. "A prostitute. Or a woman who can act like one. I'll get my girlfriend."

"You're still seeing Zara?"

I told Eddie to leave Zara alone after the last incident. I don't want to deal with another domestic problem.

"Why should I stop? She always takes me back."

"At least she makes a believable prostitute," Enzo says, shrugging. Eddie laughs, not even bothering to defend the woman he claims to love. Yes, she's a foreigner, but that shouldn't matter if he's chosen her. Love. This is what papa wants me to fight so hard for? Whatever he has for this family isn't love, and I have no intention of repeating his mistakes. I'll leave love for the younger generation, although Eddie doesn't leave me with much hope.

"Show some respect," I growl. "We're not using Zara."

Eddie puffs out his chest, but he's careful not to push me too hard. I'm just as likely to put out a hit on him as anyone else.

"Why not? She's mine to use," he says defiantly until I raise my eyebrow and silence my nephew.

Unfortunately, my idiot brother speaks up in Eddie's favor.

"We don't have a choice," Enzo says. "Unless you have someone else for us to use?"

The smirk on his irritating fucking face tells me he knows exactly who and what he's asking for. Bastard.

He knows what Cass did for me. Either that, or he

suspects. My face betrays nothing. Unlike my father and Matteo, I don't let Lorenzo get under my skin.

"I have nothing for you."

"Except the unconscious immigrant in the back of your car," Enzo replies calmly, stealing another cigarette from Eddie's shirt pocket. All they fucking do is smoke and run women. Maybe my father's right and I need to take control of this family. My stomach lurches at that thought, combined with the knowledge of the woman in the backseat of my car.

"Why bother drugging and kidnapping a prostitute if we can't even use her?"

"If he doesn't want her, I'll have her," Eddie snickers, taking the lit cigarette from Enzo and taking a huge puff.

"Put out the fucking cigarette. We don't need a lure, we need patience, something you stupid fucks know nothing about. We drive to the Jew and we wait for him to exit alone. We trust he will exit alone. If we can't get him tonight, we get him tomorrow night. Understood?"

My tone sets them straight this time. Enzo puts out the cigarette. They can't disobey direct orders. Even if they might not fear me, they both fear papa. Then again, judging by Eddie's averted eyes and sheepish glances, perhaps I'm more terrifying than I thought. Matteo would have whipped them into shape. I hope Albania is worth it, you stupid fuck.

The boys get into Enzo's car and he drives away first. I want to take my time out here on this beach, with this woman, and assess this mess of a fucking situation. Never trust a Greek bearing gifts. How many fucking times has papa warned me about the Pagonis family? They're tricksters. I wipe my sweaty hands on black jeans and open the back of the car.

Fuck you, Cass.

She couldn't have made a bigger effort to deviate from my exact specifications for what I wanted in a woman — and, more importantly, what I wanted in a womb. How am I supposed to produce an heir with... her? I specifically said blonde. This woman couldn't possibly come anywhere close to blonde. And her skin color...

My stomach twists in an incomprehensible knot as I stare at her unconscious body, a tight party dress barely covering her thick thighs. Her thighs are... large. Everything about her is larger than the typical Amalfi Coast club girl. She doesn't look like she's afraid to eat anything denser than lettuce, to start. She has curves. Very full curves. She's not my type, but my cock doesn't appear to get the message. I feel like a fucking teenager.

She isn't suitable for this job, but perhaps she'll have her uses. I'll examine my prize later. I have to kill the Jew before the woman wakes up. Considering how little Cass obeyed my instructions, I may not have much time. I follow Enzo's route to the bar where the Jews hang around, shooting dice and drinking like the rest of us. I have nothing against the religion — it's the people. It's tradition.

Our families have been at war for generations. They blame the past on our people, even if two generations ago, they were the ones bankrupting humble Italian families and taking ears and noses as collateral for unpayable loans. Without the family, without the protection and organization under papa and his trusted advisors, they would have owned all of us, kept us no better than slaves.

So no, I don't hate the Jews — but I have pride in myself and my family. I am an Italian man. Nobody owns me.

Enzo texts me when he's in position. This is the boring part. I stop the car and allow everything to settle into pure silence — except for a soft sound in the back seat. Snoring. I find the sound unsettling. I spend nearly every waking moment that I can alone, so her soft noises remind me that there's a stranger, another fucking problem, lying in my back seat.

The crowd around the Jewish bar thins shortly after our arrival. It's late enough that couples and foreigners and groups of students on vacation spill out of the bar and onto the cobblestone streets. Foreigners don't care who owns which bar or which club. They just want to spend their money, blissfully unaware of the work that goes into keeping Italy their playground.

I know the man I'm going to kill. We're friendly. In public, us Italians hold nothing against the Jews and they hold nothing against us. Our war happens in secret. I attended school with David. We played football together in high school. Tonight, I'll chop him up into several pieces and... well, you'll see how it goes.

After an hour, Enzo finally messages me. Eddie saw him and he's leaving through the back, drunk and stumbling home alone. Eddie has eyes on him, but we'll need to move the cars to get him. Easy. I command Enzo to pick him up since he has Eddie on the street. We'll take him to the beach. It's the best place for a born and raised Italian to die.

We drive thirty miles up the coast to the beach where we work. You don't shit where you eat, right? The woman sleeps peacefully in the back seat the entire time. It's for the best. Enzo and Eddie wait for me to get there, only pulling the Jew out when I leave my car. They might be fuckups, but when it's important, they make an effort at obedience.

He doesn't struggle and not just because of the gun Eddie presses into his stomach. He knows his time has come. Everyone in the life knows this is most likely how we're going to die, a bullet to the fucking head that's had our name on it for years.

"Take his hood off. He knows who we are."

Enzo obeys, but Eddie keeps a tight grip on the Jew before removing the cloth hood from the man's head. He raises his gaze instantly.

"I don't want to do this," I tell him.

"Don't give me the speech, Van," David chokes out. "Just finish it. Don't draw it out."

"You know what you've done and why this is happening. We have to send a message."

"I have money, Van. Enough money to set the three of you fucks free. You could leave Italy. Forever. Money. Information. I have anything you want."

Every man behaves differently when he faces death. Death isn't pretty. You piss and shit yourself in front of other men. You cry for your mother. You deny what's happening — and with the Jew, you attempt to strike a bargain. You attempt to give your killer what he wants, hoping he sets you free and allows you to disappear. Believe me, you get this far and free yourself, you want to disappear.

The Jew has made a grave miscalculation. I will never and would never choose money over family. Even if it's just my sister Ana, who I strongly dislike.

"We don't need money from you people anymore."

"I know. I know... But Van... we have history."

"Fuck, I'm tired of this. Uncle, can I shoot him?"

"Eddie, no. That's not how we do things."

Enzo puts his hand on the man's shoulders and nods. "Yes," he says. "We give them time to pray to their God and whisper any last words before we gut them and stuff their dicks in their mouth."

Now the man takes a piss. I swear I could fucking kill Enzo for scaring him. That's the last thing we need.

"I promise we won't desecrate your corpse. Now pray if you must."

"I have a request," David pleads.

"Hm?"

I don't like the idea of a dying man making requests, but considering Enzo just pushed him to the edge of fear, I feel a touch generous. Just a touch.

"My chain. Give it to my daughter. Please. That's all I ask. I want her to know that I was thinking about her."

"Your daughter is three. She won't remember you," Enzo says. Fucking hell, I want to kill my brother.

"Don't listen to him. Eddie, take the chain. We'll do what the man says."

"Take my gun off him?"

"He won't run," I say to him, but of course, I can't exactly make these assurances. It's just a guess. He's alone with three armed mafiosos on the beach. He would have to be an idiot to run. I make a very incorrect judgment about our captive's intelligence. As Eddie lowers his gun and begins removing the man's star hanging around his neck, he shoves his elbow into Eddie's side and throws a hard kick toward Enzo before taking off down the beach.

Stupid fuck… I take off after him, pulling out my gun as I

run. The poor bastard isn't quick — something I would have considered in his position. He played football with me. He should know who he's dealing with. I throw my leg out and catapult the Jew to the sand. He cries out as his body goes flying. Enzo and Eddie catch up with me as I trip and roll over, holding my gun aloft. I can't stop what they're about to do now. The Jew made a mistake by running.

Enzo throws a hard kick into the man's side. Eddie laughs as blood spurts from the man's face. They beat him for a while until he can't make any other sound except a whimper and a prayer. When he prays, I stop them with my hand.

"Before you die, we'll be needing that information you promised?"

He looks up at us as if he won't say anything. Then I watch the defeat flow from his face. Information. He'll give it up to us. The Jews have strong bonds, but not as strong as ours. They don't kill the way we do, so their people don't fear giving up information. At least I can justify this to myself.

I killed a man for information sits better with my conscience than killing a man for Ana. If I don't follow orders, I'll be the one kneeling on the beach next. I can't have that happen.

This isn't exactly going in the order I planned it, but I still need that information. The man gazes up at us, blood in his mouth, his eyes glued shut and swollen. He's already half dead.

"What do you need to know?"

Enzo whispers the question in quiet Italian. The man shakes his head.

"You're messing with the wrong people."

"Thanks for the advice," Enzo says. Before I give the

order, he empties his gun. Two in the man's head and one in his chest. My stomach tightens. Even Eddie's eyes spark open, stunned. The worst part of all happens after the gunshots — a loud, blood-curdling scream. The three of us turn around to see her standing there, wide-awake and screaming her head off like a banshee.

My woman...

*FUCK.*

# Another Preview 🎁

*Sample these chapters from my Greek Mafia Brotherhood romance series while you wait for the next mafia romance series.*

*If you enjoy dark & twisted mafia romance stories, you can binge the entire completed series on your eReader.*

*Enjoy the free chapters.*

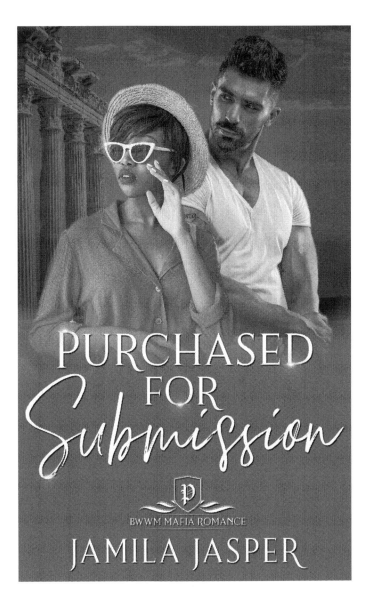

# PURCHASED FOR Submission

BWWM MAFIA ROMANCE

## JAMILA JASPER

# Description

He purchases her foolishly, impulsively... guided only by his
**unyielding lust.**
Stavros never wanted to hurt her.
He meant to set her free...
But Fallon's freedom comes with a steep price.

**Stavros loves hard. Too hard.**
As he falls for the woman he purchased for submission, he
understands the darkest truth:
He can't ever let her go.

# Series Titles

*Purchased For Submission*
*Purchased For Pregnancy*
*Purchased For Seduction*

# Content Awareness

# Chapter 1
## Auction Block

E ight auctions a year. That's how many of these papa forces me to sit through.

"It's important you understand the men we deal with," he answers gruffly when I complain.

I loathe auctions, but when you're a part of this family, you get used to doing shit you don't want to do. At least the women are always beautiful. Too beautiful. You'd think someone would notice beautiful fucking women missing around the world.

Khalid has a knack for what he does — luring beautiful women lusting after fame or power into his clutches. Once he has them, he brings them here to the auction. You get the location the day before. The invite arrives as a mysterious text message sent to your phone with a link. You can't trace the number. Once you click the link, the web page looks like a spam website unless you expected a text message. Unless you know how Khalid operates.

Type the PIN and the location flashes on screen for 120

seconds. You can't take a screenshot without turning your phone into a brick. Khalid can pack a room wall to wall — especially when he gets back from places like Vegas or Dubai, where he finds the prettiest girls. He holds the auctions in a private club, normally owned by a friend or someone who owes him big time. Fifteen girls a night once a month.

Papa sent me here to bring back my sister. It's the only reason I'm smiling and drinking vodka with the sick mother-fuckers at my table — an oil magnate and his bastard son — instead of brooding in a corner like I normally do. The auctioneer rattles off details about the first girl like he's talking about a Ming dynasty vase.

"Meet Kim, she's Korean, loves a big dominant man but willing to work for a woman. She's been pregnant once but would make a great surrogate or breed mare for individual gentlemen. We begin the bidding at €20,000."

Kim got herself on Khalid's nasty side because she has a black eye and she's whimpering, showing visible signs of distress that Khalid hates people to see. Men here like the illusion that women give a shit about them, like any chick in her right mind would get on that auction block without coercion. They tell themselves the women want it, that Khalid only finds sex freaks.

I'm here to rescue my sister from this horrible fate. But my mind ambles. Always.

If Kim's trembling and now loud whimpers affect the price Khalid and his team get for her, she might make it to her new master's house with a broken bone. My mouth is dry. There's not enough vodka in the world to desensitize you to this shit. Only time, my father tells me. I don't know if I ever want to be sick enough to enjoy these places. I hear someone call my name and look over my shoulder. But there isn't anyone there.

I've had too much vodka. Either that or I haven't had enough.

I glance over at my father and he shakes his head. We're not in the habit of buying sex slaves, although once or twice, we've purchased a girl or two — for re-sale. We mostly have Loukas to blame for that.

"We have a bidder! €20,000. Can we get €21,000?"

The bidding continues until Mr. Reichenbach buys Kim for €40,000. I wonder what happened to the girl he bought last quarter. He has a newer, younger floozy on his right arm now, desperately straining on his sleeve to tear his gaze away from the woman he's purchased. *Tick Tock, gold digger*. She may be his date to this auction and think she's not like these other chicks, but women are all disposable to him — the ones he buys and the ones he keeps as pets.

A gaunt server with a black collar around her neck approaches and offers a drink. One of Khalid's personal harem. A little "K" hangs from her neck, marking her as his personal sex slave. Her voice is raspy and strained. There are purple bruises around her neck and a placated look in her eye. Dilated pupils too.

"Vodka martini, Mr. Pagonis?"

"Dry."

"Just the way you like it," she whispers.

I grunt thanks and she seems surprised that I acknowledge her enough to say thank you.

I finish the martini in one gulp. If I have to watch female

after female parading out there with horror on her face, I get sick to my stomach. Don't these women have fathers and brothers to protect them? Yiayia is the only person who enjoys these events. Not even my father enjoys them, and he's technically the boss man. Everyone knows Yiayia really calls the shots.

A Thai girl who looks nineteen sells for €14,000 because she isn't a virgin. A Duke from England buys a blonde-haired, blue eyed American from South Carolina for €65,000. He likes Southern accents and women twenty years younger than him. My father raises two fingers and I'm the only one who notices his signal. It's simple. We bid on her, we get her out of here and our year of hell ends. We all want Helen home again. Even me.

But the night doesn't go according to plan because Khalid's man on stage announces, "Sapphire. A beautiful, fertile African American with perfect proportions. She'll need a handler with a firm hand, someone willing to engage in frequent discipline. This fresh-faced adult female has never had a baby and skilled enough for domestic labor. We recommend keeping her outside the United States."

She stares ahead, unflinching and proud. Khalid hasn't broken her yet, which means he mustn't have had her long. I can't take my eyes away from her. Straight shoulders. A slender neck. Dark skin. I lick my lips.

She's not the girl I'm here for. I'm here for my sister. Helen. Khalid's a bastard and making us buy her back. One year searching for her and tonight we finally rescue her. My instincts draw me away from my purpose. Sapphire. She's beautiful, with a raw umber skin tone and perfect lips. She's fierce and sensual in a way that scares me. I can't take my eyes off her.

"Bidding starts at €13,000."

An eighty-year-old man with mottled skin raises his card. He looks older than the first Smith and Wesson.

"We have one bidder at €13,000. Anyone for €15,000?"

I raise my placard. Foolishly. Impulsively. Because I want her. Neither my father nor Yiayia can control what I do with my money, and from the second Sapphire steps onto the block, I want her. She must be an American girl.

I can tell from her proud expression, the disgust quivering in her lower lip and barely concealed. She doesn't have visible markings on her which means whoever she is and wherever she came from, she was wise enough not to piss Khalid or any of his men off. She has one bruise on her shoulder but it's healing. A week. She must have been with them a week. And Khalid's eager to rid himself of her so she must be trouble.

I stroke my stubble, poor Helen temporarily forgotten. *I'm winning this auction.*

"€15,000. Anyone for €20,000?"

That aging bastard raises his placard again. Breaking protocol, I stand and blurt out, "I'll take her for €45,000."

My hand rushes to the handle of my weapon and everyone in this room knows that you don't fuck with a Pagonis. The aging bastard might be a billionaire, but a billion dollars can't stop a bullet. I'm crazy enough to pull the trigger. Everyone in this room knows. The old man clears his throat and raises his hand.

There's one way to win a battle.

"Sold!"

Khalid sends one of his girls over with a card containing handwritten instructions on what to do next. I've been through this before. My cousin bought a sweet Syrian girl off Khalid two years ago. She stabbed him a week later. Bastard deserved it.

I glance over at my father once I sit and he's scowling. But relief floods the room because I have what I want and my hand isn't on my weapon.

I don't know why I did this, but now I owe Khalid €45,000 and he hasn't trotted my sister out yet to force my family to bid on her. It's been too long since I've seen Helen. She comes on stage after Sapphire. She's bruised and bloody. Khalid's head would end up on a platter if he was the one who did this to her. Ironically, he's the one who saved her, but the bastard refuses to give Helen back without making us pay.

"Helen Pagonis. Bidding starts at €10,000."

No one in the room is stupid enough to bid on my sister. I raise my placard. My father strokes his chin and observes the transaction silently. I've done what I came here to do. Once the auction ends, I follow Khalid's instructions to the waiting room. After a brief wait, he sends the girls in. My sister strides over to me and wraps her arms around me. I don't hug her back. I haven't seen Helen in a year and the last time I saw her, she wished me dead.

"My brother..."

Sapphire stands against the door, terrified, like she's thinking about running but smart enough to realize if she does that, she's dead meat. At a private club like this, I'm not the scariest or most powerful guy in the room. Helen pulls away from me and I think she's going to say something deeply sentimental.

I have the words balancing on the tip of my tongue. *I forgive you, Helen.*

Then, my sister slaps me across the cheek. Hard.

❖

## Chapter 2
# The Girl I Bought

"**W**hat the hell was that for?" I growl.

After a year sold around Southern Europe, you'd think these men would have tamed Helen by now. She's like Yiayia — unchanging.

"Bastard," she hisses, "Why did you take her?"

She gesticulates madly at the girl I bought, cowering against the door, terror in her eyes as she considers her options. Typical loud-mouthed Greek woman involving herself in my business. I remember why I don't get along with my older sister...

"I wanted her," I answer, smirking at my sister as she gazes at me in disgust.

"Fool."

"Careful, sister. I might find you another buyer. Did the ones who had you ruin you entirely?"

"You've always been a filthy chauvinist, but buying a woman..."

I push past Helen and look my new purchase in the eyes for the first time.

"Sapphire. Come."

She glances at Helen, who nods approvingly, and then she follows me. How well do they know each other, I wonder? I don't need to drag her down the hall or look to see if she's following me. By now, she knows well that escape isn't an option. And I'm far scarier than a bastard like Khalid — without a weapon.

"Where are we going after this?" Helen inquires, nearly tripping over herself to catch up to me. She's thinner than I remember, and weaker.

"We're going to the boats."

"The boats?"

"Yiayia wants to see you."

"I don't want to see her," Helen complains.

Nobody does, I want to tell her. But I don't want to encourage Helen's dissent. Yiayia will be furious enough considering I explicitly disobeyed my father by bidding on someone else. We have business to attend to and when I'm working, they want me focused. I put Helen into her car. Papa sent a driver. I turn around and take a full look at the girl standing behind me. She's younger than me. And pretty.

The girl I *bought*.

"Sapphire. I will not hurt you. I'm taking you to my family boat. Do you speak English?"

I thump the door to Helen's car and her driver pulls away, leaving me on the curb with my new ward. Maybe my family is right to question my decision making lately. I'm in no position to drive. I'm drunk and I think this girl can tell.

"Yes. I speak English."

"Do you know where you are?"

"No."

I ask her, "How do you know Khalid?"

Most of the women he finds go with him voluntarily — at first. He buys some of them like he bought my sister. But Helen's trouble differs from my beloved's trouble. The Italians got their hands on my sister after an incident in Bosnia. Her idiot ex-boyfriend Demetrius got two in the head from all her brothers for letting her out of his sight. That was a fun night. When we find Nikola, the second ex responsible for this, he's guaranteed a bloodbath.

Sapphire doesn't answer. She glances over her shoulder once and I clear my throat.

"What are you —

She runs. Fuck. I should have known she'd try. She doesn't get far, even if she makes a solid break away from me to run. I wrap my arms around her and pull her close to me as she screams and thrashes.

"No, you don't," I growl, subduing her flailing limbs and clamping my hand over her mouth.

No one who witnesses a Pagonis putting a girl in a car would dare say a word. It's pointless to scream and most people here don't speak English.

My car isn't far, and she's easy to carry. I thrust the door open as she bites down on my hand. Hard. I'm screaming as I shove her into the back seat and lock the car doors. Then I hurry into the front seat while she screams and thrashes in the back. I start the car and she lunges forward, screeching and trying to climb into the front.

I take a sharp turn, throwing her off balance. She yells and I step on the gas.

"SETTLE DOWN! NOW!"

She screams and pulls on the door handles, but she doesn't lunge forward again. She gasps and shudders and appears to reconsider, settling into a silent sobbing in the backseat. I am in so much fucking trouble with this one. I don't have a plan for what to do with her.

I'm at the docks in ten minutes. Loukas and Gal already left on Loukas's boat. I assume my younger sister's with them. Helen and Yiayia stand on the dock in front of Papa's boat. Yiayia's blue eyes flame with rage. I park the car and look over my shoulder at Sapphire. If I was a younger man, Yiayia would never let me keep her. She'd make me throw her overboard, or worse.

"I need you to behave yourself," I tell her gruffly.

"You're a sick fuck," Sapphire hisses, "Is your dick so small that you need to kidnap women to get laid?"

I raise an eyebrow. Khalid would have broken her jaw for speaking to him like that. I wet my lips and realize I'm too drunk to come up with a clever retort. I need to get her out of the way so I can meet my grandmother.

"I'm taking you onto my boat. You'll be safe there."

She doesn't answer.

"Sapphire, I need you to answer me."

"My name isn't Sapphire," she hisses, "That's a cruel, racist joke your sicko friend played on me. My name is Fallon."

"It doesn't matter what your fucking name is," I growl.

But it matters. And now I know, I want to call her Fallon out loud and say her name until she gives a shit about me. *This is why everyone thinks I'm insane.* She quiets down.

"If you want to make it out of here alive, you'll be respectful. I show mercy, but no one in my family does. I swear, I don't want to hurt you."

She whimpers and nods.

"Come."

I lead Fallon onto the boat and lock her in my spare bedroom before I hop back off onto the dock. Yiayia sneers at me, "Is there a good reason you've purchased an African?"

I correct her calmly and tell her that Sapphire is American. The less my grandmother knows about her, the better. For now, that includes her name.

Yiayia folds her arms as a breeze blows her shoulder length grey hair off her face. She's a beautiful woman, especially for her age, but she looks as mean as she is. You would think it would make her less beautiful, but she only looks cruel.

"If you want women for sex, you can have any Greek woman you want. There isn't a woman alive who would turn down a Pagonis."

She smiles and fixes the collar on my linen shirt, smoothing it with a perfectionist's hand. She's proud of all of us — especially her grandsons, known for their success with the ladies.

"Yes, Yiayia."

"You're looking frail, Stavros. You need to eat."

"I'll feed myself on the boat."

Yiayia. She's not like other grandmothers, but she still keeps us fed.

"Good. I need you to work tonight once we get back to Thessaloniki."

"Eh?"

She dismisses Helen and pulls me aside. When Yiayia

says I have a job, she means that she wants me to kill someone and I always do what my grandmother asks. She's too old to be in charge of anything, and she's a woman. Women don't lead mafia families. Not in Greece. Helen retreats and Yiayia touches my shoulder gently, when she knows she's going to ask something I don't want to do.

"Who is it?" I ask gruffly, stroking my facial hair.

Yiayia sighs.

"Your father will not be happy with me. He doesn't understand what I do for this family."

"Tell me, Yiayia. I will always do what my grandmother asks."

Her soft expression turns harsh.

"Manipulative bastard," she hisses, "I don't need you to patronize me."

"A name."

She touches my forearm again and smiles. My grandfather would always tell us that her smile made men weak.

"Arturo Castillo. He's coming to Thessaloniki for the week and I expect him in the water before tomorrow morning."

"Yes, Yiayia."

She presents her signet ring for me to kiss. I kiss her ring.

"Good boy," she whispers.

I strut onto my boat and lean over to untie it from the dock. I don't bother saying goodbye to my grandmother.

Yiayia knows I went to university with Arturo. She could ask Loukas to do this — and it would be nice if my idiot younger brother Gal did something for this family for a change.

When there's dirty work and bodies to put in the water, they always call me. Stavros Pagonis — the Executioner.

❖

# Chapter 3
# Foul-Mouthed Woman

The trip to Thessaloniki would have been nice, but Fallon's screaming ruins the mood. She bangs on the door the entire time. Her gusto for escape picks up when she realizes we're moving to yet another country and I'm bringing her there with no passport, no identity, just the brand Khalid put on her nape and the chip millimeters beneath her skin on her neck. Helen will have hers deactivated once we get her home.

I hear my brother Gal calling from below deck.

"Gal!"

I remember that he isn't on the ship. I didn't hear his voice. Fuck. It's happening again. I imagined my brother's voice. I hear him calling clearly when he's nowhere around. And I believe it's real at first. Voices. Music too. But mostly voices. I ease the boat into my spot at the dock.

The girl must be hungry, but all her damn yelling pisses me off. I'll feed her later. And what was that lip back there? Doesn't she realize what a worse man would have done to her by now? I get my weapon ready on the deck, whistling as I work.

Unlike my brothers, I don't have a fetish for guns. To kill someone, you don't need a machine gun or anything fancy. I work with a police issue hand gun. I bought it off a drunk American cop and sold him enough crystal meth that he scrubbed the serial number off the gun himself.

It's a standard weapon, not traceable, and I could kill Arturo in front of a crowd of fifty and not a single person would witness it. I don't want to do that. Unlike my brothers, I don't enjoy the way people look at us. I don't want to be a Demi-god. I do this work because it's the only thing I know how to do.

I put my family first, even if they're fucking crazy because that's who they raised me to be.

Arturo walks out of the bar with a Slavic looking slag on his arm. A tight black corset pushes her enormous breasts together, and she's hanging onto his arm like she plans to milk him for every dollar he's worth — approximately $25 million, which everyone knows since he brags about it all the time. I wait for them to turn around the corner. I cock the gun.

Arturo stops walking and the girl shrieks.

"Get out of here and shut your mouth, or I will kill your entire family."

She runs. She doesn't even attempt to get Arturo out of it. Ouch. He should be grateful I've revealed the tramp for her shallow interest in him.

"Fuck."

"Yes. Fuck. That's what you did to my sister."

"I never touched Helen," he stammers, "I swear. I never knew where she was."

"I'm not talking about Helen."

He turns pale. I take a step closer.

"I don't want to do this. But... you know the rules. You don't lay a finger on a Pagonis girl. Cassia's beautiful. I understand that. But she's my sister."

"Let me go and you'll never hear from me again. Tell them I fought back."

"Pray," I tell him, "I'll give you time to pray."

He whimpers and starts, "Dear God —

I shoot him in the head. We're close enough to the water that I drag him down the docks and get him on the boat. It's close to three in the morning. No one else is here and that girl won't say a word to anyone important — not if she wants to survive to see Christmas. I load Arturo onto the boat and put a blanket over him on the deck. I'll take him far out to sea where he can sink in peace. He was always good at cards.

"You were a human once," a gruff voice comes across the deck, like it's coming from a creature crouching on Arturo's body.

The voices will never stop, no matter how many people I kill. I walk below deck. I'm not in a hurry to leave and I want to make sure Fallon hasn't found a way out of here. I knock on the door.

"Who is it? Who are you?"

"It's me. Stavros."

"Stavros," she repeats.

I never told her my name before. And she's not from around here so she probably has never heard of me. It's possible she's heard of Gal, but not me.

"We're going for a little ride and then I'll open that door... and we can talk."

"Talk? Is that what you call it?"

"Call what?"

She doesn't answer. I rap my fingers across the door again.

"You're going to rape me," she whispers.

I stop tapping.

"I'm going to take this boat for a ride. And then we'll talk."

I walk away before she can respond. I take the boat out for an hour and drop Arturo's body in our spot. I hose the deck down with vinegar and say a prayer after I lug him overboard.

"He was a good man," I whisper, taking the ring I peeled off his finger and dropping it in the water after him, an offering to the old gods. I go downstairs. Fallon won't run away from me here. She can't. I open the door and she screeches, crawling across the bed to the corner of her room and squeezing her legs together tightly.

"I'll shit all over your dick if you try to do it," she yells, "You like that? Sick pervert? I swear, I will *shit all over your dick* if you try to rape me."

I ignore her emotional outburst. Her cursing at me doesn't bother me, although she's foul mouthed for a woman.

"Fallon. No last name?"

"I have a last name."

"Does Khalid have your documents?"

"No."

"Where are they?"

"Burned."

"You're fucked."

"Thanks," she snaps.

"Take your clothes off."

"W-what?"

I fold my arms and lean against the wall. My impulses lead the way again. I'm testing her obedience more out of instinct than any proper reason.

"Do as I say. Take your clothes off."

"No!"

"I want to see what I purchased."

"I will never let you use me like a whore," she snaps.

"If I wanted to rape you, I could have done that easily. You are mine and we are in the middle of the sea on my boat. Every inch of your body belongs to me already. I don't want to rape you. I want to see you."

"Let me go," she begs, "If you have any ounce of humanity, you'll let me go."

Her lower lip trembles and I want to kiss it and comfort her. She'd probably try to kill me if I dared. Which makes me want to kiss her more.

"Beloved, I would enjoy setting you free, but without any identification but the brand on your nape, Khalid would have you back within a week. He has people everywhere. But... I can help you."

"I don't believe you."

"I don't care. Now take your clothes off."

She takes off the clothes Khalid gave her and shivers before me entirely naked. My cock stiffens instantly. I don't know why I thought I had the strength to do this — to observe her naked body and not erupt with unimaginable lust that nearly pushes me to commit the very vile act I promised myself I wouldn't do.

"You shouldn't wear slave's clothing," I tell her, "I must keep you confined... but you are not a slave, Fallon. I won't have you dressing like one."

I reveal a surprise I brought for her. It was in my other spare room — a dress that belonged to Helen that my ex-girl-friend never returned to her. I kept the dress because I never thought Helen would come home. And it still smelled like Ana-Maria. At the time I enjoyed returning to the smell but it made me nauseous now. Fallon sniffs.

"I love this perfume."

*Visit this link to continue reading…*

smarturl.it/4submission

# Extremely Important Links

ALL BOOKS BY JAMILA JASPER
https://linktr.ee/JamilaJasper
SIGN UP FOR EMAIL UPDATES
Bit.ly/jamilajasperromance
SOCIAL MEDIA LINKS
https://www.jamilajasperromance.com/
GET MERCH
https://www.redbubble.com/people/jamilajasper/shop
GET FREEBIE (VIA TEXT)
https://slkt.io/qMk8
READ SERIAL (NEW CHAPTERS WEEKLY)
www.patreon.com/jamilajasper

# JAMILA JASPER

*Diverse Romance For Black Women*

# More Jamila Jasper Romance

# Patreon

# Patreon

Instantly access all six seasons of *Unfuckable* (Ben & Libby's story) with 375 chapters.

For a small monthly fee, you get exclusive access to my all this & my recently completed serial Despicable (275 chapters) ⬇

www.patreon.com/jamilajasper

**Patreon has more than the ongoing serial and previous serial releases...**

⚡ INSTANT ACCESS ⚡

- NEW merchandise tiers with **t-shirts, totes, mugs,** stickers and MORE!
- **FREE paperback** with all new tiers
- **FREE short story audiobooks** and audiobook samples when they're ready
- #FirstDraftLeaks of Prologues and first chapters **weeks** before I hit publish
- Behind the scenes notes
- Polls and story contribution
- Comments & LIVELY community discussion with likeminded interracial romance readers.

LEARN MORE ABOUT SUPPORTING A
DIVERSE ROMANCE AUTHOR

www.patreon.com/jamilajasper

# Thank You Kindly

Thank you to all my readers, new and old for your support with this new year.

*I look forward to making 2022 an INCREDIBLE year for interracial romance novels. I want to thank you all for joining along on the journey.*

**Thank you to my most supportive readers:**

Christine, Trinity, Monica, Juliette, Letetia, Margaret, Dash, Maxine, Sheron, Javonda, Pearl, Kiana, Shyan, Jacklyn, Amy, Julia, Colleen, Natasha, Yvonne, Brittany, June, Ashleigh, Nene, Nene, Deborah, Nikki, DeShaunda, Latoya, Shelite, Arlene, Judith, Mary, Shanida, Rachel,Damzel, Ahnjala, Kenya, Momo, BJ, Akeshia, Melissa, Tiffany, Sherbear, Nini, Curtresa, Regina, Ashley, Mia, Sydney, Sharon, Charlotte, Assiatu, Regina, Romanda, Catherine, Gaynor, BF, Tasha, Henri, Sara, skkent, Rosalyn, Danielle, Deborah, Kirsten, Ana, Taylor, Charlene Louanna, Michelle, Tamika, Lauren, RoHyde, Natasha, Shekynah, Cassie, Dreama, Nick, Gennifer, Rayna, Jaleda, Anton, Kimvodkna, Jatonn, Anoushka, Audrey, Valeria, Courtney, Donna, Jenetha, Ayana, Kristy, FreyaJo, Grace, Kisha, Stephanie E., Amber, Denice, Marty, LaKisha,

Latoya, Natasha, Monifa, Alisa, Daveena, Desiree, Gerry, Kimberly, Stephanie M., Tarah, Yolanda, Kristy, Gary, Janet, Kathy, Phyllis, Susan

Join the Patreon Community.
www.patreon.com/jamilajasper

Made in the USA
Coppell, TX
16 January 2023

11214506R00188